ERICKA EVREN

ECHOES OF DESTINY

ARCHARIAN SERIES - BOOK 2

Dedication

To those who overcome.
When all hope seems lost.
When power and choice loses its voice.
And all that's left is the darkness.
Look up.
The light of hope glimmers.

Archarian series

Mission of the Ro'arck

Echoes of Destiny

Rise of Legends

Spin offs

Trials of Honor

Short Stories

Fugitive of the Stars – Honor a Sci-Fi & Fantasy Anthology

"For we wrestle not against flesh and blood, but against principalities, against powers, against the rulers of the darkness of this world, against spiritual wickedness in high *places*."

Ephesians 6:12 King James Version

CONTENTS

Key Terms

Dexsortes: The name of the galaxy that Archaria and the Alliance reside.

Arkross: A device created by the Archarians that allows instantaneous travel from one world to the next via bent time and space.

Solar rotation: The definition of one year.

Rotation: The definition of one day.

Creative Clan: One of the three clans of Archaria that specializes in the creative arts whether technological or artistic.

Farmer Clan: One of the three clans of Archaria that specializes in growing crops and tending to animals. Regarded as the lowest clan.

Warrior Clan: One of the three clans of Archaria that specializes in rigorous physical and cognitive development for battle and operation of starships. Regarded as the most respected clan.

The council: The council comprises three appointed Archarian members by the civilians of Avsilan. Each council member is a representative of their respective clan, Warrior, Creative, or Farmer.

Avsilan: The capitol city of Archaria.

Grand Tower: The capitol building of Avsilan where the arkross is kept, the Warrior Clan has their command center, and all meetings with the members of the alliance take place.

Ranks: The highest to lowest as follows. General officers: admiral, vice admiral; senior officers: captain, commander, lieutenant-commander, lead operator; junior officers: lieutenant, sub-lieutenant, acting sub-lieutenant; subordinate officer: cadet.

Narvent: A station near Archaria that facilitates the refueling of starships and performing extensive repairs. A lead operator oversees the coming and going of vessels and manages them.

Drorse: Horse-fox-like creature that inhabits the mountainous regions of Archaria.

Cordabo: Home planet to the Cordabo, seized and claimed by Lord Khelveliz. The planet of Slake, the high chief to King Saielis Shad.

Lost Race: Name given to the Archarian race.

Relapse Vision: An occurrence when a servant/slave has undergone a long period of separation from their controlling Nevo via a pheromone. Causes the victim to experience their lord beckoning them back with promises of power.

Two Souls: An unknown process by which the Nevo are able to infect their host and eventually take over.

Symbiote: Referred to a Nevo's second phase of its life cycle. Symbiotes are able and old enough to infect a host and take over after an amount of time, depending on their host's resilience.

Spawn: Referred to as the direct a-sexual continuation of a Nevo, the first stage in their life cycle.

Acknarians: A white-skinned alien race residing on the haunted jungles of Acknaria.

Acknaria: Home to the Acknarians, a council of knowledge keepers.

Pieces: The currency of the galaxy.

Colorz: A strategic card game with different colors. First person to deplete their hand, wins.

Liar's Life: A game of chance and lying with heavy consequences if you get caught lying.

Shargan: Energy being of untold abilities.

Drenna: The planet of Alissia Rabb, an important planet of agriculture before its destruction.

Cordabo Wolf: An intellectual animal that bonds telepathically with individuals.

High Guard: Trained warriors of the Cordabo who serve the appointed king.

Phase: A means by which individuals pass into another realm to become undetectable to others for a duration.

Varanus: A lizard race known for their size, strength, and temper.

Rehnna: A planet with several spaceport cities Sikik and Chalra.

Pieces: The currency of the galaxy.

Common: Humanoid in appearance but not related to the beings of the Milky Way.

Castoff: Derogatory term referring to those who are slaves or unwanted.

Dovtor: A creature resembling an Edmontosaurus but with horse and cat qualities. An animal commonly found throughout the galaxy used for riding and farming.

Nevo: A symbiotic race that destroys the Archarians in the Last Stand.

Chapter 1

REBORN

In Kaytrix's sleep, blurs of moments and memories floated through his vision.

Faces.

Feelings.

The pleasantness of these visions vanished, swirling like a black hole until they disappeared. What replaced it came as a sharp prick to his consciousness. Pain stabbed his legs, arms, stomach, and spine. He jolted awake. Every vein through his extremities burned as though laced with acid.

Something cupped his face. Dry air forced its way into his mouth, turning his tongue into a dry sponge. Bubbles danced past his blurred vision as fluid drained around him. A sucking sound filled the glass chamber with a deafening noise. Now exposed to the frigid air, chills raked his body. With each breath, his lungs ached. He slumped to the bottom of his slimy prison. A preservation tank. What terrible incident did he survive to be kept in here?

Kaytrix ripped off the breathing apparatus as the last of the fluid drained by his feet. Beyond the foggy glass, only darkness stirred. Where was he? The dark room yielded minute details of tables and trays when the silhouette of a figure appeared before him. Kaytrix recoiled in surprise as a knife pierced the containment, breaking the glass into shards that tinkled to the floor.

A hand reached in, grabbing for something near his stomach. Kaytrix struggled to avoid the hand when it latched onto him. Something in his abdomen tugged free, shooting pain through his side. Warm fluid pooled from the opening in his stomach and over his thigh. This person was going to kill him.

"Stop," he said, his voice croaked like he hadn't spoken in ages.

"Be quiet," the voice demanded, feminine but deep and harsh.

Another tug followed, and something smacked the floor beside his hand. In the dim green light, he identified the object as a tube. Out of it, a brown sludge oozed onto the floor. He gagged and threw up.

"Remain calm."

The shadow eased him from the container. Their hands floated across his slimy wet skin, and he slammed onto the floor. He groaned, his tailbone hitting something hard.

"What's going on?" This time he didn't sound like an old man.

The warmth of the person's hand returned, and the comfort of a heavy blanket wrapped around him. He tried standing again.

"I'll explain in a moment, but first we must leave this place. Can you walk?" The person whispered, casting glances around the room. They wore black robes and a face covering.

His mind felt weird, empty, as he formed a reply. "Uh, yeah. I think so."

He took a step and wobbled. Weakness jolted through his bones and he clung to the person for support.

"I've got you," the voice reassured.

A strong arm wrapped around his waist and another held his arm over their shoulder. A sweet smell wafted towards him.

"Who are you?"

Their footfalls clanged through the room on eerie metal as they approached a door. The woman inserted a small device into the door reader.

"Who I am isn't important right now."

After a moment, the door clicked and whizzed to the side of the black metal frame. That's when the sound of miserable voices rose all around him. The voices carried on in broken screams and wails.

"What is this place?"

"A place we need to leave."

The woman tightened her grip around him and ushered him forward through the doors. A lone figure stood, filling the hallway as they entered. Green eyes blazed at them.

"Hey!" the soldier boomed, unraveling its metal arms. It drew its weapon—a short-barreled blaster—but hesitated to attack as though it recognized her.

One of the woman's arms retreated from around Kaytrix's waist, withdrew into her cloak, and launched a blade. Without a sound, it sliced the air, hitting the bullseye of her target. The soldier fell to its knees with the blade lodged in its eye.

"Wow, where'd you learn to do that?"

"We need to hurry. Come on!" The woman slipped her hands around him and guided him to the mouth of a dark tunnel.

They traveled up the steep terrain and entered the darkness. Cobwebs grabbed at his facial hair and pulled against him in the cramped space. The strong earthy scent of dirt filled his nostrils, a better smell than what greeted him outside the doors. Underfoot, the soft soil caught between his toes, then transitioned to harder stones.

At a certain point, the warm air turned frigid. They traveled through the last of the air supply tunnel and arrived above ground. The air hit his lungs with a deep chill and the grass beneath his feet cut like blades.

Beyond not knowing who this person was, something important was missing: his memories. Kaytrix had no recollection of his past. Sure fragments, but they were unreachable, like peering through a frosted glass.

"Why can't I remember anything?"

The woman turned to him. Amber eyes stared at him through thick eyelashes surrounded by warm mango skin.

"You don't remember?" She studied him for a second, when a loud racket drew her attention.

From an underground structure beside them, dark figures poured out of the entrance. The hangar soon crawled with them. The woman pushed him down into the grass when blasts of green energy flew past their heads. *Thwap thwap.*

"They have learned of your disappearance! Come, my ship is over here." She led him through a field of tall grass and towering trees.

Wherever he was, the planet was dark, but glowed. Each step stirred a bright luminescent dust, and a ring arced through the sky. Ahead, ship engines roared to life and a powerful gust of wind rushed to meet them.

"Hurry!" The woman pulled him along, frantically looking over her shoulder.

From the belly of the ship, a ramp lowered. A bright light cascaded down to guide them inside. With a firm tug, the woman secured him in a harness and rushed for the cockpit above the cargo hold. The ramp retracted with creaks and groans, as if the demand of swiftness was too much effort. Outside, blasts from weapons flew by the ship. Other blasts entered through the slowing cargo door, striking metal with sizzling heat.

The ship rumbled beneath him, and he braced himself. The vessel was tiny, with rust inhabiting unused door hinges, wet floor grates, and a concerning patch job above where the cargo door receded.

From his seat in the cargo hold, Kaytrix observed the woman as she flew the ship, her motions fluid. Beyond her chair and out the cockpit window, the planet streaked by in a blur. Stars graced the viewport as the craft entered space and then a hyperspace jump.

The stench of stale fluid was overbearing now and mixed with the scent of maintenance oil and metal. For the first time, Kaytrix dared to look at himself. Dirt and foliage covered his pale skin. Strange markings ran along his right arm. He followed the thick bands and intricate circuits up to his shoulder, where they changed from black to red. Kaytrix ran his hand along their raised surface and paused.

A fluid bled from his wounds and into the blanket wrapped around him. Streaks of blue-clear liquid also ran down his legs and pooled on the floor. A chill swept through him as the ship's metal beneath his bare cheeks reminded him of his nakedness.

"I don't suppose you have any clothes that will fit me?" He doubted it.

The strange woman's chuckle echoed down to him from the cockpit. "Of all the things to worry about, clothes make the top of your list?"

Kaytrix wiped a gob of slime from his forehead. "Sorry to disappoint."

"Where we are going will have everything you need."

The momentum of the ship slowed. Through the cockpit window, the surface of a green planet with large deserts loomed.

"What planet is that?" Names popped into his mind.

Drenna.

O'ber.

Varanus.

Shrovon.

These were planets he'd seen.

"Rehnna," the woman answered. Her voice turned icy, calculated. He assumed she was concentrating on the landing sequence.

Kaytrix didn't know this planet, Rehnna. A memory of white mountain peaks flew through his mind. He recognized them, but so much mystery clouded their meaning.

"You said you'd tell me," he began.

"Tell you what?"

She was coming down the ladder to the cargo hold. Her sandaled feet revealed a soft mango skin, with the odd aquamarine marking. Through her black face covering, her amber eyes observed him.

Kaytrix swallowed. "What was that place?"

She shook her head. "All in time. You'll stay on this planet to regain your strength."

That answer wasn't satisfying, but he wasn't about to argue. She saved his life, so it appeared.

"And where will you be?" he asked.

The crinkles at the edge of her eyes suggested she smiled behind her silky black face covering. "I'll be around."

The ship shuddered and shook for a few seconds until its flight smoothened. Trees moved past the large windows of the cockpit. The ship slowed and jerked as it moved into position. They were landing. A long groan reverberated through the ship as it finally came to rest. A whirring noise filled the cargo bay as the door lowered.

Humid air stole Kaytrix's last cool breath as plains of desert hills and trees rolled out before him. To his left, a settlement lay situated with ships coming and going above the city. Tents of assorted sizes stood on the outskirts, their owners scrounging in the sand.

"This is Rehnna, huh?" Kaytrix turned to see his masked savior eyeing the terrain carefully.

"Yes, a part of it," she said when she turned to him. "Come, there is someone I would like you to meet."

He glanced at his current attire. "I don't think this is appropriate for a first-time meeting."

"You look much more appropriate than when I first met you."

Kaytrix winced, remembering the tube smacking the floor and his nakedness. "I didn't catch your name?"

A moment of silence.

"I didn't share it."

Protectiveness laced her tone. What was she trying to hide?

"Right. I think I should at least know your—"

"It isn't important. Not when you need to be kept safe."

She exited the cargo bay, and he fumbled down after her. The sand scorched his toes.

"Be kept safe from what? Or who? I don't even know what is happening."

She didn't turn her head like he expected her to. Instead, she continued to walk towards the city. He struggled to keep up as the sand gave way to the weight of each footstep.

She sighed and stopped to face him. "When you are ready, I will explain everything. For now, I have little time before my absence becomes suspicious."

Her answer only aroused his curiosity, but it was clear she hated questions.

She stood for a moment more, her amber eyes lingering on his face.

He nodded in defeat.

"Traven will see to it you receive anything you need," she said and indicated to the faint mirage of a man traveling towards them.

"Traven. Got it."

Kaytrix wished she would tell him what was happening. Finding himself in such strange circumstances, then being left alone with another stranger, didn't ease him. The man named Traven closed the gap between them and paused. A scarf shielding his face left his features hidden.

"Traven," the woman greeted.

The man sputtered and coughed, revealing his age as his goggle-covered gaze shifted towards him. Traven lifted the goggles and pulled down his scarf, revealing a toothy grin and a scruffy, dirt-smeared face.

"Why is he naked?" Traven's amused tone provoked a sigh from the woman.

"I don't have time, Traven. Can you fulfill our arrangement, or must I pay someone else?"

Traven raised his hands. "No, no. We're good. Clarr and I would love to have him."

"Remember," she warned, "no one is to know anything. Your job is to keep him safe. If I return and find out otherwise . . ."

The old man reset his goggles on his eyes. "Yes, I know, I know." He crossed his arms. "Don't worry."

The wind ruffled the woman's silky robes. Much of her skin was bare. Sheathed daggers lined her thighs, and a complex system of straps and other devices followed the contours of her body. Whoever she was, she dressed to kill.

The situation perplexed him. Here he was, saved from a mysterious place only to be left on a planet with a strange man. Should he celebrate or worry?

"Thank you, I guess?" He offered her a small smile.

"Don't thank me yet. This is far from over."

With that, she turned and boarded her ship, leaving him in the desert with the old, disheveled man. A gust of wind hit them from behind as the ship took off and disappeared into the deep blue sky.

Traven cleared his throat—a croaky, hoarse sound. "Well. Are you coming? Can't stay wrapped in a blanket forever."

Kaytrix grimaced and loosened the blanket from his sweat-slicked back and torso. It stifled him in this heat, but worse was the scratching against his open and bleeding wounds.

"Come on then, let's get going. Dressed like that, you will draw unwanted attention." Traven grunted and retrieved the bag from off his shoulder.

Kaytrix looked down at the worn blanket and his dirt encrusted feet. Of course, Traven was right. His appearance was less than appealing. Becoming less conspicuous was important.

Traven pulled out a set of clothes and tossed them at him. "Here," he said, his tone annoyed. "These should fit." Traven secured the bag back across his shoulder.

"You're going to watch?"

"Can't have you running off, now, can I?"

Though reluctant, Kaytrix dressed. With Traven watching, he tried to hurry. Nothing like getting dressed while someone watched. He heaved the pants on, noticing a black band tattoo encircling his right wrist. He ignored his curiosity to investigate, opting to slip into the tunic, which aggravated the pain in his spine and shoulders.

Traven whistled. "Man, whatever you are here for, we better be careful. Ain't seen someone the likes of you for a while."

A pang of anger radiated through him. Was it the heat, his current situation, or the increasing need for food?

"Look, I am grateful for your hospitality, but don't antagonize me."

Traven scowled and began walking, leading the way through the blistering wind and the scorching heat. Before long, they entered the outskirts of a village. A scarce population lived here, with a few tents billowing in the wind. Posts with ribbons of assorted colors stood in the deep sand, serving as markers to guide them into the settlement. The ruins of structures grew taller as they traveled further inward. The buildings comprised white stone marred by dirt from many solar rotations of wear.

Across the street, a building with scorch marks came into view. Makeshift patches of metal sealed open areas to keep wind and sand out. Stones of assorted sizes lay scattered through the surrounding street. A knowing punched him in the gut. Aerial attacks destroyed these buildings.

"What happened here?"

Traven's body stiffened at the question, his brows furrowing. "I promise we will chat in time. Not now," he said, casting a concerned glance around to ensure no one heard them.

A chill swept through Kaytrix, numbing his spine. He didn't like how secretive Traven had to be, even in his own city.

They walked through the marketplace where many vendors sold goods, and villagers begged for scraps. The noise of the crowd filled the street, muddling the vendors' shouts of their daily deals. The overstimulation of his senses drove a pain through his forehead.

They rounded a corner between the ruined buildings of the street, and the noise quieted. The dim street provided temporary relief, but something about it made him uneasy. Trash lined the foundation of the stone structures and the air smelt stale with sweat and filth.

A crowd of men of rich stature gathered, raising their hands as words were called out. What were they bidding on? What was so important that drew them to the filth of this place?

As the crowd thinned, he caught sight of an arena where a bound figure stood, their head held low. Behind them stood others of different races, waiting for the same fate. They stood chained together, forced to stand in line with cruel tools.

More words were called out and a wave of hands rose, raising the bid. A loud clamor of banging tin rang through the crowd once the bid closed and the new master paid his dues. The chained figure did nothing to fight the fate decided for them when another stood in the middle of the ring to take their place.

A fire boiled in Kaytrix's stomach as the merchants sold the life of one to another for profit. He clenched his fists and pushed into the crowd. He may not remember much about himself, but slavery was immoral in his books.

A firm hand grasped his shoulder, pulling his still weakened form backwards. Kaytrix resisted the hold as he tried pulling away.

"Let me go! This is wrong!"

"Shut it!" Traven hissed, winning the tug of war between them. Then, in a muffled voice, he said, "There's nothing you can do. Slavers aren't the worst filth around here. No worse than the bounty hunters. Around here, the Nevo are the predators. The rest of us are the prey."

Kaytrix panted, exhausted from the exertion. "Who are the Nevo?"

A look of bewilderment seized Traven's cold gray eyes. "You're kidding? Look over there," he said, jutting his scraggly chin in a direction.

Kaytrix followed Traven's subtle gesture. Standing apart from the crowd, two massive entities stood.

"Those black soldiers there. Metal and death combined to create murderous, merciless machines. No soul, those things. Kill because they want to. They are the Nevo, rulers and conquers of every planet we know." Traven snarled. "Come now. You will learn soon enough how to pick battles wisely."

The busy streets gave way to fewer buildings and more sand, but instead of desert and dead trees on the horizon, a pleasant view of rolling hills and bushes greeted them. However, the serene landscape did little to squelch his growing irritation. Slavery. Bounty hunters. Cruel conquerors. None of it made sense, but most irritating of all was he couldn't remember why.

"My house is nestled just beyond those slopes," Traven said, adjusting the rough strap across his chest before proceeding.

When they reached the hills, a large tent came into view surrounded by grids of tilled land. Small shoots of plants lined the centers of the rows and darker soil around them suggested they'd just received water.

"So this is what you do when you aren't harboring outlanders?" Kaytrix asked, still bitter from the scene at the market.

Traven laughed a hearty laugh before choking. "You're lucky you ended up here. Sure, I get paid for what I do, but it's risky. The bounty hunter pays well, and I do my part to keep her clients hidden. But you also must *listen*. You almost got us killed back there!"

Kaytrix paused. His fists tightened as he contemplated hitting Traven across the face. But what good would that do? Traven was right. What did he know of this strange world or the woman who saved him? So she was a bounty hunter. That couldn't be good. Perhaps Traven might answer some of his questions now they were out of the village.

"This bounty hunter. Why does she need to keep me hidden? How do you know her?"

Traven removed his scarf and scratched his balding head. "I don't ask questions. She doesn't like it."

Kaytrix crossed his arms and huffed. "I've noticed."

Traven wiped the scarf across his sweating forehead, pausing outside his house. "Look, before you give me anymore trouble, come in and get cleaned up. And respect my wife, or regardless of the bounty hunter's wishes, I'll end you myself."

"Fair enough."

Kaytrix followed Traven into the large tent. Various posts throughout the tent kept it situated. Tight woven material hung throughout, creating rooms and sections. Before them, a fire burned in the main section of the tent. Carpets of poor colors and upkeep lay on the floor near a wooden table off to the side. A woman stood over the fire, retrieving a boiling kettle.

"Clarr," Traven began, clearing his throat. "We have another visitor."

"Kaytrix," he corrected.

Clarr turned and smiled, but only half of her face moved. The other half remained frozen, disfigured, and scarred from severe burns.

"Wonderful. Our meal is almost ready. I will set another place," she said cheerfully.

Kaytrix observed her work with a joy he could not place. The feeling felt like a stranger in his soul, much like how he felt amongst Traven and Clarr.

"Uh, Clarr," Traven began. "He's going to need that kettle of water and a bar of soap first."

Clarr stopped her task to peer at Traven and then Kaytrix. A quick once-over and she nodded.

"Very well, I will ready a place for him to wash."

Kaytrix grimaced and rocked on his dirty heels.

Clarr motioned him over to a private part of the tent, pulling the draped door aside to reveal a small area. It bore only the essentials: a rug on the floor, a small stand with a washbasin, and a cracked mirror which hung from a beam. A round hole in the tent's side with missing threads served as a window.

He turned to her and smiled his thanks before she left. How was she taking having strangers come and go from her home? Traven mentioned he was another visitor. It couldn't be easy on her, always being at risk for Traven's activities.

The thought stuck with him as he prepared to wash from the small metal basin fashioned out of a ship's hull. As he drew the cloth across his body, the soap stung. On each of his forearms and biceps, a small hole. Clear fluid and blood oozed out of them; the scabs washed away by his cloth.

On his abdomen, another wound the size of his thumb. Along his legs, wounds from incisions marked him. His hands quivered as he continued to wash away the dirt and slime. Weakness ate at him now.

In the cracked mirror, several scars dotted his spine. He froze. All along his right neck muscles and down his shoulder ran a red circuit marking. A unique structure in black formed on the inside of his right forearm, ending in two thick bands before his wrist.

He twisted his arm, marveling at the intricacy. Somehow, these markings belonged to his culture, his race, but he couldn't piece together their significance. Wherever he was from, why was his presence on this planet to be kept a secret, and from who?

Chapter 2
CADE

The sound of the wind teasing tree leaves and flapping the tent walls woke Kaytrix. The sun's light filtered through the material and into the room, creating a bright and peaceful atmosphere.

He closed his eyes and breathed in the earthy canvas scent of the room. He dreamt last night, but the images appeared fractured. One moment he stood on the bridge of a ship, the next he was peering into the eyes of a dying woman he didn't remember. A keen sense of urgency was present in his dreams, coupled with failure. The imagery was so real, but without knowing his past, how could he tell the difference between a dream and a memory?

The soft murmur of voices filtered through the tent walls. Kaytrix sat upright, stiffening as he listened.

"Is he awake?" came Traven's gruff voice.

A pause of silence followed.

"I'm not sure," responded Clarr's sweet voice.

Kaytrix stood and dressed in the clothes Clarr had gifted. Last night he asked who they belonged to, but both Clarr and Traven stayed silent on the subject. Their reluctance to answer only nurtured his suspicion they belonged to a person of importance. Or a past visitor?

He fastened the belt to his pants and dressed in the loose tunic.

"I'm awake," he called, drawing the door to his room aside.

Traven and Clarr stood facing each other and turned to look at him. Traven's face was ghostly, his hands clasped together in front of him.

"What is wrong?" Kaytrix paused outside his room and waited.

Traven turned, his body rigid. "There's been some developments regarding your stay here," he said, his voice weak, worried. His risen brow flattened as he gathered the courage to speak.

Kaytrix's stomach twisted, his palms sweating. The thought of having to leave so soon upset him.

"What do you mean?"

Traven's shaking hand pointed to the table. "Have a seat. I'll explain."

"I'd rather stand."

Traven nodded. The fat gathered under his chin jiggled with the motion. "Please, it's better you sit."

Kaytrix shared a glance with Traven and Clarr before sitting down. "Cut to the chase, Traven."

Traven crossed his legs on a worn cushion at the short table. He was still shaking. Had the mysterious woman threatened him?

"Look, I know you have many questions," he began, "and I don't have answers for you."

"But?"

Traven swallowed. "I overheard some of the townsfolk talking. The Nevo are increasing their patrols for the first time in many solar rotations. They are searching through ships, inspecting crew manifests. There are more patrols in the city . . ." His voice trailed off as he made eye contact with Clarr.

"So?"

Traven stiffened. The muscles in his neck tightened as he clenched his jaw.

"Where are you from, stranger? An increase in Nevo patrol is never good for anyone, *especially* for you. We're at risk here. If they discover you—" He stopped abruptly, wiping his dirt encrusted hands across his face. "We must change your name. Hide your markings."

Kaytrix ran his fingers along his right wrist, feeling the raised markings there. "I have no fear of the Nevo."

Traven scowled. "Well, you should."

A tightness lodged itself in Kaytrix's throat. "What's the point of hiding? Won't everyone know I am a stranger here, anyway?"

"Not if you pretend to be our son," blurted Clarr.

"Clarr!!" Traven hissed.

Clarr rushed to Traven's side and wrapped her arm through his, her eyes glazed.

"He fits his clothes, Traven. They even resemble each other. We can tell the townsfolk that Marek—"

"No!" Traven stood and stormed towards the fire. "I will not pretend our son has returned home."

"How else will we keep Kaytrix safe? This is the only way. The bounty hunter promised this was the last time and she would look for Marek." Clarr rose and faced her husband, trying to look into his eyes. "If we don't do this, we will never know what happened to him."

Traven stormed away from her, making his way to the tent entrance.

"It will raise too many questions, bring on too much attention. We need a different story. What about a slave?" Traven cupped his bearded chin, his posture relaxing. "Everyone knows we've needed an extra hand around here and no one would bother getting to know who you are. It's against the policies of the slave trade."

Images of yesterday's walk through the city flashed before Kaytrix's eyes.

"No. I will not pretend to be yours or anyone's slave."

Clarr tucked a loose strand of hair behind her ear, ignoring him. "We still need to call him something other than his real name to be safe."

"How about Cade?" Traven suggested.

Clarr unraveled her arms and placed her hands on her hips in protest.

Kaytrix ground his teeth. "Did you not hear what I said?"

"Fine, Cade." Clarr sighed.

Traven smiled the same toothy grin, pleased with her acceptance of the name. "Unfortunately, I wasn't joking about needing help, *Cade*. The dovtors in the field need a commanding driver and since my shoulder injury, I haven't been able to get them to listen."

Kaytrix raised an eyebrow at him. "I don't think you understand what I am saying, *Traven*. I refuse to pretend to be anyone but who I am."

"Which is who? The bounty hunter told me you don't remember squat. You gotta earn your stay here and keep the fabricated story real." Traven huffed, sitting back down as Clarr poured the morning tea.

"My memory loss doesn't mean I have to agree to anything you decide." Kaytrix crossed his arms. "And if we're playing 'keep your word,' you still need to answer my questions, or I'll leave. Will the bounty hunter keep her word to find your son if you lose me?"

Traven and Clarr both scowled. His threat opened a wound.

"Very well. What do you suggest? Have the Nevo come in here and destroy everyone because of your pride? Many of us have lost more than our memories. We've lost loved ones, communication, freedoms. We're prisoners here. Until you get that through your thick skull, you'll see just how quickly you will lose body parts as well."

Kaytrix scowled. "It seems we are at an impasse."

Traven breathed in deep, the color returning to his face. "Let's each agree to do our part. Just change your name and keep your head down."

"Fine."

Clarr forced a smile but never said another word as they ate their small meal and drank their stout tea. Becoming Cade would be easy, but he still needed to know who he was. Traven was his only hope of discovering the truth, that is, if he was still willing.

"Is the town in ruins because of the Nevo? Did they do that?"

Traven dabbed the tea that dribbled onto his chin with a piece of his shirt. "Yeah, and those damn Archarians, too. Pffah. Promising to protect us. Load of dovtor manure. The war was shorter than it should have been.

Spineless whelps pulled their forces to defend themselves and look at what it got them. The Nevo destroyed their entire planet. Not only that, but they crippled the alliance."

Kaytrix swallowed the bitter tea. "Who are the Archarians?"

Traven pointed a finger at him, his eyes going cold. "Never ask that question to nobody. Especially here. You want to die needlessly? You mention that name."

"Cause of what happened after the war?"

"During, after, before. The Archarians were terrible all away around. If their politics didn't choke you to death, their entitlement and arrogance would. The Nevo are far worse. Instead of words, they use violence. Taking what they want from whomever. In the beginning it was unimaginable carnage, but as time went on, they needed us and acted more civil, in a manner of speaking."

"This war? How long ago was it?"

"Long enough that we should forget it, but the Nevo's icy grasp makes that hard. No one can live in peace. Every day they remind us to look for these Archarians, to give them up. Sad lot. I feel for them now. Who didn't die on their planet are now hunted for their skin. We resisted the Nevo's orders once. I told them I wanted no part of it, but there's no on-the-fence with the Nevo. That evil bastard of a scientist took our son as punishment. We haven't seen him since his twentieth birthday."

Clarr shot them a glance. "You've said enough, Traven."

"Have I? Maybe this fella will make a difference. Or you're just like everyone else, trapped in this maze with no way out."

Kaytrix narrowed his eyes. "Maybe and maybe not. Mazes have exits. You just need a different perspective."

"Ho, ho, look at you being wise. Come, I'll teach you what a grueling day in the field will do to a wisecrack. Then we will go into town and buy parts. Provided you make it through the day, you can put that brain of yours to use and fix my damn ship."

The idea of working on a ship filled Kaytrix with a child-like enthusiasm, but the conversation left a bitterness in his heart. The world he woke up to was full of pain and evil. Someone needed to stop it.

Chapter 3

BOUNTY

Kaytrix sat in the pub's corner with Traven, his back to the wall. The dark bar provided a slight reprieve from the burning brightness outside. The air smelled of smoke and grease. Travelers and drunks came and went without a look in their direction.

He relaxed. The ruse of him being a laborer for Traven went unquestioned. Imagine that. No one cared. Unless, of course, an individual wanted to make a profit. Most people desired to be left alone.

Since becoming Cade, it became easy to disappear into a new person than rediscover who he had been. The scare of the Nevo patrols died down over the hotter season, allowing the inhabitants of the settlement to relax.

He endured the harvest season and ornery animals but wasn't any closer to finding answers. Of course, Traven didn't let him go asking questions either. Any clues to his past came at night in his dreams. They started out peaceful, but ended in night sweats and screams. Several times he'd frightened Clarr and Traven, leading them to think a stranger entered their home. And if the night didn't haunt him, daytime found a way.

At random, terrible pain shot through his head, originating from his chest. Perhaps some sort of heart problem or trauma, but he wasn't sure. He didn't tell Traven, especially not Clarr. The less fussing from her, the better. For now, his only clue to his past were the strange markings on his right arm and shoulder, which Traven warned never to leave uncovered at any point in time.

"Are you okay?" Traven asked, startling him. "You are doing it again. That thing where you analyze everything."

Kaytrix focused on the man before him. Somehow, the dirt in the creases of Traven's face wrinkles and under the edge of his nails made him feel comfortable, at home even.

"One can never be too careful."

Traven snorted. "Ah, no one in here cares about anything but drinking and women." He chuckled, taking a swig. "Thought you would have caught onto that by now."

Traven's smile was yellower than when he first met him. The season hadn't been kind to him, or maybe it was stress.

He smiled before looking back at the crowd. Coming to the local pub after a day of working in the field became a bit of a habit for them. Traven was right, of course, but ever since he agreed to change his name and appear as a worker, his alertness only heightened. Every rotation was the same after: wake up, work, repair the ship.

On the days when heavy rains fell, they worked on repairing a ship Traven won in a gambling game of Liar's Life, a miracle Traven still couldn't explain. They'd found most of the parts from a local parts shop. Now only one piece remained to get the ship from flyable to space worthy. Traven promised they would buy the part today, but they stopped by the bar and any chance of finishing it today was unlikely.

"You trust me, right?" Traven asked.

The question raised the hair on Kaytrix's neck. "Depends." He arched his eyebrow and took a swing.

He'd known Traven for half a solar rotation, but that didn't mean he trusted him. After all, Traven only kept him alive until the bounty hunter returned, if she ever would. If that didn't speak about Traven's true character, nothing else did.

Traven slammed his drink down and let out a guffaw that put the late afternoon gathering of rowdy drinkers to shame.

Kaytrix ground his teeth. *Not so loud.* Traven lost all sense of self-preservation when he was drunk, the caution he displayed the first day they met, replaced by a boisterous man.

"You're funny," Traven went on.

"You're drunk. It's time to leave. People are noticing us."

Traven cleared his throat and leaned back against the worn padded bench to stretch. "Yeah, you're right. Let's head back."

Kaytrix waited for Traven to rise first. A quick glance around reassured no one paid attention to their movements.

Traven rose and stumbled into another customer.

"Watch it," the gruff alien spat.

"Pardon me," Traven said, his words slurred.

Kaytrix rushed to save Traven from a potential fight as the alien glared at them. Traven lost his balance multiple times before they made it outside, almost falling into other grouchy customers.

The cool evening air struck Kaytrix with a fierceness, bringing back memories of the dark planet he awoke on.

Traven let out a sigh. "I guess we will have to get that part tomorrow."

Kaytrix scoffed, forgetting the memory. "What? We can't risk someone else taking it from the dealer first. I'll get it. You go home without me."

Traven exhaled through his nose. "You are right, but you shouldn't go alone. It's too risky."

"The merchant has seen us there together multiple times. I am sure it will be fine."

Traven paused, eyeing him. "Do you still have the blaster I gave you?"

"Of course. I always keep it on me, just like you said."

Traven shook his head and wiped a grimy hand underneath each of his eyes. "I'll come with you just to be safe."

"Alright, then we better go before the sun gets any lower."

The trip to the opposite side of town was uneventful. Kaytrix learned the best part about Rehnna was the simple life, but he couldn't stay here. Since arriving, he'd grown comfortable as Cade, but the bounty hunter hadn't been back like she promised, which worried him.

He'd waited long enough for answers, answers he needed now more than ever. Who put him in a hyperbaric chamber? Why? And what did the markings on his skin signify? If he was going to discover his identity, it required leaving Rehnna. Traven always resisted the notion, keeping the ship's flying key safe. Whoever the bounty hunter was, her promise to find Traven's son was strong.

They entered the small doorless shop, the dusty building barren of the usual customer buzz. Kaytrix strode to the shelf where the part always sat, his boots scuffing the dirt floor with a familiarity he was used to. As he neared the shelf, a sinking feeling settled into his bones. The part they needed was nowhere in sight.

"You're too late," a heavy gurgling voice said from behind him. "I have added it to the auction tomorrow."

Kaytrix closed his eyes and made a fist at his side. Sure, they were late. Traven warned him of this merchant's dealings. Yont was the reason people found themselves stranded here. Once he learned you needed a part, he'd double the price or put it up for auction. No one could afford the ridiculous prices or to get caught up in a bidding war. These people were commoners, not crooks.

It never occurred to him it would happen to them. He exhaled. He wouldn't let it happen. He turned on his heel for the sales counter when Traven caught him by the shoulder.

"Let me handle this," Traven warned in a low voice.

Kaytrix ground his teeth and relaxed his fist. Something about Traven's calm voice reassured him.

"Now look here, Yont," Traven said. He stalked towards the counter and slammed a fist on the counter. "You were supposed to hold that part for me. Either you sell the part to me at a fair price, or I will take my money elsewhere."

Yont's disgusting yellow eyes floated up and down his face before bursting into laughter. "There's no other scrapyard within seven rotations walk from here!" Yont exclaimed in a gross laugh. "I'm afraid you'll have to pay full price."

Something in Kaytrix snapped, his patience worn raw from the day of heat and now the irksome voice of Yont. Kaytrix reached past Traven and across the counter to snatch a handful of Yont's oil-spilled shirt. He jerked him forward. This was the last time the merchant would ever cheat someone again.

"Cade!" Traven scolded.

"Unhand me!" Yont demanded. "My shop doesn't deal with your kind, *castoff*. If you don't release me, I'll make sure the only way you are leaving Rehnna is in the clutches of the Nevo!"

Kaytrix tightened his grip on the merchant's shirt. Yont's words hung in the air like a foul smell. "For starters, the Nevo don't scare me—"

"Cade!"

"Second, the last bit of restraint to not punch your ugly face just walked out the door! Now get me that part," he said, jerking the merchant forward, "before you lose more than just a few measly pieces off your overpriced item."

Kaytrix didn't have the patience or desire to waste his energy dealing with this disgrace of a life-form. He would not leave to earn more pieces just to satisfy this cut-throat's prices.

Yont hesitated, his wild yellow eyes bulging in fear. He glanced at Traven as if begging for him to do something.

Kaytrix's temperature rose with his growing frustration, and he twisted the merchant's shirt tighter.

Yont's gaze fell, his wide, fear-stricken eyes transforming into something dangerous: greed. A revolting chuckle left Yont's greasy throat, filling the air with a horrid stench.

"What's so funny?" Kaytrix demanded. He followed Yont's gaze. The sleeve protecting his markings had fallen towards his elbow to expose them. His stomach knotted.

"Well, well, well," Yont spat with disdain. "It is my lucky day. Appears you will leave in the clutches of the Nevo after all!" Yont laughed. "They've got bounty hunters looking for you. Big reward too," he snarled.

Kaytrix stared at the merchant as his fat face bounced with revolting laughter. He hated watching the fat slug laugh about his demise and the benefits of it.

He snapped.

With a swift motion, he lifted his left fist and drove a punch into Yont's face. The merchant flew backwards, slamming into a display shelf before slumping to the floor. Parts and glass tinkled and banged, leaving everything in a disheveled pile.

"Cade!" Traven grabbed him by the shoulder and turned him around. "Do you know what you've done?" Traven's wild eyes scaled him in disbelief.

Kaytrix pulled away and rolled his sleeve down. "You heard him, Traven. I can't stay here and now I must leave. The Nevo have a bounty on me. I can't stay here to find out why."

The merchant lay still, blood oozing from his wide mouth. Kaytrix surveyed his surroundings, but no one noticed his violent disagreement with the merchant. He swiped the hyperdrive power core fuse from the case and placed it in his satchel.

Traven grabbed his graying head of hair. "What's your plan?"

Kaytrix grimaced. "I'll take the ship and leave this place."

"That's your plan, wisecrack? Even if the ship gets you into the atmosphere, there's nowhere to hide. The Nevo are everywhere!"

Kaytrix headed for the door. "I must leave now before they learn what's happened. Will you help me?"

It wrenched Kaytrix's heart, knowing what he did affected Traven. The look on Yont's face unsettled any sense of security he had. Time was of the essence. He needed to leave now.

A painful grumble left the merchant's body, interrupting his thoughts. Yont stirred, mumbling words under his breath. Glass tinkled to the floor as the alien tried to lift his massive body from its slumped position.

Traven pushed Kaytrix to move, and he quickened his stride to the exit. For the first time, he feared the unknown. People tried to use the Nevo as a scare tactic with dealings all the time, but it never worked on him. He never had a reason to let the name scare him until now. The once peaceful stroll through the small village overwhelmed him. Onlookers shot him suspicious glances as though someone painted his face with anxiety.

Kaytrix's hustled walk transformed into a panic run. Traven followed behind until they arrived at the tent. Clarr's shadow danced on the canvas as she prepared the evening meal. Kaytrix stalked past the house. There was no time to say goodbye to her.

He headed towards the ship and boarded. He knelt beside the open panel and dug into his bag to begin replacing the missing hyperdrive fuse with the new one. His hands shook as he tried placing the crystals in the correct activation sequence.

"How do you suppose you're going to outrun the Nevo?" Traven asked. He threw a bag of supplies at Kaytrix's feet and knelt to help with the last crystal.

Kaytrix stepped back, letting Traven secure everything in the circuit panel.

"I don't know. I'll wing it."

Traven stood and rushed to the cockpit. "You can't wing it. You won't last a minute against the Nevo fighters."

Traven pulled something from around his neck and placed it into the ship's ignition slot. The key. Traven entered coordinates into the navigations panel and switched on different systems.

"Alright. The computer will jump you to this planet once the hyperdrive has reached a full charge. You can't let the Nevo fighters follow you." Traven pulled on the dual control handles. "Don't forget these will guide your flight, but double as your defense system. Don't miss. Ever. If you're lucky enough to get a shot, you must be quick."

"What about you and Clarr? Yont won't be merciful when he makes his report."

Traven exited the cockpit and backed out of the ship. "You can't worry about us. You need to leave. Now!" Traven punched the lowered ramp switch and jumped off the ship before it closed.

"Traven!!" Kaytrix bolted to the closing door, but it had already sealed.

The ship came to life as he turned from the rear to face the glow of the cockpit. He rushed to the pilot's chair and sat down. Once strapped in, he pressed the ignition switch. The engines primed and ignited, whirring to life. A dust devil encapsulated the ship as it eased away from the desert. Kaytrix gripped the controls as the ship turned midway through the air and prepared to leave the planet.

The dash lit with vibrant hues of blue while other screens had accents of greens, oranges, and reds depicting malfunctioning areas of the ship. Most systems were in the orange. Except for the hyperdrive power core, which he replaced the fuse in. That system was green. His crude installation worked with the help of Traven.

Beep, beep.

On his radar, several contacts blipped to life. Information displayed on his HUD in a holo-screen, providing information about the vessels. They were Nevo.

"Should have finished that disgusting slug!" He cursed.

Traven warned the Nevo can track ships through hyperspace jumps. If he wanted a chance to survive, he must destroy them before making his jump. Or outrun them.

Gripping the controls tighter, he piloted the small vessel away from Traven's home, the settlement, and entered the atmosphere. Quicker than he expected, the Nevo fighters were within weapons range. The computer beeped, flashing red on his navigation display. They were targeting him.

Sweat ran down the side of his forehead when he took in a slow breath. A calmness filled him, and an unfamiliar feeling of focus zoned him in on his targets. A strange sensation overtook him as his hands glided to where they needed to be. The band of ships opened fire, spewing hot plasma of green energy at him.

He swayed his ship from side-to-side, avoiding most of their fire while pelting them with short, rapid bursts of his own. No matter his tactics, they outnumbered him. He couldn't hope to stay and fight.

The squad of Nevo fighters made their way around, firing as they flew past. One lucky shooter clipped his ship's left wing. The computer wailed a warning.

"Dammit," he said, avoiding the last Nevo ship.

"Hyperspace jump ready," spoke the computer as they left the planet and entered space.

Kaytrix punched the hyperspace activation button on his terminal. Black space gave way as a portal of purple and blue opened before him. The ship shot through the vortex of swirling stars, leaving the planet and the Nevo behind.

Hyperspace was beautiful, the colors relaxing—like looking at one's dream while you slept. Kaytrix sighed with relief, but guilt settled into his bones. The encounter with the merchant and the Nevo robbed him of this long sought-after moment. He wanted to leave Rehnna for a while now, but leaving Traven and Clarr in that mess was not his plan.

After a few breaths, he arrived at his destination. The ship came shuddering to a stop, shaking him. He grasped the controls, as if it would help keep the beast from falling apart. He surveyed the radar screen, scrutinizing, but nothing appeared.

"Computer, run a diagnostic of the ship. I need to know if I can land."

The ship clicked and beeped, signaling it completed the diagnostic. He pored over the displayed information. The left wing sustained damage and wouldn't survive another jump if left unrepaired. Re-entry would be a challenge, but he didn't have a choice. The wing needed to be fixed, and the only way to do that was to land.

Kaytrix guided the ship towards the planet. His primary concern was locating a spaceport to repair his ship. He wasn't sure what to expect, but he had to trust Traven. He had no other option.

After a moment, the computer offered several suggestions until he picked one. "Engaging thrusters," he uttered, switching some safety buttons off before activating the engines.

As he neared the planet, a weird feeling found its way under his skin. The oil-stained face of Yont and the words he sneered at him replayed in his mind. Kaytrix grit his teeth. He hated not knowing what his markings meant. The Nevo paid bounty hunters to return him, then he would make it his mission to know why. With his resolve hardened, he headed for the planet Tarwi.

Kaytrix squeezed the controls as he piloted the ship through the different layers of the planet's atmosphere. He anticipated re-entry to be challenging, but he hadn't expected it to be *this* difficult.

His ship complained, sounding off various alerts and sirens the moment he passed through the thermosphere, the broken wing the primary cause for concern. If it broke free, he would end up in a spin.

Even though this was exciting, Kaytrix couldn't remember if he ever crash-landed before. The lack of memory to call upon left a knot in his stomach.

BOOM!!

Sirens wailed. The left thruster exploded from the heat of re-entry and took with it the broken wing the Nevo weakened. The ship swirled into a spin as he passed through the atmosphere.

"Aaaaaaaaaaagggghhhhhhhh!!"

He fought against the ship as it spun out of control. The centrifugal force pried his fingers from the handles and shoved his body in every direction. The cockpit blurred. His sloshing brain and oncoming nausea consumed his focus.

The ship struck the ground with tremendous force, shoving him back into his seat. A moment of blackness faded as the flashing red of his ship's broken console stirred him. He stared at it for a second.

"Oh blasted!"

The ship was going to explode any second. Kaytrix scrambled to unbuckle his harness and clambered over the broken parts of his ship, searching for the bag Traven packed him. He didn't know how long he was unconscious, but he needed to leave the ship.

Kaytrix bolted for the escape hatch and fumbled with the door. He pulled the latch open and released the pin, but it wouldn't open.

The warnings continued screaming from the cockpit.

He kicked the door. "C'mon!" It thudded in resistance. "C'mon!" He kicked it once more. This time, it bent, opening enough for him to squeeze through.

He pushed through the narrow cavity, adrenaline surging. The beeping from the cockpit continued in a frenzy. He pulled himself out of the ship. Fiery sparks flew from broken connections in the ship's hull and an immense heat wafted from the engines through the chilly evening.

Kaytrix ran for the trees, navigating dirt mounds and the trail of steaming vegetation left in the wake of his crashed ship. He was at the treeline when a violent shockwave sent him sailing through the air . . .

Kaytrix opened his eyes to the glowing pink hue of breaking dawn. Dark silhouettes of plant life lingered above him, swaying in the breeze. He drew a hand across his face and stiffened. Everything hurt.

He sat up, groaning with pain, and checked his body. All his limbs remained intact, but his head hit the ground hard. A splitting headache throbbed through his skull like a beating drum.

"Well, that was a stellar way to land." He cursed himself, reaching for the nearest broken branch to aid his attempt to stand. It would take a while to recover from this crash-landing experience.

Kaytrix slung his bag over his shoulder. In the distance, the charred remains of the ship's carcass smoked. The one thing he'd worked hard to repair, to build his life anew, and he destroyed it. And here he was again. Stuck on a planet without a ship.

"Ugh!" He fumed, kicking a pile of dirt, and wringing his hands. He turned from the ship and groaned.

There should be a way to get off this planet. Traven wouldn't have picked it unless it promised him some sort of chance. Kaytrix tore through his bag and found a gauntlet. On the top, a device with a case opened. Several buttons glared at him; their dull surface hinted at a lack of power. He resisted the urge to throw it into the jungle and attached it to his forearm. With a few quick strokes, he found the power button and located a spaceport due south.

A small sense of hope replaced his doubt. This trek through the jungle would not be easy, and the hardest part was navigating the spaceport, knowing he was a target. He re-secured his firearm and stepped forward, leaving behind all he had known for the last half solar rotation.

Chapter 4

THE CREW

"Get to the ship!" Javex grit his teeth and fired another round of energy arrows.

"I would if they did not outnumber us, *Captain!*" Aaro hollered. His helmet muffled his voice, but his anger was unmistakable.

Javex crouched across the alley behind the remnants of a wall. Their pursuers boxed them in, a mistake he could have avoided had he listened to Aaro. Deep down, he rather enjoyed this brief confrontation.

"I guess I shouldn't have asked them about the Lost Race," he said, hiding a smile from Aaro.

"I guess not!" Aaro fired his dual pistols, striking two foes. He rested his helmet against the broken wall. "A pickup would be nice right about now."

"Guys, I am right above you. Move to the exit. I'll clear a path!" Seraphina's voice melded into the ship's engines, making it hard to hear.

A round of blasts tore up the ground in front of them, clearing their way. A dirt cloud of debris floated in the tight space when blue pivotal engines lit the settling dirt particles.

"Ah, there she is. What took her so long?!" Aaro said, amusement in his voice. He fired off a few more shots to cover their escape.

The *Dauntless* eased down above the open market, its engines stirring up loose dirt and sand. The dull gray hull bore thermal gouges from fire fights in the past, its blue striping worn from multiple asteroid run-ins and questionable re-entries. Despite what others may say, it would always remain beautiful to him.

Javex leapt onto the lowered ramp as the *Dauntless* eased back into the sky. He looked back. Aaro should be right behind him. Enemy weapon fire soared through the cloud and struck the ship.

"It's time to go!"

"Not without Aaro!"

Javex peered through the cloud when a cord shot through the air and into the hull. It anchored into the ship's frame and Aaro rappelled onto the ramp to stand beside him.

"She almost left me behind!" Aaro complained.

Javex smiled and opened the comms channel. "Maybe it's your charm. We're aboard, Seraphina. Take us out of here."

"Or lack thereof . . . Affirmative, Captain. Moving off to safe coordinates by the moon."

The ramp eased shut and Javex let out a breath. The altercation tired him, an unneeded reminder of his age.

Aaro removed his helmet and tussled the brown hair on his head. While his deep blue eyes shone bright, a well-known look surfaced: disappointment.

"I know what you are thinking," Javex began, placing his hand-crafted energy bow down and removing his bracer.

"Good. Then I don't have to say it," Aaro spat, his jaw tight.

How fleeting the humor of their escape was. The echoes of them exiting the planet's atmosphere yielded to a stillness in the ship's belly.

"It won't always be this way. We can't give up on finding the Archarians." Javex dusted the dirt from his spotted fur.

Aaro shook his head. "Captain, we've been at this for how long? Ten solar rotations? That's a long time to search for something we may never find."

"I know," Javex agreed as they headed for the bridge.

Out of anyone, he sacrificed the most time on this journey. He didn't need a reminder of how long it had been, or how long it could take him.

They arrived on the bridge with not another word said. Seraphina glanced their way from the pilot's chair. Her green eyes probed them, a look of frustration on her face.

"Well, what happened?" She rose from her seat in the pilot's chair and crossed her arms. Even with a thin physique and frail-looking shoulders, her sass made up for any shortcomings.

Aaro leaned against the frame of the lift's doorway, leaving Javex to deal with Seraphina's fiery temper all on his lonesome.

"Captain mentioned them *again*."

Seraphina glanced at their empty hands, then back at their faces. Her shiny auburn hair danced with the motion.

"He said it *before* they handed over the supplies?"

"Yup." Aaro gazed back at him knowingly.

"Enough." Javex growled in irritation. "I thought we could trust them. Especially after trading with them several times."

Seraphina huffed. "Javex, you know as soon as anyone so much as hears the Archarian name, we are as good as dead! The Nevo—"

"I know! But we're running out of time. I'm—" Javex sat in his chair abruptly and ran a hand over his face. The stars beyond the viewport of the *Dauntless* passed by, soothing his irritation, but not his growing weariness. He was tired. Tired of it all. The running, the secrets, his mission. "Well," he spoke finally, more gently, looking to Seraphina and then to Aaro. "We will just get supplies on the next planet. For now, get some rest. We still owe Atara and Noro a match of Colorz after supper."

Seraphina rolled her eyes but uncrossed her arms.

Aaro hung his head with a reluctant smile.

When he adopted Atara and Noro as a part of the crew, Seraphina and Aaro assumed the uncle and aunty role of the young one's lives. What they hadn't agreed to was everything that came with it, including keeping the young teens entertained.

"Better go brush up on my skills. It's not like I haven't played in a while," Seraphina said sarcastically.

Aaro perked up. "Mind if I join you?"

Seraphina shrugged. "I guess. What about you, Captain? Care to join us? I have the *Dauntless* programmed to orbit the dark side of the moon. We'll be safe there for the time being."

"Go on ahead. I have to fine tune some details for our next mission."

Aaro hesitated before he left the bridge with Seraphina. Of course, Aaro didn't believe him. The man was too smart for his own good.

Javex didn't know where to go from here. Leads were as scarce as trust. Seasons like this had come before, but this time was different. Lately, things went wrong more than right. In his desperation to show something for his effort through the solar rotations, he'd gotten sloppy. More than once, Aaro picked up the slack.

He found it hard to believe the last fifteen solar rotations of his life were not a waste. The time spent hoping and searching for something he was desperate to find: the Archarians, or remnants of them. If he found their abandoned technology, then maybe they'd stand a better chance of protecting themselves from the Nevo and liberating worlds.

Since the Last Stand, the Nevo's tyranny through the systems dwindled until the last half of the rotation. Without warning, the Nevo reinforced their control on claimed territories, monitoring bigger, more populated spaceports, and patrolling their borders. It restricted his ability to travel, trade, and threatened the safety of the crew. Anyone who wished to keep possession of their limbs, eyesight, and beating heart knew to never cross the Nevo. So he kept his head down and carried on with his mission without being noticed.

Though up to this point his travels were unsuccessful, he didn't waste his time. Captaining the *Dauntless* provided opportunities to offer certain individuals' sanctuary. People like his crew. Sparing them from slavery, bounty hunters, and far worse fates at the hands of the Nevo. But that was just it. Lately, his failures impacted his crew. The life he provided for them wasn't what they needed. It was full of danger and uncertainty.

They deserved more than to wander space searching for something that may only be myths and legends. They needed to make something of themselves, to have normal lives. Especially Noro and Atara.

Javex lifted his gaze to the stars again. It was *his* hope they chased. It was important to let the crew decide where they wanted to be. He stood from his chair and stretched, apprehension knotting his stomach. Could he share his feelings with the crew? He feared their decision. Over the solar rotations, he grew fond of them—even the troublemakers. The thought of saying goodbye . . .

The parting doors of the bridge whizzed open, and Seraphina walked in.

"Everything alright, Javex?" She didn't sound worried, but her question hinted otherwise. She joined him on the command deck. "I hailed your comm, but you didn't pick up."

"Deep in thought." He appreciated Seraphina's concern.

"Supper is waiting. And so is Colorz." She winked.

He chortled. "I was just on my way. Tell me what you did after we got back."

Seraphina smiled and told him about how she whipped Aaro in the first round of Colorz, the latest diagnostics she ran for the *Dauntless* and the outcomes of each. But as she talked, the information became lost in his muddled thoughts.

They rounded the bend in the faded and dirt-stained corridor. What was he was going to say? Hearing Seraphina share her day added to his anxiety. What if they all left him? He wrung his hands behind his back to avoid Seraphina's eyes. Did he have the strength to let them go?

The automatic doors whizzed apart to the dining hall, revealing his beloved crew, his family. The sounds of their laughter filled the small room with cheer.

"Captain," their voices rang in unison.

Noro rushed him, hugging his hips. His beady eyes gazed at him. "How was the planet? Aaro said you got shot at?"

Aaro turned away from Javex, hiding his guilt.

Atara hugged him from the other side. "Seraphina also mentioned we'll be having rations soon."

Seraphina shrugged, not afraid to meet his gaze.

Javex nodded. "Yes, this is also true. Now, enough about my day. What did you do?"

Noro and Atara left his side to sit at the table. They began talking, fighting for a chance to share their day, often interrupting the other. While their squabbles increased in sibling hostility, he reminisced about how he met them.

He adopted Noro and Atara as his own children eight rotations ago. Though they differed in race, they shared a bond not easily broken. Noro, a short brown Lanks from Lenamo, resembled a child but with fur and ears. His love for anything technological saved them on more than one occasion.

And his adopted sister Atara, a beautiful young spirit; humanoid but graced with cat-like ears, tawny skin, and blond and purple locks. All revered her skills in the kitchen, but her other passion guided her to healing as the med bay doctor.

Laughter split his focus for a second as Seraphina snorted. Aaro's disgruntled face and Noro's fit of laughter meant Seraphina revealed Aaro's shortcoming as a Coloz contender.

Seraphina covered her mouth now as she tried to hide her amusement. She came aboard twelve solar rotations ago after he'd saved her from a slavery of a more perverse type. Aaro joined them next. The rugged man had grown soft since the kids arrived.

A pang of pity washed through Javex. Once a decorated Shrovon general, Aaro lost everything when his own people betrayed him. Aaro's choice of mercy banished him from his planet, unable to return lest he face the death dual of his race. Now bounty hunters seek to bring him back to his planet's leaders to make an example of him.

The laughter subsided as the last member of his crew sauntered into the room, a Varanus named Grootie. A natural enemy of his species, Javex found it difficult to bring him aboard. Grootie joined them two solar rotations ago and, by far, was the most troubled individual. Having served at the right hand of a Nevo lord, he suffered withdrawals, cursed by their lust for power. The large lizard beast seeks seclusion nowadays, suffering from post-traumatic stress his servitude caused.

Their excitement for a new mission electrified the room. Many rotations passed since they received a tip preceded by endless waiting and restlessness. The hope they would press on glimmered in each of their eyes. Javex hesitated for a moment, wishing the moment of laughter would remain forever. He took in a deep, calming breath. The moment had come.

"I know you expect me to have new information, another mission planned, but that is not the case."

Noro and Atara stiffened while Aaro and Seraphina shifted in their seat.

"As you know," he continued, "I have searched many solar rotations for remnants of the Archarian's technology, hoping to fight against the Nevo." His brow furrowed as he fought the fear in his stomach. "This journey is getting more dangerous and because of that . . ." He paused, gathering his strength. "I want you to know you can leave the *Dauntless* if you so choose."

Atara and Noro shared a glance. Atara resisted the urge to cry, embracing her matured years with grace. Noro remained youthful at heart, even at fifteen. Tears brimmed his eyes.

"Captain," Aaro spoke, standing from his seat. "I don't think I could live with myself, leaving you alone in this aging ship. Who will help you repair the engine thrusters when they conk out again? I recall, it takes two men to lift one of those compartments to get at the circuits." His tone, while humorous, concealed his true feelings. Like the rest, Aaro had nowhere to go.

He smiled and placed a hand on Aaro's shoulder. "Thank you."

"Javex," Seraphina began, "I . . . I . . ." she stuttered. "Aaro is right. You need us."

Noro and Atara attacked him in another embrace. "My sister and I wouldn't dream of being anywhere else, Javex."

"This is our home," Atara said softly, grabbing Noro by the shoulder and bringing him close to her side.

Grootie remained unmoving. The Varanus never said much at the best of times.

"And you, Grootie?"

The Varanus lifted his piercing reptilian eyes to where he stood, meeting his gaze more intently. The fine blue tendrils atop his head swayed in a calm, rhythmic disarray. As he prepared to speak, his jaw slacked and the muscles in his neck deflated. His blue forked tongue slithered out to moisten his leathery-scaled lips before he spoke.

"Captain," Grootie spoke with reverence, his husky voice sending chills down his spine. "I wish to remain aboard the *Dauntless*."

Javex nodded, relieved, but also afraid. Aaro made an excellent point of them needing each other, but that didn't lessen the danger. The desire to persuade them to reconsider tightened his throat.

Able to read his emotions, Seraphina said, "Alright, that settles that. So, where are we off to next?"

He smiled at her. "Well, I think before we set out, we need to get more supplies and the next planet is Tarwi. Only a few rotations away."

Everyone grimaced. No one ever daydreamed of the bland taste of rations. There would be rations until they bought or traded for actual food.

Aaro said, "Tarwi? Good call, Captain. Nevo presence there is minimal, so we shouldn't have a problem with check stops." Aaro glanced at Grootie.

The Varanus provided brawn to their mission, but the Nevo shrouded Grootie's history. It was rare for the Varanus to leave the ship if ever. This pained Javex the most, but Grootie made no show of desiring anything more.

"Very well, we will set a course for Tarwi, but first," he paused, "We have something else to resolve."

The crew studied him. Worry filled the creases of their brows.

"We have to determine the new champion of Colorz."

Aaro and Seraphina's gaze fell while Atara clapped her hands and cheered. Noro pumped a fist. Noro appeared to be the only one eager for a rematch. After all, he was the best at the game.

"I will plot a course to Tarwi," Seraphina said when with a teasing but serious glance she declared, "Then I am going to kick all your asses."

"You wish!" Noro yowled as he dealt the cards.

With fondness, Javex observed his family gathering for supper and the upcoming game. Even Grootie, who played to lose, watched as Atara passed the food around. Noro dealt the cards and readied his hand.

Soon, the fear turned into joy as the evening carried on. He only hoped it would not haunt his heart in the future.

Chapter 5

TARWI

Javex tensed as the *Dauntless* dropped out of hyperspace. Before him, the planet Tarwi spun perfect in its orbit, its face beautiful compared to the sea of ships and satellites sprawled around her. One in particular made his hackles stand on end. A Nevo patrol ship.

"So much for not running into them," he said.

"They appear to be searching the larger passenger ships, sir," Aaro muttered from across the bridge.

Seraphina toggled a few switches. "Selecting a less populated spaceport, Captain?"

She turned in her chair to look at him when he didn't answer. The dark bridge of the *Dauntless* compared to the bright planet made reading her facial expressions difficult.

"Yes, someplace less populated. I'd rather not draw attention. We buy what we need and leave. No distractions."

Seraphina curled a strand of hair behind her ear. "Understood."

Aaro cleared his throat from his station on the bridge, a subtle hint not to mention the Archarians again.

Javex grimaced. He did not need the reminder.

Aaro smiled. "What's our landing party look like, Captain?"

Javex considered it for a moment. "You and I will travel to the planet's surface and locate a weapons dealer. After, let's stop someplace and find out why the Nevo are here. Seraphina, Atara, and Noro are to get food supplies upon our return."

Grootie stood at the far corner of the bridge, present yet keeping himself distant from them. It's not that he didn't allow Grootie on missions, but his presence complicated their efficiency to disappear in crowds. It was also a struggle to trust Grootie enough to leave him unattended on the ship.

The *Dauntless* glided through the atmosphere and across the planet's surface. Tarwi was a planet well-known for trade and spaceports, allowing ships to come and go with resources to trade. Horizontal docking structures, transportation tubes to farther spaceports, and, of course, the commotion of civilization's daily travel riddled the entire surface.

No matter how civilized and overgrown with metal structures, Tarwi's wild nature still emerged throughout the city. Whether it be vines scaling structures, the vicious birds of prey, or the dirt of the ground, nature persevered.

The *Dauntless* slowed as it approached a docking port, a tall structure riddled with private hexagon ports that allowed multiple ships to land, creating a hive of vessels. Thanks to Seraphina's skills as a pilot, the ship settled into a smooth landing. A whine reverberated through the hull as the engines powered down.

"Alright, Aaro," Javex began, standing from his seat. "Let's go."

"Just need to grab my helmet." Aaro smiled and disappeared through the bridge doors.

Javex winked at Seraphina. "We won't be long. Stay out of trouble."

Seraphina rolled her eyes.

Javex entered the aging cargo bay where Aaro geared up. He only needed two pieces of equipment: his bracer, and energy longbow. He tightened his grip around the weapon as he admired the darker knots of wood surrounded by a lighter grain. Enhanced with technology, it brought his arrows to life with deadly energy. He slung it onto his back before too many memories surfaced. He didn't have time to deal with them now, not when a Nevo ship orbited the planet.

Aaro stood by the ramp, his blue-visored helmet already obscuring his face. Javex sensed Aaro's eyes observing him.

"Remember," Aaro warned.

Javex bent his ears back, irritated at Aaro's tone. "I know." He growled, exposing teeth. "I won't mention anything to anyone. Not about to eat rations again."

Aaro punched the lever and waited for the ramp to lower, no doubt smiling behind his helmet. While Aaro's good mood was a blessing, the constant reminders were unnecessary.

The ramp lowered to the landing pad and a wave of heat infiltrated the ship, striking them with intensity. Hotter than any other planet they'd visited, Javex braved a step onto the platform, careful not to sear his padded toes. To his surprise, it was tolerable.

Before them, a thick metal sliding door with locking arms waited. A payment consul ensured the use of the dock with no way to leave the hexagon unless they paid. Javex slid a few pieces into the consul, it beeped a cheery tone and the light above the door beamed white.

They passed through the doors and into the inner workings of the spaceport. Cool air ruffled through Javex's fur, but what they needed was on the planet's surface. No one within this structure would be crazy enough to sell weapons or talk about the Nevo.

Aaro approached a map near the center of the room, where it indicated their location.

"Here, Captain. We need to take the central elevator to the first floor." Aaro pointed. "Then we should be able to find an exit to the planet's surface."

They made their way through the crowds, avoiding Nevo patrols and busier markets. Aaro focused on the crowd, leading them through the throng of species. The capabilities his helmet possessed surpassed Javex's feline abilities, allowing them to avoid potential threats.

Among the crowds were the popular humanoids. Some harder to distinguish than others unless they carried specific markings or armor. Many of the species varied in color and sizes, heads and limbs different and unproportioned. And then some's beauty stopped hearts.

All professions mingled here from mechanics looking for work, pirates seeking ships, to the stealthy bounty hunters who blended into crowds or waited in the shadows. Never did Javex see another of his kind, a Zaguarz.

They reached the main exit and passed through the gates without being stopped. The cool air disappeared, replaced by a heat cooler than the landing pad, but not by much. The shock resulted in the unpleasantness of sweat, and the bustling crowd reeked of it.

"This planet is just full of surprises, aye?" Aaro asked sarcastically through his helmet.

A pair of unpleasant looking creatures walked by. The heat made their stench intoxicating.

Javex crinkled his nose. He detected the faintest of scents, and this place bombarded his senses.

"Harrumph. At least you have a filter."

"It doesn't do much, Captain. Trust me."

The crowded spaceport pressed in from all sides. So much for a "less" populated area. From a spacious ship to a bustling little spaceport, Javex's growing need to escape from the overwhelming group of strangers intensified. Yet, he composed himself and focused on his surroundings.

Loud chatter came from the markets. Sleight-of-hand exchanges transpired in the shady alleyways. Whispers flitted to his ears, stealing his gaze to those sharing the secrets of others.

"Finally!" Aaro cheered under his breath, distracting Javex's focus. The shorter man passed him with a quick stride.

Javex grimaced, understanding where Aaro headed. Before them stood a short building with a craggy roof. A drink promotion written in several languages blinked out front of its sliding metal doors that were patched with mix-matched pieces of metal. Of course, Aaro would want to stop here. Several aliens of different races exited the tavern entrance and fell into the gritty soil, their laughter hysterical. Javex grimaced. Not the best place to start, but anything beat the heat. He stepped around the drunks struggling to stand to follow Aaro.

The tavern smelt of rich smoke and strong drinks, pleasant compared to what the outside offered. Those within the pub busied themselves with drink and cheer, oblivious to their entrance. Aaro left his helmet on for privacy but allowed the mouthpiece to retract. He strode into the busy room, more at home here than he would ever let on.

"Where would you like to start?" he asked.

Javex examined the dim room. "How about with a drink? I need something to wash away the filth."

Aaro smiled and headed to the bar while he located a pair of seats nearer the far wall. At least this spot would allow him to observe the room better. Aaro soon joined him, placing two large vessels of drinks on the table.

Javex rose an eyebrow, wishing to see more of Aaro's face than just his foam-covered facial hair. The greedy man couldn't even wait to get to the table before taking a swig.

"How many pieces did this cost?"

Aaro slid him a drink. "It's the special. So not a lot."

Javex sipped his beverage for a few moments, trying to keep his large canines from clinking the glass.

"Need a straw?" Aaro chuckled.

"Perhaps you need one." Javex pointed to his facial hair.

Aaro dabbed his gloved hand to his face and scanned the room with him.

The tavern's atmosphere was peaceful in its chaos of bodies. Despite the busy atmosphere, the stout bartender was relaxed, as were the bouncers near the entrance.

Javex let his sensitive ears go to work, homing in on any mention of violence in the area. Not a lot was being said. If anyone knew something, it was the bartender, having the grisly privilege of witnessing the daily drama. Javex studied the short man who constantly wiped the sweat from his brow. Trust to share information needed to be earned, or bought, but he didn't have pieces to waste.

Javex continued to watch and listen to the relaxed room. Aaro, however, sat rigid, his shoulders back, his arms crossed now that the joy of his beverage was gone. Lately, Aaro's outlook was less jovial. Was the ex-soldier deep in thought? Aaro's behavior did not concern him, given the history of the helmeted man. Perhaps being in the presence of so many hostile people made him nervous? He couldn't tell.

Javex recalled the day he met Aaro on Acknaria. He was busy in a conversation with another, explaining his desire to locate the Archarians' technology. Disinterested, the other person left the table when Aaro slid into the seat, expressing a curiosity for the mission.

Aaro later shared his story of how he'd been a man of power on his planet, and then the punishment he incurred by standing against the influence of the Nevo. His rulers stripped him of his rank and banished him from Shrovon, his home world, warning him to never return or face execution. After receiving this judgment, an old friend warned Aaro about the public execution the Nevo desired; that the leaders of Shrovon placed a bounty on him for his retrieval. From that day forward, Aaro ran.

Javex took a drink as he reminisced about ten solar rotations prior. Then again, he may be mistaken about Aaro's rigidness. The female at the bar was quite attractive. Aaro's gaze in that direction hadn't moved for a while, as if he were watching her.

"Time to go?" he teased, watching Aaro's rigid body relax as he readily turned his helmeted face to look at him. It unnerved him not being able to read Aaro's eyes. With no eyes to gaze into, how might he detect what Aaro thought?

"We just got here," Aaro answered, a hint of a smile in his voice. "But I also wouldn't want to stick around and get into any trouble."

Javex let out a growling chuckle. Aaro would have winked at him if his helmet were off.

"There's not much being said. We are clear to proceed with the rest of our plans." He took another swig and placed his mug down.

As they exited the pub, Javex made eye contact with the bartender and nodded. A slight gesture to let him know that the drink was satisfying. The bartender grimaced, pleased enough, but didn't keep eye contact for long. He wiped his brow and poured another slew of drinks. Plenty of customers required his constant attention.

"We're coming back tomorrow, aren't we?" Aaro guessed, as they exited through the tavern's doors.

"Yes," he said. "Maybe I'll bring Seraphina."

"Yeah, she needs to get out more." Aaro grumbled.

Javex observed the shorter man beside him, detecting bitterness.

"You must let go of what you cannot control. Some things take time," he said.

They were outside now in the blistering sun. In places like these, the dealings always took place in the back alleys or in the darker, dirtier parts of the city.

Aaro rounded his shoulders and cracked his neck. "It's complicated and, to be honest, frustrating. Just as we get close, she withdraws again. Is she afraid I'll hurt her? You know how I feel about her, Captain. I'd do anything for her."

Javex weighed his words. "Seraphina is lovely, but given her past, she is also a sensitive creature. She's like the sun. Brilliant and warm, but get too close too soon, and you will burn to a crisp."

They entered a darker alley filled with trash.

"That's an accurate analogy." Aaro paused beside him, observing the alley. A few potential sellers stood further ahead, eyeing them up and down. Their quick glances evaluated whether they were buyers or the local authority.

Javex pointed his ears forward and tapped his right thigh, communicating his interest in buying ammunition and weapons.

"Aaro, if you wish to get close with Seraphina, you must realize not all flowers come without thorns."

When Seraphina gushed her feelings for Aaro, he was happy, but since then, it'd been a rollercoaster of emotions for her. He hadn't forgotten where he found Seraphina—being sold from one master to another, surviving the cruelest of circumstances. It made sense why she would be hesitant about accepting Aaro after being abused, but even he was tiring of the drama.

"Captain, respectfully, I don't need the *talk*," Aaro bristled. "I've dealt with several women in my time, but I can't seem to get past her shields. Will you speak to her for me?"

Javex flattened his ears. The last thing he wanted was to get involved.

"I can assure you nothing I say will help her ease out of her trauma that quickly."

The weapons dealers approached them from the shadows.

"I know. It's just she needs to be cared for the way she deserves—"

"In the way she *needs*," Javex corrected in a whisper. "And for her, what she needs may be more patience from you."

Aaro didn't respond and instead approached the waiting man in the alley, who kept to the shadows. The air here was thick with heat and strong with decay, the buildings worn from sandstorms and gouged with weapons fire from deals gone wrong. While Aaro talked, other figures appeared down the street as shadows. Javex allowed himself to relax when they remained distant. No doubt they were the seller's backup.

Aaro returned to his side. "They have what we need and will bring it by the ship once the sun sets, but they demand half the payment now."

Javex knit his brows. "They get a third of the payment now and the rest upon completion."

Aaro stalked over to the man and relayed the information. The seller remained silent and glanced at his counterparts for guidance. When they nodded, the dealer stuck out his skinny wrist to receive payment on his transaction device.

Pain shot through Javex's heart. The man was no older than Atara.

"We're at platform Z4387," Aaro said, his voice faint. "You have until sunup to deliver the goods. Then we will rescind the payment."

With the deal concluded, the seller nodded and disappeared into the shadows with his companions. Aaro waited a moment before turning his back on the barren alleyway.

"No life for a kid," Aaro muttered once by Javex's side.

They headed back to the ship without another word. If Aaro took offense to his guidance, he didn't say. In the end, Aaro would decide. The only thing he didn't need was unrest and friction between Aaro and Seraphina.

The suns were close to setting by the time they returned to the *Dauntless*. According to the update on Aaro's transaction, the delivery of their ammunition would arrive soon. The two of them stood at the edge of the landing pad, overlooking the growing lights of the city while they waited. A sultry breeze carried the smell of stale ship exhaust, but the view was peaceful. The multiple sunsets with their layers upon layers of color, unlike anything Javex witnessed.

They continued to stand in silence. As the darkness of night grew, the colors of the last ray of sun intensified and melted below the horizon. A blanket of stars twinkled above them now.

"Captain, look," Aaro said, pointing.

A bright light entered the atmosphere and blazed across the sky. The magnification on Aaro's helmet zoomed in on the object.

"It's hard to really distinguish what it is, Captain, but given the debris flying off, I'd bet anything it's a ship."

"Shot down?" If the Nevo were shooting down ships, they best leave before the planet entered a lock down.

Seeming to detect his worry, Aaro said, "Possibly, or engine failure. I didn't see any pursuing craft. Should we check for survivors?"

Javex hesitated. "Let's finish our deal and carry on with tomorrow as planned. We should leave as soon as possible." They all itched for some adventure beyond the life of the *Dauntless*, but they couldn't afford complications.

"Aye, Captain." Aaro exhaled and crossed his arms. His gaze focused on where the ship crash-landed in the hillside, its impact near to the small city they'd visited today.

A pair of bright lights appeared above the edge of the landing pad as a small rectangular ship landed. The thin dealer in his tattered robes exited the side panel of the vessel with another figure, lugging a large container between them.

Javex remained where he stood, observing the crash site. The air grew still as Aaro double-checked their purchase before concluding the deal with the rest of the pay. The young men returned to their small ship and disappeared over the platform and into the city.

Javex kept his gaze fixed on the spiraling smoke among the hillsides, content to listen to the crew.

Seraphina descended the ramp with Grootie, her light footfalls approaching from behind. Aaro exchanged a few words with her before lugging the ammunition cart onto the ship with Grootie.

"How was the trip? Productive, I see," Seraphina said as she stood beside him.

Javex turned his back on the star-filled sky. "Yes. Eventful, but plans have changed."

Seraphina glanced at him, then spotted the smoke over his shoulder. A light breeze tussled her auburn hair and streaked it across her face. Her green eyes met his gaze as she waited.

"You and I will go for supplies tomorrow and let Atara and Noro remain aboard with Aaro. A ship crashed, and I don't know if the Nevo are responsible. I'd rather take you with me than have the younger ones go."

"Understood, Javex. Rations again tonight." She crinkled her nose and smiled.

He smiled but cringed on the inside. "Yes, again. Sorry."

Seraphina turned with him as they headed towards the ship. "Is Aaro okay?" she asked suddenly.

Javex's ears bent backwards. *Oh, no. Here we go.* "As far as I can tell. I can't read him when he wears his helmet. Why?"

"He tried telling me a joke." She looked up at him as they walked. "It wasn't funny," she admitted.

Javex nodded. "He must have heard it in town."

"Probably did, because I have never heard such a terrible joke." She snorted.

He smiled as they boarded the *Dauntless*, relieved. "What was the joke?"

Seraphina turned to face him, her eyes narrowing with seriousness. "What does a six-legged insectoid have in common with the sun?"

"What?" he asked, feeling as though this may somehow relate to their day.

Seraphina punched the button to the ramp and stared Javex straight in the eyes. "They both emit methane gas."

Javex resisted the urge welling up in his throat to laugh.

Seraphina stared him down. "It's not funny," she declared, crossing her arms. But deep down, he thought it was.

Chapter 6

GOLDEN EYES

Kaytrix reached the southern spaceport of Tarwi with a dry mouth and aching limbs. He welcomed the noise of the spaceport, but being wanted by the Nevo deepened the fear in his stomach. He analyzed everyone who walked by with a suspicious eye.

His first line of business was getting a damn drink. Of course, he'd forgotten to grab his cantina before the ship blew up, and not a single damn drop of water on the walk in. If he didn't know better, he'd swear his tongue turned into a stiff sponge.

He made his way through the swell of varying races and kept his head low. A quick burst of wind drove the heat through the crowded street. Much to his relief, a busy tavern waited up ahead. He hesitated only for a second, keeping his hand on his hidden sidearm. Grab a drink and go. The plan was simple enough. Then he'd need to find or steal a ship, whichever came easiest. Or gamble for one. Shouldn't be that hard.

He entered the tavern, and a strong smoke struck him. Everyone in the hazy room kept their eyes on their drinks, the buzz of their voices steady. One pair of eyes, however, stuck out from the crowd, their golden color locked on him.

He looked away. Heat coursed through his body, bubbling in his chest. He shoved it down and took a seat at the bar to monitor the feline, determined to quench his thirst before an altercation broke out. Their connection only lasted a second anyway, but one of the creature's ears remained pointed in his direction.

Kaytrix let his thoughts fade, but the sense of his surroundings peaked. The tavern was full of all kinds of faces. One caught his attention. A young female humanoid sat across the room having a discussion with a few gnarly fellows. They appeared to be of the scavenging-type. What was she looking for?

"I assume you're here to drink?" asked a gruff voice from behind the bar.

Kaytrix pretended to glance at a menu. "Yes, of course. I'll have your special," he said, having just overheard one of the other customers exclaim how amazing it was.

"You're not from around here, huh?" the bartender asked, raising an eyebrow as he poured a drink.

It was impossible to fool this bartender, but the conversation wasn't finished.

"Most people in a spaceport aren't." He raised his glass to toast the bartender.

The stout man paid little attention to his reply, already busy with another customer.

Kaytrix sipped his drink, trying to look content, and observed the room. Gambling groups hung out in the back, their roar of winning the cause of most of the noise. He focused on the woman again. She was beautiful, fine-boned. Fierce looking. Whatever her race, with the pointed ears and auburn hair, a look from her green eyes stopped his heart.

"You should clean up," the same gruff voice said again.

Kaytrix resumed his gaze on the bartender. *Ah, so he was paying attention.* He rubbed a hand across his face and cursed himself for not thinking to wipe his blood from his cut brow.

"Thanks." He grunted. "Guess the other guy got me better than I got him."

The same look in Yont's eyes flashed in the bartenders.

Kaytrix ground his teeth and swallowed the last of his drink. Time to go. He stood to leave when the same pair of brutes heckling the woman sat down on either side of him.

"Hey there, stranger," one breathed gruffly, shoving him down. He stunk of liquor and held a knife casually in his hand.

The other thumped his glass on the bar. Half of his face appeared scarred with revolting bulges carelessly sewn together.

"Another one!" he barked at the bartender before he turned to grin at Kaytrix. "After today, I'm going to be rich!"

Kaytrix held his breath, his hands beginning to numb. How was he going to get out of this? He wasn't a trained fighter. Sure, he can punch, but brawl?

The bartender slid the drink to the scarred man. "Ozhin, leave the mess for outside." The bartender glanced to Kaytrix, then to the other with the knife. "You too, Gluviz. We need to be discreet." He winked and turned his back to them, serving other customers.

Kaytrix glanced around the bar for a way out. Only then did he notice the woman leaving, stooping to exchange a quick word with the golden-eyed creature whose eyes locked on him.

"Okay," Ozhin murmured, grabbing a hold of his arm. "Time to cash in your bounty."

"Yeah," Gluviz said, raising his blade. "Let's step outside. No mess inside the boss's bar."

Kaytrix stiffened in his seat, tightening his fists. He wasn't letting these castoffs boss him around, not so soon in the game.

"Let's go," Ozhin said, his breath flying into Kaytrix's face.

Gluviz pressed the knife to his throat.

That was it.

In an out-of-body experience, Kaytrix brought his right arm up and pushed the blade away from his throat. He crashed his elbow into Gluviz's face and dodged a punch from Ozhin, then kicked the stool out from under him. Ozhin scrambled to stand, his face red.

"Why you—"

Kaytrix grabbed the drink from the bar and threw it in Ozhin's face, then kicked him in the stomach. Ozhin crumpled to the floor, his heavy frame dragging him down. Sensing someone behind, Kaytrix chafed to the left, just missing the thrust of Gluviz's blade. He grabbed Gluviz's wrist and twisted. The bones cracked, and the blade dropped to the wooden floor. Gluviz wailed, cradling his wrist, and ran from the bar.

Kaytrix stood for a second as the crowd gaped at him. He turned to the bartender while adjusting his cloak. "That wasn't necessary."

"H-h-here, have another. On the house." The bartender poured another drink and set it down. Beads of sweat dripped down the side of his ghostly face.

Kaytrix eyed him, wary. The bar grew loud again as drunks continued to drink and continued their gambling games. He grabbed the drink and slammed it back. Just as he placed down the mug, a furred hand placed another beside it.

"Mind if I buy you another drink, stranger?" someone asked in a low, calm voice.

Kaytrix turned to see the golden-eyed creature grabbing a stool to sit. Depths of gold surrounded purple and blue iridescent patches, creating a distinct pattern on his body. A tail followed behind him with spots and thick markings. Large paws with retractable claws supported his weight as he sat down. Through the feline's fur, the sinews of muscles stretched across his frame.

"Thanks, but I was just leaving," Kaytrix replied, his tone harsh. He cursed Traven. This place was nothing but a hub for trouble. He needed to leave, ship or no ship.

The individual stared at his cup. "Well, all right. Where are you heading from here?" His ears perked forward.

Kaytrix wasn't in the mood for small talk, yet nothing about this creature's body language and tone suggested he was a threat. Still, he could not trust him.

The creature said, "You look to have been in a crash."

"You should mind your own business."

"Perhaps, but I think we have more in common than you think, stranger. That was your ship that crashed last night near the mountains. I reckon you will need a new one. If you know where you are going?"

The creature's golden eyes pierced his soul. Kaytrix froze, numbed by their presence. Or was it a predatory tactic? He lightened his tone. He didn't need to get tangled in a brawl with a six-foot something feline.

"If you could point me toward the nearest shipyard, I would be grateful, mister?" he said, trying to divert this stranger's interest.

"The name is Javex. And you are?" he asked casually.

"K—," he hesitated. "Cade."

Javex's eyes darted from him to the entrance of the bar. The tension in Javex's slim form amplified—the fur atop his head and neck raised. He glanced over his shoulder and a deadening chill traveled his spine.

Three Nevo soldiers entered the tavern. One would have been enough, but three? The Nevo stalked through the entrance and the buzz of the room resumed. The Nevo were only on patrol, something the citizens were used to.

Kaytrix threw his hood over his head. "Shit, shit, shit," he fumed. He eyed the nearest exit, but too many people crowded the area. Behind the bar, he spotted a delivery service door. Not the best option.

"They are here for you, aren't they?" Javex asked, his face close.

"Shut up!" Kaytrix hissed, using the reflection of a bottle to watch the Nevo. He focused, hearing the sick clicks come from their bodies of bio-mechanic armor.

With raspy breathing, they heaved their unnatural bodies through the crowd. The heavy clunk of their feet across the old floor roused disturbing images. How did they discover he was here? Once they were far enough from the entrance, he would try to slip out.

A hand clasped Kaytrix's shoulder, and he jumped.

"Come with me," Javex whispered to him as he placed the payment for their drinks on the counter.

"I don't even know you."

Javex ignored his words and, instead, grabbed his arm to guide him out of the tavern. He then mumbled something into a device on his wrist.

"Wait a damn minute," Kaytrix demanded in a hushed tone, suspicious of Javex's intentions. "I said I didn't want to go with you!"

Javex didn't respond.

Kaytrix escaped Javex's loose hold and drew his weapon, his back to the tavern. They stood among the bustling street of travelers. A gentle rain fell, dampening the ground and dripping off building awnings. Exhaust from machines swirled around them as they analyzed each other.

"What do you want?" Kaytrix demanded.

Strangers rushed by in search of shelter as the rain fell heavier.

"Nothing. I am merely trying to leave." Javex growled, forcing his voice over the growing roar of rain. He drew his own weapon, a beautiful wispy bow carved with precious wood and intricate mechanisms. "But you don't have long to decide," he said. Javex drew the bow to its full capacity and took aim.

"What makes you think I need your help?" Kaytrix stood, unwavering. Javex wasn't making a compelling case while aiming at him.

A green blast from the tavern whizzed past his head and towards Javex. The shot missed by a margin, igniting a barrel of fuel. Javex ducked into a roll, recovered, and knelt to fire his bow.

Another set of green blasts tore from the tavern, vaporizing the rain on contact, and pelting holes through the buildings along the street. Kaytrix turned to kneel beside Javex and fired off a round. What was he getting himself into now? A shootout was the opposite of stealth!

Javex fetched another arrow from his quiver and drew his bow. The muscles in his arms accepted the burden with grace. Javex released the string. The arrow disappeared into the tavern's darkness and a rolling black cloud drifted out of the entrance. A blue hue pulsed over a green sparking field. It popped and cracked as the energy resisted each other.

"Get to the alley behind me!" Javex ordered, his voice stressed.

Kaytrix caught his breath as a Nevo exited the tavern. It removed the arrow from its arm with a swift yank and tossed it to the ground. A low hiss seethed from its grated mouth, its eyes flashing with revenge.

He froze when Javex grabbed a hold of his cloak and launched him into the alleyway. Kaytrix landed on his knees, thankful for the soft soil. Several rapid succession shots struck the building and split the wooden market stands. He ducked, then aimed his weapon.

Blue energy ripped from his gun, but he missed. The shots struck the tavern, colliding with several victims. A lump caught in his throat. He didn't intend to kill anyone. More men rushed from the tavern to fire at him. A blast struck his shoulder, hurling him backwards into the dirt. His guilt disappeared.

"Scoundrels!" he cursed and rose to attack.

The three Nevo stalked across the clearing, stepping over bodies. Their black skeletal carapace shone in the rain as their machined parts whirred and clicked together.

Kaytrix furrowed his brow in concentration and fired another round at them, but the blasts rolled off the Nevo's shields. He peered over the crates to where Javex hid. How were his shots getting through but not his?

"Now what?!" he yelled.

How were they getting out of this alive? He waited for Javex to reply as the rain drenched his clothes and constricted around his thighs and legs. The rolling black clouds and heavy rainfall soured his mood.

"Now we get into the ship!" Javex fired off another energy arrow.

"What ship?" he asked, confused, when a growing roar encompassed them.

"That ship!" Javex yelled, pointing.

There above the alley hovered a battered but striking ship; blue pivotal engines lit on its undercarriage allowed it to remain motionless.

Out of the cargo bay, a helmeted figure appeared, firing two dual pistols. The soldier swung down on a tether while firing at the attackers in the tavern. He leveled anyone who approached and became a target for the Nevo soldiers.

"Get in! Hurry!" Javex said.

Kaytrix hesitated. The Nevo stood too close to where he took cover.

Javex leapt to where he crouched in the alley and, with a tinge of impatience, shoved him in the right direction. The ship lowered closer to the alley. Javex followed stairs up the side of a building to the roof where he boarded the ramp and shot at the Nevo. The Nevo soldiers returned fire as the ship eased into the sky. Kaytrix backed up the ramp with the dual-wielding soldier.

"Anytime now, Ser," Javex said. "And get us into hyperspace before the Nevo come calling."

The Nevo disappeared, obstructed by the closing cargo bay doors. The helmeted figure turned towards him, not lowering his weapons.

Kaytrix took aim and stood ready.

"Who's this?" the soldier asked with a smoky accent.

"This, Aaro, is Cade. Lower your weapon."

Aaro held his aim, the tension between him and Javex escalating. "Wanted by the Nevo? Sounds like trouble," Aaro said, his tone thick with blame. "We have enough trouble as it is."

"No different from the rest of us, *Aaro*." Javex growled.

The tension lingered when Aaro finally holstered his weapons. "Right. Holster your weapon. The danger is long behind us."

Kaytrix waited. This wasn't an ideal situation to be in: aboard a vessel outnumbered by armed and equally strange people.

"Welcome aboard the *Dauntless*," Javex said formally, reaching out his hand.

Kaytrix held his weapon firm. How fast did he have to be to outrun these two?

Chapter 7

MISTAKE

Alissia Rabb stood in the corner of the Nevo bridge, waiting in the silent darkness. As a bounty hunter, she had little time for herself. She was a servant, a slave to her master, and awaited his daily commands.

A chirp from the bridge's communication terminal awoke her from her standing stupor she'd allowed herself to slip into. Sleep was a privilege she did not have.

An angry hiss seethed from between the metal plating on Lord Khelveliz's face as he stared at the displayed holographic message. The green light glitched away, leaving in its wake the viewport of his ship. The giant lay overgrown with trees. Dormant for as long as him, no doubt as rusty and ineffective as well.

The Nevo lord grew slower over the solar rotations, but not stupid. Even if his appendages tried to fail, his brain remained active, scheming, growing. The rotations came and went, like each of his breaths. It took her a long time to find out what put him on edge. Contrary to her initial belief, remaining on this planet wasn't what angered him. The slow progress of his scientist, Vhulse, caused his irritation.

Whatever the message said, it put Lord Khelveliz in a mood.

Khelveliz rose from his seat and huffed at her to follow. The view of the dark planet disappeared as they left the bridge and entered the fog-laden halls. Often, Khelveliz bragged about how he'd commanded the last of his race to victory in destroying his ultimate enemy, but often left out the part he needed them to survive.

Alissia didn't care about the story. It only reignited her flame for vengeance every time he shared it. She wasn't always a slave, a servant. Once she'd been free, but that was a long time ago. The day the Nevo murdered her family, they stripped away the timid young woman she was and unleashed her fury. The only reason she stood close to her enemy was to enact her vengeance. Khelveliz wasn't her target. His scientist, Vhulse, was the one she wanted to see begging for his life.

She'd been waiting for the right opportunity to avenge her family and return to her second home, Cordabo. Many solar rotations passed, but the moment never presented itself.

They entered the corridor, and she disappeared behind Khelveliz's tall mechanical figure. Sick clicks and whirrs came from his body as he walked, each of his steps labored with a heavy breath and a loud slam as the claws of his feet collided with the metal corridor floor.

The hazy green halls with dim yellow lights made her skin crawl. If a hell existed in the galaxy, this place was it. And it wasn't bad, yet.

They exited the ship and entered a gate to the underground base they built. She hid her disdain. Built. More like stole. Anything here the Cordabo constructed. In time, it would be theirs again if she had anything to do with it.

Khelveliz's mood darkened as he moved through the corridors of the underground, his tattered cloak following him. Alissia quickened her pace to keep up with the brooding lord. They were heading to the lab. She memorized the path, having traveled this exact route a hundred times.

The door to the Nevo scientist's lab slid open and Khelveliz charged in. The Nevo lord crossed the room with a speed he hadn't demonstrated in many rotations, putting her on edge.

Alissia recognized the look of fear in Vhulse's eyes and leaned against the dirt wall. The Nevo lord struck Vhulse across the face, sending his head to the left. The collision created a grating, shrieking sound as metal scraped metal.

"You fool!!!" Khelveliz screeched angrily. "How were you so careless?"

Vhulse backed away. "Of what do you speak?"

Khelveliz's anger intensified, shining through his eyes as he glared at Vhulse. His metal fingers contorted into fists, ready to strike again.

"Don't play the fool! I know you've lost the Archarian!"

The Archarian. Khelveliz's trophy from the war—the man she saved and placed on Rehnna. She was thankful her mask hid her smile. Watching Vhulse squirm was delightful.

Vhulse straightened himself. His gleaming eyes and proud posture hinted at being insulted by the suggestion he had failed anything.

"I did not lose him, my Lord. See for yourself."

Vhulse drew his arm up and indicated to the far wall where several of the canisters stood anchored. Inside one, the silhouette of a figure floated, suspended in liquid and tubes.

Alissia's heart quickened. She glanced at the hyperbaric chambers. The broken one was still there, the other two remained intact. She wrinkled her nose and relaxed. The body wasn't the Archarian. Even from where she stood, the figure appeared lifeless.

Khelveliz screeched. "If he is there, then what reports am I hearing of an Archarian disrupting order on Rehnna, escaping in a ship? And now on Tarwi!"

Vhulse hesitated to answer, enraging Khelveliz.

Alissia allowed herself a swell of glee as Vhulse fumbled for a viable excuse, but then her heart stopped. Rehnna? She hadn't been back to see Traven in a half solar rotation. She cursed herself. Did the man she save, leave?

"Your soldiers are reporting nonsense," Vhulse said.

Khelveliz towered over the short frailty of the scientist, watching him.

Vhulse dared a retreating step back, disturbing the fog that swarmed their feet. "I will hire some bounty hunters to investigate. If it is an Archarian, its DNA will speed up our tests. I have nearly completed the acceptance serum."

Khelveliz didn't appear to be convinced. Through the past solar rotations, Vhulse played on the fear of the Nevo existence depending on him. His arrogance, however, was growing bolder and even Lord Khelveliz reached his wit's end with Vhulse.

Khelveliz's dagger-hands quivered at his side, the rage building in his body. Oh, how she wished for Khelveliz to end Vhulse's life right here and now. With her revenge complete, she would leave this mess behind. But alas, she had to keep dreaming.

Khelveliz flashed his eyes with a fierceness. "I hope you understand what consequences you face if you fail to capture them." Khelveliz exhaled, a reverberating growling sound. "If my soldier's reports are correct, we need them . . . *alive*. I need not remind you what is at stake."

"Yes, Lord Khelveliz, I am aware," Vhulse replied, calm. "Your bounty hunter would do an excellent job of bringing them to us."

She unraveled her arms to stand straight. Part of her hoped Khelveliz would say no. However, this would be a perfect opportunity to complete her mission and escape this dungeon, but she hated the idea. The last thing she needed was to be taking orders from Vhulse. She would have to produce results or face Lord Khelveliz's wrath.

Khelveliz eyed the canister that held his prize, lingering in the laboratory's stench. Finally, he nodded.

"Very well. She is to aid you in the investigation on Tarwi."

Alissia's chest tightened. So it begins.

With one last huff, Khelveliz left, leaving her in the stench and foul company of the most revolting Nevo of all.

Vhulse exhaled. "Finally. After all this time, we get to work together."

"I hope it's the last time," she said.

Working with this creep was the last thing she wanted to entertain, but she could achieve her goal much quicker this way.

Vhulse tsked. "Still living in the past, Alissia?"

"You have no right to say my name." She growled. "Not after you killed my family and took me from the Cordabo."

He moved closer to her, but she kept her cool.

"You listen to me now," he breathed, his exhale an old waste basket stench.

"I serve no one. It's one thing to fool Lord Khelveliz. It's another to get caught."

"What do you know about it?" he sneered, allowing himself a chortle.

"For one, I know a dead body when I see one." There it was. Her anger boiled in her belly. Oh, how she wanted to kill him.

Vhulse stalked towards the door and commanded it to shut. He returned his gaze upon his life's work, a large room filled with tables, trays, tools, submerging tanks, and secured cells for victims of his research and experimentation. The arrogance dripped off him, a completely different Nevo than who he pretended to be around Lord Khelveliz.

"I don't suppose you know who's responsible for this tragedy then?" he spat.

She released Khelveliz's prize from his slimy prison, but Vhulse didn't know.

"How would I? I never leave Lord Khelveliz's side unless on a mission."

Vhulse stalked up to the body submerged in a liquid-filled tank with a life support system providing it air. Another tube, filled with a mix of life-sustaining ingredients fed into its stomach to keep its body alive. She recoiled, remembering how she struggled to remove all the tubes out of the man she saved.

"Don't you reveal our secret," Vhulse threatened the corpse in a mocking tone. He pointed his finger at it. "Or it is the end for us both."

The scene repulsed her.

Vhulse turned to his tabletop with an array of vials and tubes and picked one up to gaze at the complex contents inside.

"What is it you are working on, anyway?" She suspected something intricate but wasn't sure.

Vhulse scoffed. "It is a serum, but I haven't perfected it yet. I need my results back before it is complete. No matter how the Archarian escaped, his blood holds the key to my rise in power. I thought the other bounty hunters would have returned with him by now. They are useless it seems. That is where you come in."

Alissia tightened her fists. What bounty hunters did he hire? If the man she saved wasn't on Rehnna, then she must find him and quick.

"What makes you so sure I will find him?"

Vhulse stared at her. A wicked flare lit the orbs of his eyes as he squared his shoulders. "If you don't, someone else will."

Fear's icy grip latched onto Alissia. If Vhulse needed this Archarian to complete whatever he was working on, she must prevent the other bounty hunters from getting to him first.

Chapter 8

THE DAUNTLESS

Kaytrix stood in the cargo hold of the *Dauntless*, examining Javex's outstretched hand and the soldier. Aaro, as he was called, stood with his feet apart, his hands floating by his sidearms. One wrong move and Aaro would shoot holes through his body without the slightest hesitation. Not ideal. Regardless of the situation, keeping a level head was the best plan. He holstered his gun.

"Thank you," he said and grasped Javex's forearm. "That was one hell of a rescue. Not that I asked for it."

"I hope my forwardness doesn't alarm you. I am passionate about saving people from the Nevo."

Kaytrix shrugged. "I would have found a way, but I appreciate it."

Javex turned towards Aaro beside him. "I said not to make an entrance." He chuckled, exchanging a look with the helmeted soldier.

"Yeah, yeah, you're welcome." Aaro sneered, his tone hinted a smile on his lips. "What's so special about this one?" he asked, nodding towards Kaytrix.

"There will be enough time to discuss that later. First, we need to leave this place. I'll be on the bridge," Javex replied, putting away his bow. "Standard procedure with Cade, Aaro. And be hospitable."

"You got it, Captain," Aaro said, his voice still muffled by the apparatus on his helmet.

Javex left Kaytrix standing alone in the cargo hold with the stranger. He braced himself, unconvinced Aaro wanted him here. Who was to say Aaro wouldn't jettison him out the airlock?

Aaro removed his helmet, his rugged face scarred by a life of strife. Several smaller scratches dominated the left side of his face, but they hadn't healed ugly. Whatever violence this man encountered in his past; exceptional healers patched him up.

Aaro's gaze was icy, his eyes a harsh, dark blue. Was he sizing him up?

"So, you are Cade."

His wariness of his presence aboard was clear with his standoffish demeanor. Kaytrix felt the same about being aboard their vessel.

"And you are Aaro," he countered.

Aaro grimaced. "Right. Now that introductions are over," he began, slamming a fist to his heart, "let's carry on."

A moment of silence followed the gesture when Aaro's voice reverberated off the cargo hold.

"I only have one request before you enter the *Dauntless*," he said, taking a step towards him.

Kaytrix's fingers twitched, ready to grab his weapon. "That is?"

"I need your weapon to remain here. Protocol."

Aaro's request didn't allow him a choice. However polite, it was still an order. Kaytrix hesitated, then drew his gun and surrendered it. He hoped Aaro wouldn't search him.

Aaro exhaled and put out his other hand. "The knife too, *kid*."

Shoot. It was impossible to deceive Aaro.

"The magnet will pull anything else from your body, so I suggest you relinquish it while you can, unless you want to take the chance?"

Kaytrix rolled his eyes and surrendered his blade into Aaro's waiting hand.

"Great! Follow me," Aaro said in a mock cheery tone. "I hope you enjoy your first moments aboard the *Dauntless*. They are the most memorable."

Unsure of what Aaro meant by his words, Kaytrix followed him through the bay exit and further into the ship. The rough corridors rusted at every seam while paint peeled off in hotter sections, revealing layers of assorted colors. The space was tight and crammed, nothing like what he was expecting. They rounded a corner, and the corridor grew in length. On the left and right, sealed doors staggered down the length of it.

"How big is the *Dauntless*?" he asked.

Aaro turned to observe him. "It's big enough. Sometimes the damn thing is not small enough. Bigger ships are slower. Unfortunately, there aren't many to choose from that have the speed and agility to evade the Nevo. That's why we try to keep the *Dauntless* going. When she's gone, that's it. Good luck finding a replacement." Aaro led him down the corridor and took a right. "Oh, and don't even get me started on the price of parts."

Kaytrix followed Aaro into a medical center with bright white lights and clean surfaces, but it did nothing to calm his nerves.

"We need to make sure you aren't carrying any bugs, kid. Nothing personal." Aaro stood and faced him as he entered the room. "You can strip and stand in this chamber. It will scan and clean you. I will have a change of clothes set out for you. OK? After we bandage that," he pointed to his wounded shoulder.

Kaytrix stiffened. "Thanks, but I can tend to my own wounds."

Aaro shrugged. "Suit yourself."

"After the scan, then what?"

"I'll get you for dinner. It's kind of tradition around here."

"How will I know when to change?"

Aaro smiled, his dark blue eyes hinting a bit of humor. "Don't worry, there's a timer and the chamber locks from the inside. You're safe. If you need anything, I will be right outside."

Aaro left, leaving him alone in the solitary square chamber with a med kit. He removed his tunic and prepared a bandage for his shoulder. Its deep throbbing ache was enough to make him curse. Once the bandage laid ready, he wiped his face and dressed any other cut from the crash. His face took the brunt of it, a thin scratch marring the left side of his face. It would heal but leave a visible scar.

He glanced from the mirror to the frosted glass containment. Aaro's shadow remained, as promised, outside. He sighed. There must be a catch for the nice treatment. He recalled what Traven said about 'staying in good' condition for the bounty hunter and scoffed. Nothing in this galaxy was free.

Kaytrix stripped and got into the scour when a blue laser-like scan passed over his body. He found it strange to stand there, feeling nothing. He didn't even feel clean. It must be a decontaminate laser, meant to destroy the molecular bonds holding bacteria and viruses together. Part of him hoped water was involved, but a spaceship this size wouldn't allow for water storage.

A shadow moved outside, and he tensed, ready to protect himself, but it was only Aaro. He sighed, relaxing his fist. Aaro spoke, but the sealed doors drowned out his voice except the low tones. Was Javex checking in on their progress?

Kaytrix relaxed further, letting his shoulders drop. He appreciated the fact this wasn't a physical examination. While he was grateful for Javex's help, he still didn't trust him or his motives. The mysterious markings would have to always stay hidden. They only brought trouble, and he didn't want to ruin the chance this might be something good for him.

Something else bubbled in his chest, a strange feeling he hadn't felt since fixing Traven's ship: hope. Being aboard the *Dauntless* gave him respite from fleeing, and maybe a little more than that. Perhaps he would learn to trust the crew to help him? Time would tell.

The laser stopped and the blue light turned off, followed by a beep.

A female robotic voice said, "Subject is clear. Negative tracking devices located. All bacteria and viruses eliminated."

"Good to know," Kaytrix mumbled to himself. He dressed and took in a breath before opening the chamber doors. Aaro stood there as promised, his arm extended to the left, indicating he was welcome to exit the chamber and enter the room.

"How was that?" he asked.

"It was different. Can't say I ever experienced something like it before." Kaytrix shrugged.

Aaro remained armed, his hand resting on the handle of his sidearm.

"Javex wants to see you, now that you are clean," Aaro said with the hint of a smile.

If Aaro meant to be funny, he didn't get the joke.

"Very well, and off to dinner after?"

Aaro chuckled. "Yes, that too. Though I can't promise anything delicious. We kind of missed the market this time around. Again."

He detected the disappointment in Aaro's voice. The ache in his stomach intensified, and he sympathized with the man. A few times Traven's crops did poor, and they succumbed to purchasing rations. He recoiled from the memory. Rations were never delicious. Just dry powder held together by ingredients the body needed to survive.

He followed Aaro out of the med bay. The clean scent dissipated, replaced with the smell of machine parts, grease, and body odor. Parts of the ship appeared off limits or restricted. Whether from a safety standpoint or his presence on the ship, he wasn't sure.

Aaro led him to a door that whizzed apart, revealing the small bridge of the *Dauntless*. Kaytrix recognized Javex's tall form standing in front of the viewport. Bouncing off his silent posture were the colors of the hyperspace window, leaving Tarwi. His golden fur glistened in the light, while the dark patches gleamed a purple-blue hue.

"Cade, welcome to the bridge of the *Dauntless*," the captain greeted with a smile on his feline face.

"Where are we headed?" He asked, standing hesitantly just inside the doors, aware Aaro stood within arm's reach.

"To an empty pocket of space," Javex answered. "No one travels in that sector. We will be safe until we can help you."

That wasn't the response he was expecting. The pilot's trajectory was visible from here. He was telling the truth.

This had to be the strangest day. From almost captured by the Nevo to whisked away to safety. The generosity he received from Javex conflicted with his fight-or-flight response. It was impossible to believe their 'good intentions' were pure. Why would Javex offer him refuge on his ship if the Nevo were after him?

"Not to seem ungrateful, but why?"

"You appeared to be in distress."

"I'm not the only one in the galaxy with troubles. Why help me?"

The pilot stood from her chair and crossed her arms. "Javex helped you like he helped all of us. Maybe you should be grateful."

He recalled seeing her in the tavern on Tarwi.

"Maybe I am, but maybe I don't trust you." Kaytrix noted the exits and profiled the other faces in the room when a chill went up his spine. His gaze froze on a figure.

Stood menacingly at a station was a Varanus. Enough talk passed through the settlement for him to know the Nevo favored the Varanus as their foot soldiers for their unconquerable rage and strength.

"What's he doing here?"

The Varanus's tendrils bristled, vibrating in irritation.

"Easy Grootie," Javex said, putting a hand up. "It would serve you well, Cade, to show him respect."

"Why? Isn't his kind responsible for enforcing the will of the Nevo?"

Javex scowled. "Grootie is a member of my crew, as is everyone you see here. Aaro Riffo is our security and weapons expert. Atara, cook, medic, and communications. Noro is our engineer. I am the captain. Seraphina is our pilot. Everyone here has suffered from the Nevo. This ship serves as a refuge for us."

"Just drop me off at the nearest planet with an arkross. I'll use it to go where I need to," he said, testing Javex's intentions.

"If that is your wish," Javex said, nodding at Seraphina. "But I fear the Nevo will find you no matter where you go."

Kaytrix held back his relief. "Thanks, but I think I'll be alright."

His gaze settled on Seraphina. She hadn't moved to follow Javex's orders. Instead, her green eyes probed him with a fierceness.

"Like you were *alright* on Tarwi? Aren't you on the run from the Nevo?"

Kaytrix scowled. He'd only just discovered the bounty on his head. He just didn't know why the Nevo hunted him.

"Seraphina," Javex warned. "It is not our business."

"I think it is. We're sticking our necks out to help him. Why are they on your tail?" she asked again.

Kaytrix hesitated to answer, conflicted by their generosity and his natural instincts to keep his secrets safe.

"I don't make it a habit to stop and chat with them," he said, subconsciously pulling his sleeve down.

"How long have you been running?" Aaro asked next.

Kaytrix's brow furrowed as his first memories of waking in the chamber surfaced. "Long enough," he answered coldly. "Is there a planet in range?" He asked, changing the topic. He was not about to play Q&A with people he didn't know.

Seraphina glanced down at her screen. "There are several options here," she said when she looked at Javex. "Shall I put them on display?"

Javex nodded and Seraphina pressed a few commands. A blue and orange hologram appeared, projecting the systems with an arkross.

"These are the only ones?" He crossed his arms, skeptical of Seraphina's honesty.

"You can check if you'd like," she countered.

Her clipped tone spoke volumes of her worsening mood. He stepped towards the hologram. Beside each world were passages, noting the Nevo activity. They were crawling everywhere. He held his chin, and the atmosphere of the bridge grew silent.

"If you like, you can stay here until you decide," Javex offered from behind him. "Maybe it will give you a chance to collect yourself before moving on?"

Kaytrix scrutinized the planets. Without a ship or a clear sense of direction, the Nevo and the bounty hunters were sure to capture him. He wouldn't last a day.

"I will think on it, but I would like my weapon back," he said, focusing on the gentle gold of Javex's eyes. "I'd feel better if I had it."

Javex smiled. "You are my guest, not a hostage, but I will keep your weapon for now. I have learned the hard way I can never be too careful. This is no exception."

"Fine. Is there someplace I can stay until I decide?"

He examined the crew. Although Javex expressed enthusiasm for his presence, the crew's crossed arms and scrunched faces suggested they felt differently.

"Yes," Javex answered. "Aaro will show you to your quarters. I understand you will join us later for a meal?"

The tension on the bridge intensified.

"Perhaps. Thank you." Now, more than ever, he needed a moment to sort through his thoughts.

Chapter 9

CONFLICT

Once Aaro and Cade left the bridge and the doors shut, a bombardment from Javex's crew begun. He'd risked their lives and the *Dauntless* interfering with the altercation on Tarwi. A risk, a rotation prior he wasn't willing to make.

Seraphina's fiery green eyes locked onto his. Not only did they reflect anger, but also disappointment.

"What happened down there? We barely escaped that mess."

Javex pinched the bridge of his nose. "Something about him, Seraphina. He's not like the others."

"You mean other people don't have the Nevo actively chasing them? The Nevo don't even hunt down their lost property like this." Her voice wavered.

Grootie grunted, seeming to agree with that comment.

"I couldn't leave him there knowing his odds were slim."

Seraphina's lip quivered, but she reigned in her emotions. "What about our odds, Captain?"

Javex breathed in deep and exhaled. He found it difficult explaining his instincts. Something felt right about intervening, but it came across as selfish to the crew.

Noro left his station and approached them.

"Not to disagree with Seraphina or you, Javex, but we did actively decide to stick it out on the *Dauntless*."

Seraphina crossed her arms at Noro's point.

Atara approached the group, fidgeting with her hands. She was always the last to add her thoughts as the least controversial person aboard the ship.

"He seems like a decent person, but the fact remains the Nevo want him and badly. I'd hate to think we've painted a bullseye on our back."

Javex met the faces of his crew and sighed. Of course, this is the reason they were hesitant about the idea of Cade remaining aboard. It put them all in immediate danger. As if their mission to find the Archarians wasn't dangerous enough. Now he added this to their shoulders.

Aaro returned to the bridge and met his gaze. He could foresee the coming conversation and braced himself.

"What did I miss?" Aaro asked. "And what exactly are you thinking, Captain? This is a mistake of a lifetime."

Javex pinched the large bridge of his cat-nose and shut his eyes. He was exhausted.

"I didn't think this through. He was in trouble, and when the Nevo arrived. I didn't think," he admitted in frustration. "But now that he is here—"

"We should let him leave as he requested," Seraphina interrupted, her gaze cold. "We're risking our safety and our mission with him here."

Javex's brow furrowed, his gaze at Seraphina intensifying. "We don't know that for sure. What if I turned you and so many others away because of the Nevo? It is the reason you are here. Why I am here. Why I do what I do."

"His situation is different," Seraphina said.

"His story does not differ from any of ours. Destiny has brought us to his rescue." Javex growled again.

"Or lead us to our demise," Aaro spoke lowly. "Captain, we need to know why the Nevo are after him. The negative outcomes of trusting this stranger are endless. I scanned the bounty hit list. There's a request with a description matching his. Bounty hunters are actively hunting, and you can't avoid them forever."

So Aaro also feared for his safety. Bounty hunters and Nevo were never an ideal mix, but with them thrown into the mess, their problems doubled.

Javex shook his head. "Was there a name? An image? It can be anyone."

"No, but the description is the same," Aaro countered. "The only thing is the post date is a half solar rotation old."

"How did he outrun the Nevo and bounty hunters for that long?" Seraphina scoffed.

"I have," Aaro began when he swallowed. "But I had support. Cade is a rogue, which doubles my interest in how he's made it this long. Also, the pieces for his return would purchase a new ship and provide food for an entire solar rotation. That's heavy coin. Only the Nevo can afford that. So this must be him."

Javex snarled. He'd rather not admit it, but his crew was right. However, something about Cade made it impossible to turn away. Something regal in his form and disposition. Something ancient and familiar.

"I don't think he should stay at all," Seraphina persisted. "It's clear he is uncomfortable here. Coercing him to stay is wrong, regardless of how he may need our help."

"I think we should let him decide," Aaro said. "He appears to have received rigorous military combat training. He might be an asset to us if the Nevo weren't on his tail."

Seraphina scowled at Aaro. "Are you purposefully disagreeing with me?"

Aaro raised his hands. "I only stated my opinion. That is all. You seem uncomfortable with him here, as am I. I think Javex is right. He deserves a chance, but only if he shares his story."

"Don't assume what I am feeling." Seraphina snarled. Her words cut through Aaro, leaving his face emotionless.

Javex growled. "Enough. We don't know him well enough to trust him to stay, but he also deserves a chance to prove himself. We also can't assume he is the same person on the bounty hit list, but if he is, isn't that enough reason to help him?"

"So, what then?" Seraphina spat. "We risk everything for a stranger?"

Seraphina crossed her arms, her eyes glazed. Indeed, she was upset, but at what? Aaro being argumentative? The stranger aboard? Hunger? It was never clear when she became snappy. He took in a breath to allow patience to guide his future answers. This was unfamiliar territory for all of them. She had a right to be upset, but not to lash out.

"Seraphina, I want you to remain open-minded about the possibility of him staying," Javex said.

"Like how open-minded Aaro was when Grootie came aboard?"

This time, Aaro scowled. "Easy there," he warned. "This isn't about the past. Grootie and I are on good terms now. Whatever you are going through, you need to take a step back."

"Don't order me around," Seraphina said, taking a step forward.

Javex sensed it now, her anxiety. She was fighting not because she was angry, but because she feared what might happen.

Seraphina glanced at him, anger prevalent in her crisp green eyes, but they hid something else much deeper: fear.

"Let's you and I take a walk," he said to her. "Atara, prepare our meal as planned. Noro, help Aaro and Grootie double check all our security. Ensure all failsafes are in place."

Aaro nodded, glancing to Seraphina, before he left the bridge in silence. Noro and Grootie followed him.

"Where are we going to walk?" Seraphina asked, her tone still sharp.

Javex guided her arm and placed it in his. "The destination matters not, but what happens while on the journey."

Seraphina rolled her eyes, but her hand tightened around his forearm, and she followed him out of the room.

"Seraphina, what is wrong?" he asked, as they entered the corridor.

She hesitated to speak, a tear falling down her cheek.

"I will have Aaro watching Cade the entire time if he stays. You trust Aaro, right?"

Seraphina snorted. "I guess. Yes."

Javex patted her hand. Seraphina was like a daughter to him. It mattered she was comfortable, but also trusted his instincts. "I am glad to hear that. I feared for Aaro's life the way you glared at him."

Seraphina appeared amused when her face grew somber, and a sob choked out. "I'm scared we're risking too much this time, Javex. What if the Nevo find out we have him? They'll take us away from each other." Tears fell from her eyes. "I don't want to lose what we have here," she choked. "Not for one person. My home, my family . . . They're gone. I have nothing without you, without the *Dauntless*."

He wrapped an arm around her shoulders. "I would never allow such a thing to happen," he said. Yet as he spoke, something pierced his heart. Could he promise such a thing in the world they lived in?

<hr>

Kaytrix rested his head on the bulkhead wall. An eternity passed before someone summoned him for dinner. After the first hour, boredom and restlessness set in. He stared at the marking on his forearm, trying to distract himself from the growing stomach ache.

Javex's offer to stay aboard the *Dauntless* was generous, even if his crew didn't like the idea. If he stayed, he might be safe for a while, but he didn't know who these people were. As for finding answers about himself, well, that wasn't going great with everyone recognizing him from the wanted poster. Did he need answers? Wouldn't it be easier to use this opportunity to start fresh? Perhaps, but he would be bound to the *Dauntless* for the rest of his life. If he was ever going to be free, the Nevo and every bounty hunter out there had stop hunting him. But how?

Dedeep, dedeep. The ringer to his room chirped.

"Come in," he called, standing.

The door whizzed to the side, revealing Aaro's calm face. His eyes, however, were cold. Kaytrix tensed for a potential fight.

"Is something wrong?"

"Not at all," Aaro said, forcing a smile. "I've come to announce we are ready to consume our last meal of the day."

"Finally. I was starting to think I was a prisoner."

Aaro's lips formed a thin smile as he crossed his arms. "You haven't done anything to be treated as such," he said, then added, "yet."

Kaytrix recalled the tension on the bridge beforehand. Suddenly, he wasn't so eager to eat.

"Understood. I will try to have some manners."

"Everyone would appreciate that." Aaro chuckled. "Except Grootie, of course. He doesn't care about manners. He's a Varanus. Now we best get going before the food goes cold. Our chef Atara is passionate about serving dinner warm."

He followed Aaro to another area of the ship. They passed the med bay, the bridge, and took a right down a corridor. Aaro entered a room through an arched entryway. The walls were a dull gray, a contrast to the brighter lights that lit the room from the ceiling. A few tables and chairs filled the space with a smaller meal prep area nearer the back. Paint peeled at the edges of the metal hull, signifying its age and attempts to rejuvenate the space.

The crew sat around one table with a few worn seats belonging to varying sets. He wasn't ready for this kind of personal setting. Aaro offered him a seat and sat down. The Varanus, Grootie, sat a few feet away from him. Their eyes met for a second and Kaytrix diverted his gaze.

"Never sat beside a Varanus before?" Grootie's deep voice rumbled.

Kaytrix recalled his rudeness to Grootie from before and met his penetrating, reptilian gaze. The Varanus's blue forked tongue slithered in and out of its mouth.

Kaytrix swallowed. How easy it would be for the Varanus to rip him limb from limb?

"Never, this is my first."

A guttural chuckle left the Varanus, sending the tendrils atop his head into a frenzy.

"Well, then you're in for a treat. And contrary to what you may have heard, we don't eat *everything*." Grootie's eyes shined a wicked flare. "Unless our food makes us angry."

Kaytrix feigned a smile and placed his hands on the table. Seraphina snorted and, by the sparkle in Noro and Atara's eyes, they liked the direction of the conversation.

"Come on, Grootie, leave the kid alone," began Aaro. "Your presence usually causes a bad first impression. And when has sitting beside you ever been a treat?"

Grootie turned on Aaro, his jaw tightening and his tendrils stiffening. His white teeth gleamed in the light.

"Beat me in an arm wrestle, then we'll see who calls the shots." He hissed.

Aaro grinned. "I don't play by the rules, Grootie. I enforce them." Aaro twirled his gun before holstering it.

Grootie's nostrils flared as he lifted his massive head in protest. His lips split into a snarl.

"True, Shrovon."

Kaytrix's stomach dropped. The two held each other's gaze for a long moment when they burst out laughing.

They were toying with him.

"You should have seen your face," Grootie rumbled, his tendrils on his head swaying.

Aaro pinched his eyes as he laughed, trying to hide the exhaustion. Seraphina let a chuckle slip and Noro cried tears.

"Jerks." Kaytrix growled.

Instead of being greeted with hatred, he'd turned into their evening sport. What a relief they found comfort in making jokes at his expense. He settled in his seat and tried to ignore any other prodding.

When Javex entered the room, the atmosphere calmed. He'd never witnessed this kind of reverence before, at least not that he could remember.

"Captain," they said in unison.

"Javex," he acknowledged.

The captain sat down and smiled.

"I hope you've been comfortable while waiting, Cade." Javex eyed the crew as they suppressed mischievous laughter.

"Not the treatment I am used to, but I've had worse," he admitted, allowing himself a smile. Anything beat being submerged in a tank with tubes sticking into his body.

A young, charismatic voice broke the silence and the anticipation building in the room.

"Time to eat!" Atara's said from the entrance of the kitchen. When did she slip away?

A wonderful smell filled the room as she walked in and placed a large pot of steaming food at the center of the table. Atara was young, but in the prime of her young adult life. Her individual blond and purple braids swayed as she placed down metal bowls and spoons in front of everyone. Their eyes met, and a warmth filled him. She was so joyful as she dished the meal, starting with the captain.

A poke on his left shoulder made him turn. Grootie leaned towards him, and he shuddered as the fine canines in Grootie's mouth came into view.

"Whatever you can't eat, I'll take care of."

Grootie's breath repulsed him. It took everything in him not to gag.

Atara tapped Grootie on the head with a spoon. "Ignore him," she began with a shake of her head. "Grootie helps me clean the dishes. Believe me, he's not hurting for food." Her skin crawled at the admittance. He could only imagine.

Javex raised his short glass. "Let us welcome our guest with a toast. To our new friend, Cade! May whatever light you seek find you among the ever-growing darkness."

"To Cade!" everyone toasted.

Silence followed as they took sips. Grootie, however, drank his entire glass and slammed the mug on the table, provoking a displeased look from Aaro.

"Please eat," Javex said.

As they took small bites to savor the flavor, the warm food released any tension between them. Reluctant at first, Kaytrix took a bite. The stew melted in his mouth, relaxing his shoulders. He hadn't tasted something so delicious. No offense to Clarr.

"This is definitely not rations." He wiped his mouth, glancing around the table as the others ate.

Atara scrunched her face and smiled at the compliment. "Thanks. It's the last of our real supplies. We will eat rations tomorrow."

Kaytrix lowered his spoon. They shared their last proper meal with him? Did he know anyone else who would do that?

One by one, each of them finished, stacking the empty bowls in the center of the table until the captain placed his on top. The youngest, Noro, eyed everyone with a mischievous gaze when he smacked a thick deck of colored cards on the table.

"Loser washes the dishes!" he declared.

A glimmer of happiness entered the Varanus's eyes.

"Grootie, you're not playing Colorz if you don't try to win," Noro said again, lifting an eyebrow.

Noro's bravery towards the large lizard astonished him. Noro was the shortest of the crew but made up for it with his big personality and brains.

Grootie scowled and crossed his massive arms at the declaration. How was it possible for a Varanus to hold cards without poking holes in them?

"Oh, you're going down this time," Atara said. She sat beside Javex and motioned for the dealing to start.

"Pffft as if." Noro smiled as he counted out the cards.

He'd never heard of such a game, but the sudden competitiveness of the crew intrigued him.

Someone cleared their throat.

"No cheating allowed," Aaro said, grabbing Noro's wrist and removing a card from his sleeve.

Noro's eyes protested. "But you taught me how!"

A sheepish look passed over Aaro's face as the rest of the crew scrutinized him.

"Is this true?" Seraphina's mouth gaped, her eyes wild with surprise. "That's why he's been on a winning streak! Cause of you!" Seraphina playfully threw her cards at Aaro, who ducked out of the way.

Aaro grinned, shrugging his shoulders. "Well, yes, but I didn't think he would use it against us."

Everyone shook their head in mock disbelief, except Javex. His wise gold eyes rested on each of the crew when he said, "Perhaps Aaro should wash dishes with Noro tonight."

"What?!" Noro and Aaro said in unison.

"A lesson, and a break for poor Seraphina."

Javex chuckled as Seraphina swatted him. She clearly lost more rounds than won them.

"I guess that's what happens when we get caught." Aaro shrugged and ruffled the small furry mohawk on Noro's head.

"I wouldn't have if you didn't intervene," Noro said, laying his hand down and pushing away from the table.

"Then I guess you're still learning. If I can see the card, so can others." Aaro grabbed the dishes and followed Noro to the kitchen, much to the disproval of Grootie, whose stomach was bottomless.

The game paused while they waited for Noro and Aaro. Now was the perfect time to have a word with the captain. He cleared his throat and Javex tensed.

"Javex, may I speak with you?"

Seraphina, Atara, and Grootie looked at him. In each face was an indiscernible hope. Did they want him to leave or stay?

Javex stood. "Of course. We can speak in the corridor."

Kaytrix got up from the table, feeling guilty as they excluded the others from the conversation. The doors whizzed apart and closed behind them, creating a silence.

"I've considered your offer." Damn, he hoped this wasn't a mistake. "I have decided it would benefit me to stay, but only for a while. I know I will have to face the threat of the Nevo eventually."

Javex's smile was genuine. "I am pleased. We'll do what we can to help you. There is one other thing, Cade. A security measure."

"What's that?"

"To ensure the safety of my children and crew, Aaro will be your security detail," Javex said, his white whiskers flowing with the movements of each of his expressions.

Security. He could live with that. "Okay, then."

Javex turned to the door, hesitating when he didn't move to join him. "Won't you join us for a game?"

"I dunno. Competition seems intense." He chuckled.

Javex smiled again, his golden eyes warm and peaceful. "I have yet to win my first game, but I enjoy the theatrics. Come join us. Noro and Atara would benefit from spending more time around you. Lessen their fear."

Nothing of what he witnessed tonight suggested the younger ones feared him.

"Alright, but I'm only watching."

Javex clasped him on the shoulder and entered the dinner hall. Aaro and Noro sat at the table once again, their sleeves still rolled from the labor of washing. A look passed between Aaro and Javex. Aaro nodded and relaxed, but the security officer's hand remained close to his holster. They were welcoming, all right, but not naïve.

The evening progressed with laughter and the game of Colorz. As time passed, it proved difficult to keep his guard up, even with the family dynamics and jokes. Surely Javex was truthful about bringing him aboard, but only time would tell.

Chapter 10

QUESTIONS

Dedeep, dedeep. The ringer chimed on Kaytrix's door.

"Who's there?" Damn, it was early. Couldn't he sleep in on his first day?

"Wakey, wakey," came Aaro's recognizable voice. "Time for a quick breakfast. Rations," he chided.

"Alright, I'll be out soon." Kaytrix pulled his hand across his face and breathed in deep.

"Try to hurry. I'd like to show you around the ship before our official duties begin," Aaro said, his voice muffled through the door.

"What? Official duties?"

Aaro chuckled, amused. "Well, you didn't think the captain would let you stay for free, did you?"

"I guess not," he mumbled, pulling on his pants and boots.

He dressed in his tunic and fastened his belt. He opened the door. Aaro leaned against the side of the bulkhead, still armed.

"Are you going to wear that the entire time I am here?"

Kaytrix didn't expect Javex to trust him right away, but damn. He didn't like Aaro having the advantage should something unexpected occur.

Aaro grinned, his eyes sparkling. "Well, maybe I won't have to. All I need to know is if I can kick your ass in a sparing match. If you're better, the weapon stays."

Kaytrix lifted his eyebrow. "Really? That's all?" He thought back to the bar. He'd handled himself okay.

Aaro nodded. His chest swelled with confidence. "That's right, kid."

Kaytrix scowled. "I'm not a kid," he said as he joined Aaro in the corridor.

"Really? Well, how old are you then?"

Kaytrix hesitated, faced with another inconvenient fact he should know about himself.

"I lost count, to be honest, but I know I am not a kid."

"Mhm." Aaro muttered. "Mind telling me what training you've had? You carried yourself well on Tarwi, also seen your bio-scan. Someone trained you in some form of military combat. Care to share who?"

The information piqued his interest. How did the scan tell Aaro that much? Had the scan revealed his clan markings? Kaytrix met his gaze, meeting the rich colors of his eyes again. Why were they so blue?

"I can't tell you," he said. He couldn't fool Aaro.

Aaro stopped walking to face him.

"Look, we all have our secrets. Some we can keep; some you have to share to stay."

Kaytrix held his tongue, allowing Aaro to finish.

"It's my job to keep everyone here safe," Aaro said again. "For most of us, the *Dauntless* is all we have. Don't think I won't hesitate to protect it."

They entered the dining area and joined the rest of the crew for the morning meal. He ate in silence, allowing himself time for reflection as the crew ate around him. He studied how they behaved. Last night, everyone appeared so relaxed. This morning, reality snuck up on them. He upset their routine. There was no denying that.

After their meal, Aaro proceeded with the tour, guiding him to certain sections of the ship, explaining which areas were off limits—which turned out to be everything.

"And this is the cargo bay," Aaro said, walking into the extensive area.

The grated floor was old and worn-out. Several rings at key locations allowed for cargo to be held down. Rust encroached on well-used areas while dirt and grime caked hard-to-reach creases.

"So, where do your sparring matches occur?" Kaytrix crossed his arms. He had lots of time to think about Aaro's proposal.

Aaro flashed a smile and opened his arms in the middle of the cargo bay.

"Right here. It's a spot I picked for when Grootie came aboard. Really, we do it to stay fit and pass time when we are between places."

"Speaking of. What's our next destination?"

Aaro glanced around the room as if to reminisce. "Not sure. The captain is staying here for a bit before we keep going."

"So, that means more rations?"

Aaro grimaced. "You hate them too, eh?"

"With a passion."

Aaro chuckled. "How about we ask him later?"

"How about a sparring match first? I lose, and you don't have to carry your weapon."

Aaro paused, his body going rigid. "How about this: I get a strike, you answer a question and vice versa, deal?"

A risky agreement. He didn't know how well Aaro spared, let alone how he would answer his questions without looking like a liar.

"I'll do my best," he agreed. "First day privileges?"

Aaro beckoned him to the center of the cargo bay. "No such thing, kid."

Heat rose through his chest, his hands chilled. He was nervous about fighting Aaro, even if it was a friendly match.

"Before we begin, we need a witness. I bet Grootie would love to watch," Aaro said, reaching for his comm. "Hey, Grootie. Come on down to the cargo bay. The kid and I are having a sparring match. Should be fun."

Kaytrix resisted his need to correct the 'kid' comment and made his way to the center of the cargo bay. Aaro removed his gauntlets as Grootie arrived and settled against the bulkhead to watch. His massive frame rested as his eyes wagered the opponents, his countenance tense.

The match began, and Aaro proved to be formidable. Anytime Kaytrix fought in the past, his rivals slung their fists around like amateurs. Aaro had a type of grace about him.

Aaro attacked, forcing him to raise his forearms in defense against his barrage of strikes to his head.

"You know," Kaytrix said, panting. "After this fight you have to stop calling me kid."

Aaro engaged with another set of hand and kick strikes.

Kaytrix flew to attention, struggling to deflect each strike.

"Only if you get a strike in, *kid*," Aaro reminded him.

"What's your story? And Seraphina's? The captains? You all seem to want to know so much about me, but I know nothing of your crew."

The topic brought out a sudden intensity in Aaro's fighting. This was becoming more severe than he wanted.

"Don't forget the rules, kid," Aaro said again. He looked tired but scored a hit on his right arm. "Aha!" Aaro laughed victoriously, stepping back and raising his arms. "That's one for me. My question is: where were you born?"

Kaytrix rested his hands on his knees. Had he ever fought someone so hard?

"I was born on a planet of darkness of what I can remember."

It'd been a while since he recalled the memory of waking naked lying in a pool of liquid with tubes being removed from his body. It wasn't something he liked to recollect.

Aaro nodded, satisfied with the answer. He beckoned with his hands for them to fight again.

"Show me what you got, kid."

"Tell you what," Kaytrix began with intense focus as he deflected Aaro's kick to his head. "If I knock you on your ass, I earn a chance to ask you guys some questions," he challenged with a smile, catching Aaro's fist.

Aaro took a step back and did a double take. He chuckled. "You're pretty cocky."

But there was a hidden emotion in his tone. Was it anger?

"Takes one to know one," he fired back.

"So far you haven't shown me anything impressive, kid."

"Do we have a deal then?" he said, stepping back. He was enjoying this moment with Aaro, but his comment set Aaro's eyes ablaze. He attacked.

Aaro fended off his barrage of punches and struck him in the chest, sending him backwards and onto his ass.

"Let your skills do the talking," Aaro retorted.

Kaytrix huffed, catching his breath. He wasn't expecting such an intense move so early in their engagement. Aaro had held back, allowing him to think he even stood a chance.

"Better luck next time, *kid*." Aaro offered him his hand and hoisted him to his feet. "I tell you what, though. I am impressed. That's earned you a moment to ask some questions of your own."

Kaytrix gasped, still trying to recover from the feeling of his chest collapsing in on itself.

"Thanks, I think?"

Aaro donned his gauntlets and shot a smile at Grootie. "I still have to keep my weapon, by the way."

Kaytrix coughed, trying to find the air to laugh. "After all that? You are obviously better than me."

Grootie stood up from his position. "He doesn't always play by the rules," he rumbled.

Kaytrix rubbed his chest and followed Aaro, aware Grootie joined them. Even if Aaro didn't play by the rules, this little match earned him an opportunity to find out more about the crew. He still hadn't figured out what Javex was doing with an old ship evading the Nevo. What would drive someone to save outcasts and put themselves in danger?

"Need to visit the med bay?" Aaro teased from in front as they passed by.

Kaytrix wanted to retort with something smart, but bit his tongue, remembering how well that went over during their sparing match.

"No, I am good. I've had worse."

Aaro glanced back at him. "I bet you have."

They entered the large circular room of the bridge. The view port was his favorite feature of this, but also the sunken terminals and the equality the room presented.

Javex stood near his command chair in the center of the room, his gaze focused on a holographic display in front of him.

"Sir," Aaro greeted.

"Yes, come on in," Javex said.

Aaro approached the captain's side and whispered in his ear.

Javex's gaze flicked from the hologram to look his way. "Very well," Javex said, his tone calm as he beckoned him over.

As Kaytrix approached the captain, he got to observe the creature he knew so little about. Scars trailed parts of his face, preventing fur from growing back. His ears were round and weathered, with bits missing. His eyes, a rich gold with a depth of empathy he'd never witnessed in any creature or humanoid alike. Whatever his race, he'd never met one before.

"Aaro said you were fair in the sparing match."

"Was only practice." He rubbed his chest again. "Aaro hits hard, though. Next time I'll know better."

"And watch your mouth, kid," Aaro said from the opposite side of the bridge. Aaro stood with Seraphina and Grootie, keeping a close eye on him and the captain.

Javex's mouth curled upside down as he refrained from smiling. "Well, what do you want to know?"

Kaytrix breathed in deep. Standing on the bridge, looking at the stations, being on this ship, brought back senses and feelings he couldn't place. He focused on Javex.

"In the time I have been here, I have witnessed your bond with each other. Getting me out of trouble on Tarwi was a reckless move. These guys might have lost you. Why'd you do it?"

The crew examined Javex, curious to know the answer to this important question. Javex sat in his chair and rested his chin on his paw. It took a moment before Javex met his gaze.

"I can't explain why, Cade. The reason still confuses me, but there's something about you that reminds me of a race once revered in the galaxy."

A tense pause rippled through the crew as if they expected a negative reaction.

"Uh, huh? And the rest of it? Why fly this bucket of bolts? To what end? I guess my question is, why not pick a planet and live peacefully?"

Javex scoffed. "First, my ship is not a bucket of bolts." Javex smiled at him before continuing. "There is no peace in this galaxy until we can end the growing power of the Nevo. Or do you not know the history? Originally, I set out to save my planet . . ." he paused, as if revealing something too personal. "I wanted to find a technology that would defeat the Nevo, but my path led me to helping others. My primary mission remains, but as you have seen, the galaxy is not a simple place to navigate."

"That's for sure. So, do you have a new destination?"

Javex shook his head and paced the bridge. "I do not. With the Nevo constricting around popular spaceports and planets, it is hard to find someone who will risk their lives to share information. Not everyone will openly defy the Nevo." Javex pointed to the hologram. "For now, we decided to travel to the planet Rabori for resources. Only Seraphina and I will visit the surface. The galaxy has seen an increase in Nevo activity in the half solar rotation. It's making everything I do that much more difficult. We visit worlds in smaller numbers to avoid detection."

Kaytrix swallowed, remembering what the merchant said to him on Tarwi.

"Yeah, I have also noticed."

Javex folded his arms. "I am curious. What caused you to crash on Tarwi?"

Kaytrix hesitated. "When I jumped into hyperspace, one of my wings disintegrated, damaged from where I was coming from." A half-truth, but still true.

Javex nodded. "I see."

Another moment of silence befell the bridge.

"Aaro mentioned I have duties?"

He crossed his arms and tried not to be unenthused, but after working every day on Traven's fields driving dovtors and hiding from bounty hunters, he was exhausted.

Javex chuckled. "Yes, but they are simple. You will help Aaro move cargo into necessary areas aboard the ship and help track inventory."

"I think I can handle that."

"Good, because it's time to get started."

Chapter 11

SUSPICIONS

Javex removed his bracer as Seraphina left the cargo bay to pilot the *Dauntless*, their trip to the surface of Rabori a success. The cargo bay door eased closed, reminding him of the ship's age.

"Don't fail me now, *Dauntless*." It was more of a plea than anything, but that's all he could muster right now. A plea. His hope of freeing his people was waning. Each rotation a reminder the galaxy was to stay slated in the Nevo's control, a fate he refused to partake in.

As the warm air of the planet left the ship, the potent scent of fresh fruit and vegetables replaced it. He breathed deep, allowing the scents to fill his nose with the many sweet and earthy smells.

"Captain," Aaro called as he neared the cargo bay entrance. "How was the mission?"

Javex smiled. "It went well. Peaceful. The sun was brilliant. Many things grew and produced a rich quality of food. We will eat well tonight."

Aaro grinned, turning to look at Cade, who grimaced.

"How did things go here?" Javex asked, grabbing a sack of the produce.

"Boring as usual, but Cade is improving in his skills in organizing inventory."

Javex caught Cade rolling his eyes. They appeared to get along over the last few rotations. They were making substantial progress.

Aaro and Cade grabbed the last four sacks of food and disappeared through the doorway. Grootie entered the cargo bay not long after. Javex met his gaze, and a chill went through him. The Varanus appeared disturbed. A ghostly glare illuminated his slit reptilian gaze, much like when he first came aboard. A haunting look he recognized. Grootie had not shown that face since he recovered from serving the Nevo.

Grootie stood with his arms at his side, his hands poised, twitchy. It sent another chill down Javex's back. The Varanus were by nature an unpredictable race. Being aboard the *Dauntless* for two solar rotations wouldn't change his tendencies.

Javex found him beaten and left for dead on a remote world not well-traveled. Technically, Grootie was not supposed to be alive. According to the Varanus, the Nevo kill their servants after their use expires. Grootie's servitude wasn't a choice. He received a lot of prejudice for the atrocities he committed after being freed from the Nevo.

When Grootie first arrived, everyone found it difficult to adjust to his presence. Against the better judgment of his crew, Javex provided Grootie another chance at life. There was a time when he believed Grootie would not mentally recover, but the Varanus showed resilience to his mental and physical wounds. Given Grootie's history of Nevo servitude, he required a lot more monitoring and a lot longer to heal, spending most of his time in solitude. Once able, Grootie became an active member of the crew.

"Grootie, what troubles you?" He asked, letting go of the produce.

The Varanus halted his approach and Javex tensed.

"There's something about Cade." Grootie's voice rumbled. "That is hauntingly familiar."

"Familiar? How so?"

The otherwise flowing tendrils atop Grootie's head stiffened with aggression.

Javex's jaw tightened. He didn't like the way Grootie stood. The words he spoke troubled him as if they were some sort of confirmation of a hidden truth.

"What do you mean?"

Waiting for Grootie to answer was like trying to pull a bent nail from a board. He could only tolerate it for so long.

Grootie's large, blue forked tongue slithered out of his mouth and tasted the air. "Hard to put it into your words," he said, staring into his soul. His countenance did little to reveal his feelings.

Javex crossed his arms. He was in no mood for riddles.

"I have lived long enough to know what your words mean, Varanus. There is no estrangement between our cultures."

"He's chosen." Grootie growled. "He doesn't walk with one soul, but two."

A sinking feeling settled in Javex's stomach, but relaxed with doubt.

"Are you certain? There hasn't been an incident like that since the Last Stand." He let his mind wander. "It isn't possible. Our medical scan revealed nothing suspicious."

Grootie's eyes flickered, and he took a step closer. The Varanus stood taller, broader, and was stronger than him. The might of the Varanus was the reason the Zaguarz had fallen to their enslavement many solar rotations ago.

"I would encourage you to do another scan, Captain. For everyone's sake. Our races know the stories of the two souls. If I am right, Cade doesn't have much time."

Javex held his gaze with the Varanus. It would be unlike Grootie to have ulterior motives for this request.

"Why didn't you tell me when we first brought him aboard?"

"Things take time to grow, Captain."

Another chill ran through Javex as he recalled the terrible stories of the two souls. Varanus and Zaguarz shared them during their planet's war. How two souls happened remained a mystery. The only certainty was the victims lost themselves to darkness. Eventually the victims emerged as another creature who the Nevo would ferry away to their ships. If Grootie was right and Cade suffered from two souls, they were in greater danger than he bargained for.

Grootie pointed at the sack of veggies. "Want me to get that?"

Grootie's tendrils wisped into a more relaxed dance atop his head as he grabbed the sack with ease and exited the cargo bay.

Javex stood silent in reflection. "Two souls," he muttered, still frozen by the thought.

He had limited knowledge of the Nevo, but Grootie's understanding about the creatures surpassed it. He wanted to trust Grootie, but he fought with his own feelings towards the Varanus. The history of his people enslaved by the Varanus left a sour feeling in his heart. For him to show mercy to one challenged him daily, but he would be a fool to ignore the Varanus's warning.

Javex activated his comm. "Aaro, bring Cade to the med bay for another medical scan. Tell him it's a check up. I will meet you there."

Aaro's voice rasped into his ear. *"Everything okay?"*

"I'm not sure."

The comm went silent for a second.

"Affirmative, Captain."

Javex hoped Grootie was mistaken.

When Javex entered the room, a shadow of Cade stood in the scanning chamber. Aaro crossed his arms as he faced the chamber and the entrance.

"Captain," Aaro greeted. The creases on his forehead deepened with concern.

"Aaro." Javex viewed the information the scanner presented.

"What are we looking for?" Aaro asked.

Javex held his chin. The scan showed nothing again. "I am not sure. Grootie mentioned he sensed something about Cade."

Aaro nodded, looking back to the chamber. "Did he say what, exactly?"

Javex hesitated. "He said another soul." Even just saying it aloud made him cringe.

Aaro's face crumpled into a wince, but his military thinking kicked in.

"Perhaps he doesn't mean a literal soul? Something else. Like a tracker?"

"It might be nothing," he said, gazing at Aaro. "I am not saying Grootie's senses are invalid, but it's possible he's sensitive to Cade, especially his story."

"Hate to say it, Captain, but we haven't equipped the *Dauntless* to detect more than the standard stuff," Aaro said again.

He grimaced. He loved his ship and the idea it was old and ill-equipped wasn't something he wanted to admit. "We'll look into upgrades," he muttered.

"Or trade it for a newer model?" Aaro suggested.

Javex cringed. That was unlikely. "Never," he said. "Do you think the Acknarians can help him?"

Aaro stiffened at the name, no doubt reminded of unpleasant memories. "Can't say either way, Captain. We haven't visited their planet in a while. Is it a wise idea?"

Javex held his chin, watching the blue lights streak over the shadow of Cade in the chamber. With this recent concern brought to light, he wasn't sure what to do. The planet Acknaria was his only source of reliable information regarding the past. He must protect it. However, the Acknarians possessed extensive knowledge of many things, good and evil. They might provide some clarity on Grootie's feelings, but was Cade worth it? Taking him there could be a mistake.

"As you so delicately put, the *Dauntless* lacks the equipment for this." He pinched the bridge of his nose to fight his oncoming headache.

"What should we do? Lock him up?"

"No, that is not wise."

Aaro nodded, holding his tufted chin. "I'll monitor him, see if anything weird happens."

"Thank you, Aaro. We will find the nearest void and wait there. If nothing happens, we will proceed to Acknaria. Maybe we will see some of your friends." Javex chuckled when a pain shot through his temple. "Let me know when the scan is complete. I need to go mediate."

"Copy that, Captain," Aaro said when he caught his arm. "Try not to overthink it, sir. But this *is* the best course of action."

"Let's hope, Aaro. I could be mistaken."

Chapter 12

INCIDENT

Kaytrix sat in his room, trying to relax his mind, but many distracting images filtered into his thoughts.

The void. He found it boring. After his last 'routine scan' as Aaro called it, they traveled to a little pocket of space with nothing and no one in it. Javex said they needed to run a diagnostic on the ship with no outside interference from other vessels. While he bought that line for the first three rotations, something else was the matter.

He grew to appreciate the crew, and even trust them a little more after being aboard the *Dauntless* for ten rotations, but things were tense and the last little while they weren't acting themselves. Especially the kids.

The aspects of his duties of inventory and restocking shelves were less than appealing. What time he didn't spend working, he would devote to reflection, or he'd spar with Aaro.

Kaytrix closed his eyes and images from his dreams filtered into his memory. Some nights he dreamed horrible dreams. Things he'd never seen before and never wanted to see again. Why he was having them seemed a mystery. Did they link to his past? Were they only nightmares?

He opened his eyes to escape the bombardment when a chill ran down his spine. His stomach churned in a sudden sensation of nausea.

"Ugh, to heck with sitting here any longer." He groaned, standing from his cot.

He opened the door. Aaro peered at him from the opposite side of the corridor.

"Want to spar?" Kaytrix asked, wiping his brow. He was still sore from yesterday's session.

Aaro closed something he'd been reading.

"Are you sure? You look like shit."

He rolled his eyes. "I'm only sick of sitting in here with nothing to do."

Aaro nodded and tucked whatever he was reading into his vest.

"Alright. I'll go easy on you. Lead the way." Aaro invited him into the corridor with a gloved hand.

Kaytrix led the way. The cargo bay door whizzed aside, and he headed straight for his starting position. The nauseous feeling subsided since leaving his room, but as Aaro stood before him, his vision blurred.

Aaro attacked.

He blocked several of Aaro's advances, but one slipped through and hit his jaw. He fell to the mat and closed his eyes.

"Hey, are you okay?" Aaro asked, rushing to his side. "I thought you would see that one coming."

"I am okay, really. Let's keep going. You got lucky." He grimaced and readied himself. He blocked Aaro's next set of attacks. "See, I am okay." He forced a smile.

His vision cleared. In fact, he could see details he couldn't before, like the white hairs starting in Aaro's beard, or the dark waves of blue hidden in his irises.

Aaro attacked again.

A surge of strength flowed through his extremities as Aaro advanced forwards, beginning another sequenced assault. Kaytrix deflected each strike, keeping Aaro at bay, and then began his own barrage of attacks. He began to move and fight in a way unfamiliar to him, blocking Aaro's attacks and advancing with more aggression.

Aaro faltered, unable to keep up with the momentum and power he brought to the fight. He punched Aaro in the face and then his chest. The blows sent the Shrovon falling to the mat.

"What the hell?" Aaro's face darkened in astonishment as he pinched his bleeding nose. "What was that?" Aaro rose to his feet and eyed him with a cautionary gaze.

"I . . . ," Kaytrix hesitated. "I don't know what that was." His head was heavy, like drowning in a vat of water.

Aaro's hand rose to his comm. "Sure, kid. I think you owe me an explanation." Aaro gasped and rubbed his chest. "I have fought on many worlds outside my own and *never* experienced that level of melee."

"Should we go to the med bay?" Kaytrix countered, changing the subject. His head was still heavy.

"Yeah, sure. And you're joining me." Aaro activated his comm. "Hey Atara, meet me and Cade in the med bay. Sparing injury."

Kaytrix nodded and bent to retrieve his poncho when the nausea returned. "Ooooh," he groaned.

"Hey, hey," Aaro said. He was helping him stay on his feet now.

"Ugh, I am okay. I am not used to being in space. Artificial gravity or something," he groaned, able to regain his footing.

Aaro eyed him. "Sure, well, let's get a doctor's opinion."

They arrived at the small med bay to see Atara readying bandages. Aaro sat down on a gurney with a huff. Atara placed an icepack on the back of Aaro's neck and he leaned forward, still pinching his nose, but Aaro focused on where he sat.

"What caused this to happen?" Atara asked, her brown eyes twinkling with curiosity.

"I knocked him down on the sparing mat."

Kaytrix rested on the gurney opposite of Aaro. A machine hovered over him to check his vitals, but he made sure his sleeve covered his mysterious markings.

"Oh, really?" Atara gaped at Aaro. "You aren't showing him your *secret* moves now, are you?" She teased.

Aaro snorted, resulting in blood coming out between his fingers. "Yeah right. Some sort of concoction of melee I've never fought before. Hardly call it a fair fight." Aaro rubbed his chest again.

"He doesn't share his *special* melee with anyone," Atara half whispered, winking at Kaytrix.

"Harrumph." Aaro scoffed. "I just don't enjoy teaching you!" he teased, touching the cold ice pack to her bare arm.

"Aaro!" she squealed, twisting away from him. "Space is cold enough without you trying to freeze me to death! Get going. Nothing can cure you!" She flashed him a smile. "As for you," she began, looking Kaytrix's way before checking a screen. "Your vitals look good. Can't say what's going on, but you might be correct. Not everyone has the stomach for space."

Kaytrix nodded, feeling relieved.

Atara glanced to his shoulder where he got shot on Tarwi.

"Mind if we take off your shirt? I can check your wound. Make sure it's healing without an infection."

Kaytrix pulled away. "No, thanks. It's fine. I'd rather deal with it on my own."

Atara withdrew her hand and nodded, a fleeting, but concerned, smile on her lips.

Aaro groaned as he stood. "Are we free to go, Atara? I should get Cade back to his quarters to rest so I can recover." His tone was humorous, but Kaytrix sensed an urgency in Aaro.

"Of course. Cade, here," Atara began, placing two little pills in his hands. "Take one of these and rest. It will calm your stomach. If it doesn't help right away, take the other one for a stronger dose."

"Thanks."

Kaytrix and Aaro left the med bay and headed for his quarters on the second level of the ship. For now, the nausea dissipated, but a lingering pang resided in him, threatening to strike again. He examined the pills in his hand, unsure if he should take them. As much as he didn't want to, he could trust Atara, couldn't he? He swallowed both pills, hoping they would provide some relief.

As they traveled up the rungs to the second level of the ship for crew quarters, Aaro reported to Javex. To report all accidents or injuries that befell the crew was standard procedure. Kaytrix listened to Aaro's usual chatter with the captain, noting his cool recollection of the fight and the nausea he was feeling. They traveled the corridor that separated the crew's room from his.

"So," he began, turning to face Aaro.

"So?"

"You and Atara, huh?"

Aaro's face distorted in a look of confusion. "Atara? No, no. She's Javex's adopted daughter. I am like her uncle. No, I'm looking at a different sunset. However, the light is not always so kind to one's eyes." Aaro grimaced.

A hint of sorrow laced Aaro's words. During their time together, Aaro never disclosed his personal feelings. He'd always kept their conversations professional and about the ship and their duties.

"Seraphina?" Kaytrix asked.

"How'd you guess?" Aaro gave him the side eye.

"There's always a tension between you."

"So, because you hit me so damn hard, fess up on where you learned to fight."

Aaro's eagerness to change the topic was obvious. However, this wasn't something he'd rather talk about. The question only reminded him of the bizarreness of the situation.

"Believe me, I wish I knew."

Aaro didn't seem to catch his subtle mistake.

"Fine, keep it to yourself. Get some rest. You look like crap."

"At least I fight good," he quipped.

"Watch your mouth," Aaro warned, pointing a finger at him.

Aaro turned to sit in his usual spot across the corridor when the lights flickered out. A black haze filtered through the hall, and he froze, fear gripping him. Green lights lit the bottom rails, shining through a growing fog. Through the dim space, a set of green eyes glowed in the darkness. He reached for his weapon.

It wasn't there.

"Aaro! Stop!" he said, whispering.

Aaro turned to face him, confusion deepening the scowl on his face. "What's the matter?"

Couldn't Aaro see what was approaching? He went rigid like prey.

"There's a Nevo," he said in a hushed tone.

The corridor disappeared. He stood in a gloomy, fog-laden field. Something crushed his neck, cutting off his air. He choked, trying to breathe. Darkness closed in, and in it, the haunting Nevo eyes grew brighter. An outstretched hand, with razor fingers, reached for him. Other images appeared and disappeared in his mind's eye, flashes, faces, screams, pain. Then the eyes again, growing nearer.

Beads of sweat ran down his face, his rigid body frozen as the horror approached closer. His breathing stopped. The outstretched hand was upon him, ready to end his life.

"No!" he yelled, watching it cut through him. Just as the Nevo hand contacted his flesh to tear it apart, it vanished into a wisp of nothingness.

In the dream's wake stood Grootie, his face grave.

Kaytrix shook his head, confused, afraid. "Wait? What just happened?"

The three stood in silence. Aaro's face contorted with puzzlement.

"We must see the captain immediately," Grootie rumbled, his voice thick with alarm. His hands at his sides twitched, as if ready to attack.

"Grootie, did you see it? A Nevo stood in the corridor." Surely, he wasn't crazy.

"What Nevo?" Aaro retorted when his face fell.

Grootie shared a look with Aaro. "Call the captain, now." He growled, his pupil's razor thin. "You will dislike what I am about to tell you."

Grootie's voice was darker, graver than before. Menacing. Threatening. The Varanus's words sent chills through his soul.

"I think I can handle it."

Grootie analyzed him, while Aaro chatted on his comm.

"You suffered a relapse vision."

"What's that?"

Was Grootie making this up? The stiffness of his tendrils and the graveness in his voice were clear indicators he wasn't. This was something serious. But what was a relapse vision? Before Grootie answered, Javex and Seraphina rushed into the corridor.

"How do you feel, Cade?" Javex asked. The captain kept his distance. Was that concern or fear in his eyes?

"I feel fine," Kaytrix began, but as he spoke, he recalled the morning spar and the trip to the med bay. "Well, other than a little 'space sick' and whatever nightmare I just had. What is a relapse vision?"

A surge of nausea overcame him again. He bent over to support himself on his knees. "On second thought, I'm not feeling all that grand."

A thousand suspicions went through his mind of moments they might have betrayed him. He groaned, collapsing to one knee. Were the pills poison? He should have been more careful and just left when they offered. They were after the bounty on his head. He knew it!

He tried to stand, to fend for himself, but he was too weak. The strength from during the sparing match vanished. Large hands gripped him from behind. Two more grabbed his legs.

Shit. He should have known.

Chapter 13

TWO SOULS

Cade succumbed to his symptoms and Javex rushed in to catch his failing body. Grootie helped, grabbing Cade's legs.

"Let's get him to the med bay! Aaro, have Atara prepare a gurney with restraints."

"Yes, sir."

The four of them struggled to get Cade's body down the rungs of the enclosed ladder to the second level. Together they navigated the narrow corridor and arrived at the med bay entrance, stopping to adjust their hold on Cade's body. Atara was still rushing around the room, setting up equipment and preparing the bed.

"Hurry, Atara," Javex said.

"I am sorry. Almost done."

They headed for the nearest cot when Cade awoke. The man began pulling against them and kicked his legs free, hitting Javex in the stomach. Cade then swung a hand at Grootie, but the Varanus blocked the attack. Fear and helplessness were clear as Cade struggled to get out of their grasp.

"What's wrong with him?!" Atara asked in petrified horror.

Grootie single-handedly slung Cade's body onto the stretcher and held him down with the weight of his massive arms. Javex moved in to hold Cade's legs. Aaro was beside him fastening the straps across the newcomer's torso and legs.

"Grab a stabilizer!" Javex ordered.

Atara struggled to inject the needle as Cade thrashed, but a perfect moment didn't exist.

Cade resisted against the straps. One snapped. Javex and Grootie rushed in to hold Cade again.

Cade began shouting in another language, his voice distraught.

"Now!" Javex ordered.

Atara stabbed the syringe in the side of Cade's arm, and he fell limp, his eyes rolling into the back of his head.

Javex did not prepare for something like this to happen. And by the look of Atara's and Seraphina's face, he should have. He wiped a paw across his furred brow.

"Captain, look," Seraphina said, pointing.

A blue glow emanated from Cade's unconscious body, filling the surrounding space to create a barrier. It formed like wisps of energy, only with a definite shape and character.

It transfixed Javex in a state of awe until a shock zapped his hands. He pulled away as the blue force encompassed Cade's body. Never did he see something so incredible. Who was this man? Or better yet, what was he?

The energy subsided after a few moments. The following silence left the med bay eerie.

"Does anyone know what just happened?" Javex tried hiding his frustration, but also his fear.

Aaro stepped forward. "Sir, after I reported his weird behavior this morning, he had a meltdown in the corridor. He was saying something about seeing a Nevo. Grootie," he turned to the Varanus. "You said he was having a relapse vision?"

Grootie nodded as he crossed his massive arms. His tendrils remained fixed in their irritated position, a locked spike formation along the crest of his head.

Javex's chest tightened. "Are you certain?"

"The symptoms are not mistakable," Grootie said. "A Nevo has affected him with its pheromone."

"How strong is the connection?" Javex glanced at Cade's incapacitated form. For someone so peaceful looking, it was hard to imagine he posed a threat. Damn. He wanted to help Cade.

"Hard to say, Captain," Grootie rumbled.

Aaro cleared his throat. "Excuse my ignorance, but what is a relapse vision? Why wasn't I made aware of this?"

"Remember two souls." Javex growled. "Somehow it connects to relapse visions. Unfortunately, our knowledge on this subject is extremely limited. We need more answers."

Javex's heart sank. This information changed everything about Cade. As much as he hated to admit, he had grown fond of him. He didn't want the crew to view Cade as a threat.

"What about that blue wisp? What is that about?" Aaro asked, his hand resting on his sidearm.

"I can't explain what happened in those last moments." Grootie tensed the muscles in his arms and chest. "The blue light made me feel weak, as if it was feeding off my strength."

A look of familiarity flashed in Grootie's eyes, but the look vanished, replaced by anger. Javex held his chin. Cade posed a threat to him and the crew. He didn't want to admit it, but the time to let Cade share his story was over.

He took in a breath, preparing himself to give his next order.

"Atara," he said, breaking the long silence. "Take a blood sample and do a complete physical. I want to know if our scans missed something. There must be a clue of who he is. Grootie, you are to stay with her. In the meantime, Aaro, prepare the isolation room so we can safely monitor him. Seraphina, I want you to engage the stealth shield."

Seraphina's jaw dropped. "But Captain—"

"I know the old cells have minimal charge, but we don't know what we're dealing with. See if Noro can redirect unnecessary systems to increase their efficiency."

Javex recognized the worry in Seraphina's eyes, a fear of returning to what she was before her freedom. He would break a lot of his promises in the coming rotations, but something about Cade made it difficult to abandon him. He hoped by the end Cade was worth it.

"We will be safe while we try to get answers. After Atara completes her examination, we will jump to our next destination. In the meantime, let's get started on our tasks."

Seraphina hesitated for a moment before she left with Aaro, leaving him, Grootie, and Atara standing together, looking over Cade's still body.

"How can one person cause so much trouble?" Atara asked, gazing up at him.

He squeezed her shoulder. "I don't know. Let's just hope we can help him."

The crew worked hard to yield results with Aaro ready first. They transferred Cade to the secured isolation room. There, Atara performed the physical guarded by Grootie. Never before was he grateful to have a powerful presence on the ship.

Aaro stood beside him in the small observation room, quiet with focus. Seraphina entered and took a place beside them.

Through the observation glass, Atara motioned for him to join her.

"Must be the lab results. Stay here."

Javex entered the secure room, not sure what he should feel. Grootie acknowledged his presence, but the ordeal with Cade had taken its toll. Just like Seraphina and the others, Cade threatened Grootie's safety. Javex waved for him to leave, but Grootie hesitated. The tendrils above his head remained static. The Varanus was reluctant to leave, a type of regret in his eyes.

"Grootie, we'll be ok. Cade is still unconscious."

Grootie's yellow eyes flickered from Cade to his. A rumble left the Varanus as he shifted his weight and exited the room.

Javex approached Atara, not giving the Varanus a second thought.

"Here," she said. "It's the blood test and my report on his physical." Her brown eyes danced around his face, trying to get a read on him.

"I'm not mad at you for the med bay incident," he said, resting a hand on her. "I should have prepared everyone for an emergency like that."

Atara breathed out, relieved. The entire situation strained everyone, but no one's skills were being relied upon as heavily as hers.

Javex took the holopad and glanced over the initial information to find what he understood. His mind swarmed with questions and concerns.

"You are positive this analyzation is correct?" It wasn't that he doubted her abilities, he just couldn't believe what he was reading.

"Yes. I checked it multiple times. I'm also concerned about the physical . . ." her voice trailed off, eyeing him with worry.

He swiped to the next screen to the physicals results and studied them for a second.

"Yes, I know. Not sure how to feel about the results myself. How long until he awakes?"

"It won't be too much longer before the stabilizer wears off," Atara said. "What's your plan now that you know?"

Javex shook his head. "To be honest, I am unsure. I want to believe the best of Cade. I would hate to think I was mistaken about him this entire time."

Atara nodded. "Me too."

"Come," he said, placing an arm around her shoulders. "Let us speak to the others. Together, we will decide."

They took the stairs to the observation room, where the rest of the crew waited.

"So?" Aaro asked before they got through the door, pausing his thumb war with Noro. The anticipation in the room descended like a heavy cloud.

Javex crossed his arms and stood in front of the glass. "I have examined Cade's tests, and the results are quite confusing." He waited a moment. "His blood appears normal, but further study has revealed traces of other DNA woven into his and other substances in his body we can't identify."

The crew stared at him, the hope they held for Cade disappearing.

"Such tampering is not impossible in the galaxy," Seraphina stated. "But only one race possesses that kind of technology . . ."

Javex nodded. "The Nevo."

Grootie's eyes darkened.

Aaro's brows tightened.

Noro's ears flattened.

"There's more," Javex continued. "Atara, tell them about the physical."

Atara stepped forward. "I discovered numerous scars along multiple points of his body. His arms, legs, spine."

"Was he attacked?" Aaro asked.

"I am afraid not. These are precise incisions. Even along his upper left abdomen, there is a scar from enteral feeding. During my examination, I also discovered a bioluminescent brand on his right forearm and another on the right side of his neck."

"Is it Nevo?" Aaro asked.

"Not sure. The Nevo don't brand their victims. They use tracking chips." Atara winced. She glanced across the room at Grootie and Seraphina, regretting her phrasing.

"Do we know its origins or meaning?" Grootie questioned.

"It's beyond me. Javex?"

"There is technology in the galaxy that will not function unless the operator has a key. This could be such a thing, but never have I seen it this intricate."

Grootie shifted his weight. "What is the origin of the other DNA?"

Atara hesitated, her delay causing an irritation in the tendrils on Grootie's head. She sighed.

"It's okay, Atara. Tell them," Javex said.

"It's Nevo."

Grootie growled. "That is what I detected, then. Two souls." His voice darkened.

"What about him?" Noro asked, nodding towards Cade. "What's his race?"

"Unfortunately, his genomes are not in our ship's database. I could only identify the Nevo. But I found out his age from a sample of his bone marrow."

They all shuddered.

"And?" Javex probed.

"He's old. Older than you, Captain. My guess is, someone kept him in a hyperbaric chamber to preserve him. That explains the enteral feeding."

"So what? He's an old man hybrid?" Aaro asked. "And the relapse vision?" Aaro shrugged his shoulders.

Javex glanced at Grootie to see if he had answers.

"In my experience, you suffer from a relapse vision when you have gone without consistent connection to a Nevo lord. It is how they keep control of their servants. With a type of pheromone." Grootie's voice soured as the conversation surfaced with dark memories. "But in Cade's case, this is much deeper than lacking connection. Two souls," he repeated.

"What is that?" Atara asked, scrunching her face.

Javex furrowed his brow. He'd already pieced together the information. This was more serious than experimentation.

"He's becoming a host." Grootie hissed. "Two souls together as one. I have never witnessed such a transformation. Varanus shared stories of Nevo selecting certain individuals for this process. I always believed the Nevo in the galaxy were it, no more, no less."

"Hrmph," Aaro scoffed. "Not like we need more of the damn things."

"That explains why he is sick," Seraphina pointed out.

It was all interesting speculation to Javex, paired with some obvious truths. Still, he wanted to know from Cade what happened and why he opted not to tell them the truth.

"Now what, Captain?" Aaro asked, relaxing his hand on his sidearm.

Javex stroked his chin, his heart heavy. "We can't let this transition come to fruition. We need to remove it."

"How are we going to do that without killing him?" Aaro asked. "We don't know what we are doing."

"I know someone who might," he said. "Come, let us talk with Cade. He is awake."

Chapter 14

PRISONER

Kaytrix awoke with a start, his body tight, restricted. Bright lights shone on him, preventing him from opening his eyes. Familiar voices floated towards him among all the clicks and beeps of machines. A sting of resentment went through him as he struggled against the restraints.

"I knew I couldn't trust you!! What happened to your word, Javex!?" He forced his eyes open against the light, searching for the captain. He wanted to see his face. To look him in the eyes and confront him.

"I have done nothing." Javex's voice was cool and collected.

"What do you call this?" Kaytrix pulled against the restraints again. Irritation gnawed at his skull.

"Do you remember what happened earlier today?" Javex's voice was faint, as though he spoke from across the room.

Kaytrix wanted out of the restraints and off the ship, but he humored the request and settled.

"I remember seeing a Nevo. Then visions like in my dreams, only real . . ." His voice trailed off as his thoughts ran rampant for other reasons he was being restrained.

"What else do you remember?" Javex asked.

Kaytrix searched his memory when a chill ran through him. He closed his eyes, and the light disappeared. A dark cloud formed and through it, pain surfaced. Blackness drew him in, jolting his body.

The restraints melted from his arms. He was floating. Bubbles of air rose through the dark, wet, and disgusting liquid. Flexible tubes slithered across his body. Other sharp objects pierced his flesh, jerking in and out of his skin. The pain was unbearable, followed by a fervent desire for vengeance.

He didn't know where he was when a pair of bright green eyes met his gaze. A voice hissed words of progress while the pain tweaked through his body, and everything went numb . . .

"Cade!" roared Javex's voice, tearing the memory away from him.

Javex was near him now, blocking the light. The gold in Javex's eyes was intense, but it wasn't anger there, but pity.

"What happened? Was that another relapse vision?"

"I am afraid you are not suffering from just relapse visions. There is more going on here." Javex held him by the shoulders.

Besides the concern in Javex's eyes, the others shared a distinctive look. Then his gaze fell onto Grootie, and a weird sensation twitched inside him: recognition.

"I remember," he said, gripping the edges of the bed tightly, trying to recover from the memory. "I remember what happened to me . . ." His voice trailed off, seeing images beyond that of Javex and the rest of the room. "I was a prisoner of the Nevo."

A deadening silence filled the room. Each of them held their breath at the revelation.

"A prisoner?" Grootie questioned. The edginess in his voice added a tinge of horror to the revelation.

"I only remember they are trying to make progress on something," Kaytrix said, confused.

He had questions of his own, never mind those of the surrounding crew. Why was he a prisoner of the Nevo? What did he do to deserve such a terrible act of desecration? The bounty hunter saved him from the hyperbaric chamber, but why?

"I have to get off this ship. I was their prisoner. They did this to me. They stole my life, who I am!" He rose against the restraints, his strength returning.

"I don't think that will solve anything," Javex said, placing a hand on Kaytrix's shoulder. "Have you had visions or flashbacks like this before?"

"No, I can't remember anything before I was their prisoner." He stopped. He let another detail slip.

Javex released his shoulders and dimmed the lights.

"I . . . ," he hesitated. Should he lie? "I don't remember my life," he admitted. "I didn't know why until now. Being a prisoner must have something to do with it."

"I see," Javex said. "Cade, there is something I need to tell you. Something you may not know."

Javex's tone worried him.

"What's that?"

"There's no easy way to say this," Javex said, running his claws through his fur on his head. "After you collapsed, we completed a more thorough examination of your body."

Kaytrix looked down, his body clothed in a paper-thin medical jumpsuit. Oh no.

"We found something disturbing."

Kaytrix stiffened. "That's why I am restrained."

"Yes. It wasn't my first choice, but I had to act." Javex grimaced.

Kaytrix lay his head back. Everything he was trying to hide was out in the open now. There wasn't any point in trying to deny it, but he wasn't ready to admit everything.

"What did you find?"

Javex hesitated. "There appears to be an unknown substance in your blood and a significant amount of Nevo DNA intertwined with your own. We only know old tales about this, but Grootie assures me it is the process by which the Nevo *propagate.* Something he terms as two souls."

"What exactly are you saying?" Kaytrix wasn't sure how to process what they were telling him.

"It's turning you into one of them, kid," Aaro said, his eyebrows pinching together.

"We don't know how much time you have until the Nevo parasite takes over your body," Javex added.

Kaytrix tightened his fists, feeling sick. What does someone say to that?

"Is that why the Nevo have bounty hunters looking for me?"

Javex exchanged a look with Aaro and the crew, his ears flat.

"So, you *are* the one they are looking for," Aaro said, taking a step forward. "How'd you escape their clutches?"

Kaytrix held his breath and ignored the question.

A moment passed where no one said anything.

"There's one other thing that we have yet to discuss," Javex said, breaking the silence. His tone was indiscernible.

"What's that?" Kaytrix resisted the urge to fight against his restraints. For a moment, he feared the captain, as if cornered by a hunter. It brought back the dark memories.

Javex reached for his right arm, and, in that moment, he understood what Javex meant.

"Why didn't you tell us about *these*?" Javex pushed up the sleeve of his medical gown. There, for everyone to see, was what he tried so hard to keep a secret: the mysterious markings on his body.

"I don't even know what they are," he retorted. "I couldn't take the chance you would turn me in for a profit once you found out. Like everyone else who sees them."

Javex analyzed him. What was he thinking? The following pause was so uncomfortable with no assurance of how it would end.

"Is there any way you can release me from these restraints?" he asked. "I need to leave. It's obviously not safe here for any of us."

"I am sorry, but the restraints will stay. For your sake," Javex said.

"Or for yours," he pointed out defensively.

"When you have an episode, you get violent," Seraphina said, hands on her hips.

"Look, I just want off the ship. Then you won't have to worry about the Nevo finding me here."

"I believe you are telling the truth, but it isn't enough, Cade," Javex said. "If what we think is happening is true, we can't allow the Nevo to find you, or worse, let what is inside you complete its cycle. I need to know everything to help you."

He hid his amusement. How would he tell Javex something he himself did not know?

"How will you know I am telling you the truth?"

"I will know."

Kaytrix exhaled. He still wasn't ready to surrender his story. They might be lying to him about his situation. Then again, he didn't have an explanation for what was happening to him, either.

"What's in it for me?"

Javex's eyes dilated. "I won't let the Nevo take over your body."

A shiver traveled through Kaytrix as he pictured the less favorable scenario. "Alright, the truth."

Telling his story took longer than he thought it would. From waking in the hyperbaric chamber, to being saved by the bounty hunter, his time with Traven and the escape. When he finished, he waited for someone to say something. The way they looked at him was as if what he shared was just a story.

"Now what? I don't want this thing inside me a minute more."

Javex loosened the restraints holding him.

"Captain!" Seraphina shrieked. "What are you doing?"

"Keeping my word," Javex answered.

"What if he has another episode? You witnessed how violent he can be. We don't know what he is capable of," she said. "Or how far along . . ." her voice faded.

"I agree," Aaro added. "Captain, are you sure about this?"

Javex's back faced him as they discussed his future. He wished they would decide soon. The thought of a Nevo inside his body unsettled him.

"I am, and we will watch him closely. If we don't help him, we may never recover from the ramifications. We can't allow the Nevo to have this spawn. If he is what we think, we must prevent it from happening this time and in the future," Javex said, his tone grave. "We've only heard stories of the Nevo propagating. We need to know why this is happening to Cade and why now. Why not solar rotations before and to other races."

The crew stepped back as Javex loosened the last restraint and tossed it to the floor. He helped Cade to stand, grasping his arm and hoisting him to his feet.

"We must remove the Nevo before it matures." Javex's gaze was intense, his gold irises hidden by his dilated pupils. "We may already be too late."

Kaytrix shuddered. "Don't say that. There must be something we can do?"

Kaytrix scrunched his face as a wave of nausea washed over him. Being cold didn't help. He didn't appreciate cold drafts or being covered by a thin gown. "Maybe my clothes first?" He flinched as Javex's claws extended into his skin.

Javex motioned for Noro to grab clothes when he released his arm and pointed to it.

"This is your reminder of my trust," he began, his tone grave. "It is a Zaguarz symbol of loyalty chiefs give to tribe members when a mighty trial befalls them. It's our way of strengthening each other through one's most arduous journey. Each point marks five things: honor, loyalty, justice, courage, and compassion. But if you succumb to your trials, everything virtuous is reversed." The gold in Javex's eyes gleamed with a wild glow.

"How are the few of us going to help him?" Seraphina asked, her brow furrowed. "We scrape by as it is."

"We will start at Acknaria," Javex said, turning to face the crew.

"Acknaria? Bit of a haunted planet since the Last Stand." Aaro grabbed his chin, familiarity in his tone. "What about our current mission to find the Archarians?"

Javex took in a deep breath, the fur on his body glistening in the light with the motion. "The Elders on Acknaria may have some knowledge regarding them, but what is happening to Cade takes precedence."

"When do we start?" Aaro asked, rubbing his hands together.

"As soon as Cade dresses," Javex said, looking at him. "That is, unless you still want to leave?"

Even though the crew appeared ready and willing to help him with his issue, he caused an underlying tension.

"I'll only stay if everyone is alright with it."

Seraphina was the first to step forward. He held his breath. She was nothing but hostile towards him.

"I'm in. We can't let the Nevo get away with this." She uncrossed her arms and tucked her thumbs in her belt loops. "But I have my eye on you. I won't let what's inside you jeopardize my home."

Her eyes burned with a ferocity, and he looked away, her promise also a threat. However, a calmness settled at her words. Now for everyone else.

"We're in." Atara nodded, her arm around Noro's shoulders.

"Of course. I'm in for a little adventure," Aaro said, relaxing his hand on his sidearm. "Don't think this means I forgive you for our spar today, kid."

Kaytrix grimaced, almost unable to recall those events.

"Hey, you can't call him that anymore," Atara began. "He's older than you, remember?"

Atara's comment sparked his curiosity, but Aaro brushed it off with a wave of his hand. "Until he can prove himself otherwise, he's still a kid to me."

"He kicked your ass during the sparring match. I think that counts," Noro said, grinning.

"Don't curse," Aaro said, pointing a finger.

Seraphina crossed her arms. "Something else you taught him?"

The family moment faded. The only one left to decide was Grootie, who stood silent and distanced from the group. At last, the Varanus nodded.

Kaytrix grabbed the clothes and dressed, grateful to get out of the frigid air of the ship. He wasn't sure if he should let Javex help him. It was a lot to ask of anyone, least of all people he barely knew.

"You don't owe me anything. Really. I can do this on my own," he insisted, putting on his boots.

"Not with the Nevo after you, kid. Cade," Aaro corrected after Noro tapped him. "I know how the bounty hunting thing works. Unless you have someone watching your back, you won't last long."

"Right." The turn of events made him feel strange. "But why help me?"

"We all need help from time to time. And with most of us, it's an ongoing commitment. Unless you think you can take on the Nevo spawn alone?"

Kaytrix wanted to hurl at the word spawn, instead he tightened the belt around his waist and donned his cloak. "Thanks to you, I learned I can handle myself."

Aaro shook his head. "Right. Still a smartass, eh, Cade?"

Kaytrix took in a breath. He wanted to tell them his real name. Being Cade was tolerable, but finding answers while under a pseudonym would be hard. Clarr came to mind and what she said about a different name 'to be safe.' It would be wise to remain as Cade for now.

"Okay, so fill me in on the plan. What is Acknaria and who are the Archarians?"

"Oh, no!" Seraphina wailed, grabbing her hair. She walked to the other side of the room dramatically.

"What did I say?"

"You asked the question!" she said, still holding her head.

Everyone rolled their eyes except Javex, who beamed.

"Here we go," mumbled Aaro.

"I'll tell you. Take a walk with me," Javex purred. "Grootie and Aaro will accompany us in case you suffer from . . ." he hesitated.

"Let's just call them episodes." Kaytrix grimaced.

"Alright then, episodes." Javex nodded. "Seraphina, plot a course to Acknaria. Noro, check the charge of our stealth and shields. Our new mission starts now."

Chapter 15

ACKNARIA

Kaytrix followed Javex to the bridge, but his mind was elsewhere. The events leading up to this moment caught him off guard and, quite frankly, scared the shit out of him. Shock wasn't even the word to use. More like unease and disgust? The fact an alien cozied up inside his body left him wanting to hurl, and much worse. He wanted it out, by any means necessary. Only that wasn't possible. At least not yet. The hope Javex knew someone who could help was the last thread he had.

The walls of the ship didn't feel as strange as before, but unease followed him. Despite the crew's display of willingness to help, negative thoughts gnawed at him. What if they were too late to remove the Nevo inside him? What would he turn into? He shuddered. He would deal with that when the time came.

"So," Javex began, as he walked beside him. "You have never heard of the Archarians?"

"I have, but you know how it is. No one will say anything," he said.

They entered the bridge where Grootie and Aaro settled close by and Seraphina manned the helm. Noro sat at his station, but his large curious eyes observed them.

Javex settled in front of the main viewport, crossing his arms as he gazed into space.

"When I first learned of the Lost Race, it was from my father, who heard it from his." Javex feigned a smile, but pain hid behind his eyes.

"What happened to them?"

"Not long ago, an alliance of worlds stood strong for many millennia. My father said when the Dark Ones attacked our world, the galaxy plunged into chaos after. We later learned the Dark Ones were called Nevo. They enslaved and killed many across the galaxy." Javex paused, scratching his chin. "One Archarian stood against their violence, Commander Torex, but to no avail. The Nevo ripped the alliance apart and destroyed the Archarians. We know this event as the Last Stand."

A rumbling and angry hiss seethed from beside him. Grootie's tendrils moved in an intense disarray, his lips turned into a full-fledged snarl.

"So, if the Nevo destroyed the Archarians, why search for them?" he asked. The mission seemed pointless.

Javex's golden eyes glowed warm. "Some escaped destruction, while others never left worlds when their leaders commanded them to, thus leading to their capture or death. After the annihilation of the Archarian planet, the Nevo leader, Lord Khelveliz, made a decree: anyone who helped the Archarians were to be slaughtered. He even offered rewards for turning them in. Since the Last Stand, no one has seen or heard of them. We refer to them as the Lost Race because of this."

Aaro scoffed from across the bridge, his thin form leaning against the hull. "That's why everyone wants to shoot us when we bring them up."

Javex frowned at the interruption and continued. "After hearing the stories, I became confident I would find remnants of the Lost Race, but my ideas were less than popular. I left my home in search of them, their technology, and have been looking ever since. That is how I came across the *Dauntless* and eventually my crew, but no sign of the Archarians." Javex looked down at his hands, as if weighed by an invisible burden he carried. "There is a reason my search for the Lost Race ended with failure. Let's hope that reason doesn't jeopardize our future."

Of course, Javex wouldn't elaborate on a statement like that.

"If you were to find them, how will you know they are Archarian?"

The hyperspace window shifted before them. The array of colors glided beyond the viewport in a mesmerizing display. Finally, Javex answered.

"They are not unlike you or Aaro in physical appearance. From the stories I heard, their advancement in technology, ships, and weaponry is the only physical way to discern them from other races, much like a crest or banner. Besides that, no one really knows."

Kaytrix nodded. "This place we're going. What's it like?" He turned to look at Javex.

The colors from their warp travel shone on him, deadening the spotted pattern of his fur and illuminating him in hues of blue and purple.

Javex smirked. "Wild, like my home world, but haunted. Despite the progress of civilization, the plants, and their eerie counterparts, are the dominant ones. The plants overgrow and sometimes destroy structures. It is quite beautiful and scary." Javex's voice filled with awe, but his eyes grew sad.

"Your home world," Kaytrix began carefully. "Is it under Nevo control?"

Javex pinned his ears and shook his head. "Let us not speak of this now. We are here."

The *Dauntless* dropped out of hyperspace. Before him, where the colorful hues once danced, a dark green world spun.

"Stealth is holding steady, Captain," Noro reported.

"Very good. Any Nevo activity, Atara?" Javex asked.

Kaytrix's skin crawled at the question. He sat down to observe the situation.

"The Nevo base seems busy as ever, Captain. Scanners have multiple patrol ships sweeping a sector south of the arkross."

"That's near the temple ruins where we need to go. It will be impossible to get the *Dauntless* close without our engines drawing attention."

Aaro projected a hologram of the planet's surface and stepped forward. "The Nevo make it interesting, but it's not impossible to complete our objective. We can drop off here," he said, pointing to the orange hologram, "without drawing too much attention with our engines. That'll give us a half day to walk to the local village. I know someone there who can provide us with mounts to take us to the temple ruins."

"Indeed." Javex growled. "Good plan. Cade, Aaro, and I will go to the surface. The rest of you will remain aboard the *Dauntless* to advise us of any change with the Nevo. Seraphina, you are in charge. Once you drop us off, return to orbit. Give us two rotations. If you hear nothing from us, you know what to do."

"Yes, Captain," Seraphina replied, her answer unenthusiastic.

Kaytrix studied Seraphina, trying to place the emotion he detected in her voice.

"Come on, kid," Aaro called. "Time to suit up."

He turned from the bridge and followed Aaro into the narrow corridor that led to the cargo bay.

"What happens if Seraphina doesn't hear from us?"

Aaro approached a row of lockers and tossed on random clothing. It reminded him of how Traven dressed.

"She leaves."

"Just like that. No Plan B?"

Aaro pulled a poncho over his head. "She would risk everyone else's lives if she attempted a rescue. It's something the captain insists never happens."

Javex entered the cargo bay and secured a cloak around his shoulders and tossed him one.

"Here, you need a disguise. It will also keep the plants off."

"Thanks." Kaytrix pulled the larger cloak over his own.

An unusual feeling rushed through him as he got ready for the mission beside Aaro and Javex. He couldn't distinguish if he'd done this before.

"You alright?" Aaro asked, smiling at him.

"Yeah, nervous, or excited. I can't tell," he said.

"Oh, it'll be fun all right. Here. Take this comm." Aaro passed it to him. "It has a locator beacon in case we lose you in the drop off." A devilish grin split across his face before his helmet obscured it. Aaro's sense of humor became clearer the more time they spent together.

"Ha, ha, funny."

Javex approached the cargo bay doors and secured a thick tether to a metal latch on the ship. Kaytrix tried to find an interpretation in the eyes of Aaro, but the dark blue visor of his helmet hid them. He never rappelled from a ship before. Since his crash-landing on Tarwi, he wasn't keen on getting another face full of dirt, either.

"Don't worry," Aaro said, his voice muffled from his helmet. "The line is secure and we're going down together."

Kaytrix moved into position and followed Aaro's instructions on how to fast-rope. He held on below Aaro's hands, who held the rope just below Javex.

"Ready for drop off," Javex said into his comm.

"Getting into position now. Standby," Seraphina said.

His heartbeat quickened with each passing second.

"Lowering hatch now."

He gripped the rope tighter.

"Brace your arm across your head if you don't want a face full of seeds," Aaro said. "Disembarking on the count of five," Aaro said, beginning to count.

The hatch lowered. The tops of the massive green trees swayed from the winds of the engines. He focused on the rope in his hands. Aaro finished the countdown, and they dropped.

They glided through the air until they struck the canopy of the thick, large leaves. Sticky branches brushed past their faces. Kaytrix threw up his arm in the defensive, mimicking Aaro's technique. He almost yelled. It felt as though someone took a wide belt and smacked it across his backside.

As they rappelled, the multiple leaves of the trees gave way to their intrusion until they landed on a solid surface. Javex reached one hand for a hanging branch and brought them closer to a large mossy limb. His enormous, clawed feet anchored into the wood and he reeled them onto the branch. Once they stabilized their footing, Aaro released the line, and it disappeared.

The ship's engines faded, leaving the three standing in the overpowering eerie silence of the Acknarian planet.

Kaytrix stepped forward and peered over the edge of the large, mossy branch. "How are we getting down this tree?"

"We can rappel," Aaro said, pulling an anchor and two long ropes from a latch at his side.

"I can get down on my own. I will secure the area," Javex said and began his descent using only his claws.

Kaytrix turned back to Aaro, who stood ready with the secured rope. Aaro secured their lines and with a jump off the branch, they rappelled to the bottom of the tree.

The ground was squishy and boggy, covered in a thick mat-like layer of tiny plants all intertwined together. Every so often, the tiniest white bloom popped from the entangled mess, as if to protest beauty still existed where least expected.

Aaro abandoned their equipment and pulled his blasters from his holsters. A rustle in the foggy brush drew their attention when Javex emerged, pulling cobwebs from his shoulders.

"We can walk from here," Javex said, tossing a part of his cloak across his shoulder. "I am certain our presence remains unknown."

"We better start moving. Two rotations flies by quick here," Aaro said. He activated his gauntlet, which projected a holographic map. "The village is this way."

They set out on their trek. As time wore on, the planet drew closer to dusk and a creepy feeling weaved in around Kaytrix. Through the fog-ridden jungle, and the long dark tunnels of twisted trees above them, the feeling that someone watched them increased.

The wind howled and whistled through the magnificent trees, as if protesting their presence. Fog raided the jungle in a frenzy of mad swirls around their feet. The howl of wind faded with the thickening brush and the eery silence once again overwhelmed them. A blur to his right made Kaytrix pivot, but he saw nothing there.

"You said something haunts this place? What is it exactly?"

Javex's ears rotated, searching for the faintest of sounds. "No one knows for sure. Could be the trees, or spirits."

Javex looked back at him to smirk at his scowl. If Kaytrix didn't know better, he would think Javex tried to scare him. Why was he always the butt of everyone's joke?

Ahead of them, glimmers of orange light shone through the twisted trees. In the wake of the wind's calamity, the noise of the small village filtered through the silence. They emerged from the jungle and Kaytrix understood Javex's words about the trees being dominant.

Massive roots twisted through buildings, some even penetrated the rock and grew through. The buildings were old, made of deteriorating rock held together by the trees themselves. Orange orbs floated, bobbing up and down as they provided light to the streets below. People meandered up and down the walkways, as though purposeless, or lost.

"These are the ruins?" he asked.

"The ruins are just beyond this village," Aaro said, his voice muffled.

"We don't want to draw attention to ourselves. Let's find your friend quickly," Javex said.

They walked into the village without a look from the inhabitants. The villagers dressed in clothes that resembled rags and walked about with heavy eyes, as if someone stole the very essence of their existence.

"Who are these people?" Kaytrix asked.

Aaro's accented voice answered him in a hushed tone as he continued to lead them. "They're monks, or what's left of them. This used to be the most spiritual place in the region until the Nevo arrived in search of the temple ruins."

Kaytrix detected bitterness in Aaro, his banter replaced by the cold and calculated focus of a soldier.

"What do the Nevo want with the ruins?"

"The same thing we do," Javex began. "Knowledge. Only they aim to keep it for themselves and hide it from the truth seekers."

The three made it through the small village and were about to enter the edge of the jungle when a shout stopped them in their tracks.

"Oi! What's your business here?" slurred a man. He stood in the door-way of a small structure, a poignant aroma wafting from behind him.

Aaro holstered his weapons, but now his hands moved to draw them as he turned to face the man.

"Who's asking?" Aaro quipped when he froze.

The dirty man stood swaying in the entrance of a building, drunk. His facial features changed from disgust to a rotten smile as he gazed upon them.

"Aaro?" the man asked dubiously, stepping down the stairs only to trip and tumble down them.

Without hesitation, Aaro rushed to the man's side and helped him up. "You silly old dovtor," he said woefully. "What's driven you to this madness?"

"Me!?" protested the old man in a slur. "How about you? Why are you back here? Of all places."

"Take me and my friends to your place," Aaro said in a hushed tone. "We need to borrow a few mounts."

The villagers ceased their listless wandering to watch them. The man took too long to answer forcing Aaro to improvise. In a swift motion, Aaro bound the man's hands and threw him over his shoulder, a feat that proved difficult due to the man's heftiness.

"This man has a bounty!" Aaro proclaimed to the gawking villagers. "Now he pays with his life."

The townsfolk scuttled from the street and disappeared into their houses. Satisfied, Aaro turned and marched out of the village.

"Aaro," Javex said. "What is happening? Who is this? We can't afford to waste time."

"I know, Captain. Unfortunately, I know this scoundrel, but thankfully he's not the only friend we have here."

They came to a structure in the heart of a tree, where Aaro placed the drunk down on the steps. The building no longer represented a four-walled structure. The tree surrounding the house squished the materials in upon themselves with tremendous pressure, forcing the materials to split. Fragments of other materials appeared tacked on as an afterthought to prevent nature from further disturbing the house. A lost cause, it seemed.

"Hey!" Aaro said, patting the man's face. "Drat. He fell asleep. Wait here." Aaro disappeared into the dark structure.

When Aaro emerged, he held an old lamp and a blanket.

Kaytrix gazed upon the old man as he slept. "How does he know you?" He knew little about Aaro's past.

"Agh," Aaro spat, shaking his head. He wrapped the blanket around the man and gazed at his grubby face in the lantern's light. "After the Nevo destroyed the Archarians," he began, whispering the name, "my planet, Shrovon, embraced their rule over us. I grew up in it until I couldn't stand the corruption. My people no longer held the values and beliefs that my ancestors once fought and died for. I started a coup, but one of my own soldiers betrayed me." Aaro took a breath before continuing. "After my exile, I joined the Red Sky Alliance, a faction of rebels who fought against the violent rule of the Nevo. When that ended in their annihilation, I barely escaped through the arkross with my life. When I arrived here, Nava found me and brought me to the village. This old monk, Harves, helped me heal my wounds. But Shrovon hadn't forgotten what I did. My coup did more damage than they cared to admit. They wanted to make an example out of me. A public trial and execution. Only the bounty hunters they sent couldn't find me. I stayed on Acknaria to avoid any unnecessary violence." Aaro paused. "Long story short, Javex came through the village and that's where we met. The rest is history."

Javex trained his gaze on Aaro's helmeted face. "I did not know that about you."

"I risked a lot to join you, Captain, but I don't regret it. Harves here got me through one of the toughest phases of my life, but I couldn't stay knowing what the Nevo were executing on other systems. It's sad he's let himself go."

A rumbling snore escaped the monk's gaping mouth.

"Damn drunk."

The snoring stopped with a snort and a gulp. Harves sputtered when he coughed. His eyes remained closed, but his face contorted as he grasped the blanket and held it tighter around himself.

"You don't know what it's been like around here since you left, Aaro. I don't drink to wallow in self-pity. No. The drink helps me forget. The Nevo cannot find them. It's the only way to keep the elders safe."

Aaro froze. "Is Nava . . .? Are the elders still in the ruins?"

Harves opened one eye and looked from Aaro to Javex and finally rested on Kaytrix. "Who do you travel with?"

"They are my friends. Cade here is sick. We need the elder's help."

Harves closed his eye and furrowed his brow.

Javex crossed his arms, his tail twitching from side-to-side. Aaro remained rigid, waiting for the drunk to answer.

Harves took in a ragged breath. "I do not know. I keep the location safe. The Nevo are on patrol. Forever searching to destroy."

"We need to go, Harves. Or my friend may die. We need the dovtors." Aaro stood, taking the light of the lantern with him.

Harves opened his glassy eyes, catching the eery yellow of the light. "Will I see you again?"

"If we make it out of here with what we need, possibly."

Harves exhaled with a slight nod. "They remember the path, though overgrown. They never forget. Let them lead you."

"Thanks. Get inside. Stay safe." Aaro turned from the drunk monk and strolled further into the jungle of large trees, not looking back.

Kaytrix and Javex followed him a few paces when they came upon a tall structure untouched by the jungle. The comforting smell of hay and sweet feed filled the air. Kaytrix found himself overwhelmed by memory flashbacks. Something about this setting appeared familiar and made him at peace.

"What is this place?"

"It's a dovtor barn. Harves raised them. They will take us to the ruins before the end of the day," Aaro said.

"Is this really necessary?" Javex asked, crossing his arms. His ears bent back, his tail twitching. "I'm not good at riding."

"Unfortunately, Captain. The dovtors will save us time trying to maneuver the overgrown rainforest ourselves."

Aaro heaved the sliding doors apart. As they separated, a type of purring coo reverberated out of the darkness. The melodic sound repeated in the same pattern until Aaro walked in with the lantern. Pairs upon pairs of glimmering eyes blinked in disunity. A deep growl silenced the coos.

From the barn door, Aaro reached into his pocket and brought out a shiny object Kaytrix recognized as a whistle. Aaro blew into it and a soft sound floated through the structure.

"Hey, Strider. You remember me?" Aaro set down his lamp, and the head of a large animal extended out of a stall. The dovtor growled again and Aaro reached into his pocket to produce a treat. "Nice to see you too, boy." Aaro stroked the massive dovtor's head as it ground the treat in its teeth. Aaro secured a rope around its neck and led the animal from the stall.

Kaytrix suppressed a gasp. They were the same animals he'd helped Traven with on Rehnna, but these were more agile. The dovtor was a striking thing of beauty, its movements fluid as it pranced out of the barn and around Aaro.

Strider's neck arched in pride. The male dovtor stood taller than Javex by a hand and longer than two men. The dovtor walked on two hind legs, using two shorter forelimbs for stability. Its long tail swayed and played in the open space around it.

"What a lovely animal. I've never seen a male before. Too expensive for Traven," Kaytrix said.

Saying Traven's name caused a stab of pain. He hoped Traven and Clarr were safe.

Aaro handed him the neck rope of the dovtor. "Here, hold him while I fetch the girls."

Aaro re-entered the structure.

Kaytrix watched after Aaro with a bit of skepticism. Strider gazed at him, the bristles atop his head shuddering in a type of animal excitement. Kaytrix stroked the dovtor's soft muzzle when Strider snorted in response and released a shrilling neigh.

Kaytrix's heart raced as Strider shook his head back and forth.

"Easy," he said, patting the dovtor's thick neck.

Strider lowered his head and nudged Kaytrix hard.

"That one's a glutton," Aaro said as he exited the barn with two dovtors in tow. "He's looking for treats."

"I don't mind giving him treats as long as he takes us where we need to go." Kaytrix continued to stroke the dovtor's muzzle, the motion simple and soothing.

Waiting to be rid of the amnesia was torture. He wanted to know who he was, where he was from. But before that, he needed this Nevo removed. Being a host, or helping more Nevo spawn, was not only disgusting, but devastating.

Aaro saddled the dovtors and, after a quick lesson on how to ride, they mounted.

"Try to stay on. These guys move quick," Aaro said, turning Strider around.

Aaro rode as if he'd been born in the saddle, dawning a different sort of confidence, while Javex was awkward on the back of the creature.

They headed into the dusk rainforest, weaving effortlessly through the thick of the trees, bounding over large roots and avoiding branches with ease. There wasn't a lot to see with the fog, but he could feel every movement of his dovtor beneath him. The familiarity made his mind wander.

His thoughts flooded with images, feelings, and senses. A splitting pain brewed in his temples. The memories came too quick for him to process and the pain in the back of his neck intensified. His grip on the reins tightened. He didn't need an episode to strike now, but as the moments wore on, his symptoms worsened.

A knot formed in his stomach, and a numbness took the feeling out of his hands. He forced himself to focus, to stay present. Kaytrix observed the trees as the dovtor weaved over and under. He focused on her panting, the smell of the moist jungle, the rain pinching his face.

Rain.

A memory thrust him into the past. Cool mud soaked into his uniform, his hands shaking as he readied grenades. Voices of comrades urged him to complete the mission despite an overwhelming loss on the battlefield. He rose, drenched in sweat, mud, and rain, to complete his mission when screams of agony and metal slashing armor shattered his confidence. He delivered the payload, and an explosion erupted, raining down dirt and rocks. The victory came too late. The debris settled, revealing a lone soldier standing atop dead men he once knew. Its tattered cape billowed in the wind as its fleshy green eyes glared at him.

Pain drew him back to the present, but he wasn't in the saddle anymore. His dovtor stood munching several feet before him. The cold clung to him as he laid on the ground, the weight of his body pressing the water from the ground and into his clothes. He sat up and rested his head against a solidness unknown to trees. He turned to see a stone wall. Lichen populated the surface as it scaled up into the trees and out of sight. Deep dark groves worn away by weather etched the surface in an ancient story.

In the distance, the whisper of faint voices called his name. The rain drowned what direction they came from.

"Over here!" he called.

Through the falling rain, a blur crossed through his peripheral. He turned. Under the shelter of a large leaf, a dull white form sat perched in the darkness. Its narrow eyes blinked.

The image transfixed him. Small like a child, it tucked its spindly legs and forearms in around its crouched body and contorted its appearance. A small, toothy grin split its narrow face. A rush of adrenaline surged through his body when branches snapped nearby.

Aaro and Javex entered the clearing and rushed to his side. Relief flooded Kaytrix. When he looked back, the creature was gone.

Chapter 16
THE RUINS

Javex ground his teeth as the monstrosity beneath him strode along. Several times, his stomach lurched. He vowed not to expel his stomach, to not waste Atara's fantastic morning meal on the silliest thing, like motion sickness. He'd flown in ships most of his adult life, but the side-to-side trot of the dovtor beneath him jarred his insides.

The animal snorted, and her stride slowed. Aaro rode in front, his figure a shadow among the thick vines. He glanced to his right where Cade rode to see the man flying from his saddle as the dovtor beneath him stopped short.

"Cade!" He pulled on the dovtor's neck rope and came to a stop. Javex dismounted and leaped into the jungle.

"What happened?" Aaro called.

"I lost Cade. His dovtor threw him."

Aaro cursed, but Javex paid little attention. As he leapt over a massive tree trunk, he sunk his claws into the mossy surface and propelled himself forward. He cursed as he landed in a prickly bush. The sharp prongs pulled at his fur as he tore away. He ducked, avoiding the branches above from clawing his eyes.

"Cade!" Javex called again.

He came to a small clearing where Cade sat resting against the ruins of an ancient wall, his gaze fixated in one direction. Javex approached with caution.

"Cade, there you are. Are you okay?" He placed a hand on Cade's shoulder.

Aaro emerged out of the jungle behind him.

Cade blinked. "I swore something was there just now. Was it a ghost? I can't trust what I see."

Javex peered through the rain, unable to see anything. He took a long sniff, only detecting the wet jungle and dovtor sweat.

Aaro shook his head. "It wasn't a ghost. Nava!" Aaro called in a furious, exasperated tone. "That little gremlin's always causing trouble."

Javex helped Cade to his feet.

"Who are you calling?"

"My *other* friend." Aaro scoffed. "That's why your dovtor refused to proceed."

"You mean threw me?" Cade pointed out.

"Yeah. They don't like the Acknarians."

"Easy to understand why. If that was Nava, he's creepy."

"And a little shit." Aaro growled. "When I showed up here long before meeting Javex, my leg was all busted. Nava found me at the arkross. Told me he'd pee on my leg to disinfect it. I nearly shot him then." Aaro stared into the rain. "Forget about him. These are the ruins. Looks like your head helped us find the entrance, kid."

"Great. Doesn't look like much of a temple."

Javex strode to the wall and ran a hand over the ancient ruins. "They are all but remnants now. The jungle has made sure of that."

Eight solar rotations ago he'd been here, but he'd never forgotten the tranquility the silent and broken structure provided. Even now, the ruins calmed him, creating a sense of reverence. Though not much remained, the jungle kept it well hidden and out of the Nevo's sight. Truly, the Acknarians were wise in choosing this planet to harbor their knowledge.

"Come, let us continue. We're running out of time."

Javex entered the temple through a broken arch to find the inner structure covered in plant life. Stones, weathered by storms and covered in lichens, lay broken. Walls crippled by plants stood broken in half, their pieces scattered. Trees grew through the stone floor and through the now open ceiling.

Javex followed what used to be the hallway of the temple. Though broken and lying in fragments, it led to the center of the temple where the Great One would meet him. He rounded the last corner, stepping over a fallen column before entering the temple's most reverent gathering place.

A flash of lightning brightened a slim figure waiting for them, too small to be the Great One. The creature before them bore narrow eyes. Its skull elongated as if someone stretched it in some horrible tug of war at birth. A long, thin, bony tail coiled around its body. The alien's knees bent close to its face and its slim arms tucked under itself. It was an Acknarian, the native species of this planet.

"Nava, there you are!" Aaro strode up to the creature and squatted to his level.

Nava blinked, but his expression remained distant.

"These are friends, Nava. You don't have to fear them," Aaro said. Aaro stood and motioned for Javex and Cade to join him.

Javex approached where Nava sat perched, relieved the tree they stood under provided ample protection from the bone-chilling rain.

"Are the others coming?"

Nava remained silent.

"There are others?" Cade strode under the tree, wrapping his poncho around him tight, his skin pale.

"There are six other members that make up the Acknarian council," Javex began. "They convene together before sharing information with strangers. Nava, youngest of the council. I am Javex. I sought the wisdom of the Great One several times before. Our friend Cade is sick. We request the guidance of the Great One, for this far surpasses our knowledge."

Nava regarded Javex more closely, and his face relaxed.

"Yes, I remember you, Javex." His tiny voice was odd and creepy. "We have not had contact with you for a great deal of time. How do I know I can I trust you?"

Javex reached for his blade. "Would someone devoted to serving the Nevo offer to cut their palm?"

Nava entertained the notion when an old voice called out, "That is quite enough, Nava."

Javex turned, alerted to movement in the center of the ancient ruins. Five Acknarians, with inquisitive eyes and bony bodies, sat on the broken remains of the council chairs.

"Such a demonstration of loyalty is unnecessary."

The oldest one with the largest crest of a head sat upright. The Great One.

"You must accept my deepest apologies," the old Acknarian spoke, his voice non-wavering despite his age. "We need to be cautious these days. Nava, however, was not to go so far."

The elder's voice was thick with disapproval as the younger Acknarian took his seat on a weathered stone.

"Thank you for your time and council, Great One." Javex bowed.

The Great One took his time to answer, folding his hands together. "Your story is intriguing, Javex."

Cade bristled beside him and stepped forward, his hands clenched. Javex placed a hand on Cade's shoulder.

"Let him finish."

Cade relaxed, and a shiver rolled through his body.

The Great One's beady eyes sparkled and then closed.

"I sense your fear, and the cause of it. Profoundly disturbing what the Nevo are up to." The Great One stepped down from his chair to walk on all four of his legs around Cade. "Where were you born?"

Cade grimaced, as if unsure.

"You can tell him everything you told me," Javex said. "Only the truth can help set you free."

The Great One extended his hand to Cade. "To save you the time and words, may I see?"

Cade glanced back to Javex for guidance, and once again, he nodded. Cade extended his hand and the old Acknarian touched his finger. A pause followed as the Acknarian concentrated.

"Hmm. This spawn proves to be a dangerous problem. An increase in the Nevo's kind would change the galaxy forever. Your history is also interesting."

"Can you help me?" Cade asked.

The Great One blinked his black, narrow eyes. "I cannot. I can only see, but there is someone with power that can do the unspeakable, a sage."

Cade smiled, the first Javex had seen. "Well, that is great. How do we contact them?"

"Unfortunately, I lost contact with them, but I know of the planet they frequent."

"We appreciate any guidance," Javex said with a bow.

The old Acknarian released Cade's hand and sat before them.

"I must warn you, Javex. If you do not find the sage in time, you have a difficult decision to make."

Javex lowered his gaze, unable to face that truth. It was essential to believe they would find the sage and save Cade. He wouldn't allow himself to doubt, not without trying first.

"I understand."

"Javex, I have enjoyed sharing knowledge with you, but, old friend, I am afraid it has to end."

Javex perked his ears. "What do you mean?"

"The Nevo are closer to discovering where we are. If they find us, it will jeopardize our database of knowledge. They will steal all the truths of the past and use it against the worlds."

"What are you asking?" Aaro asked, crossing his arms.

The old Acknarian returned to his chair among the others in the circle. "I need you to destroy this temple."

Javex's ears leveled across his head. This was his only link to the past, to finding the Lost Race and freeing his people from slavery. "If we ever hope to fight the Nevo, to free the enslaved . . ." his voice trailed off.

The Great One rested his head against the cracked headrest of his chair. "There are other keepers on other planets with knowledge. Find them and they will help you as I have."

Aaro stepped forward. "What about the monks in the village? When we destroy this place, the Nevo are going to be drawn to the area and slaughter them."

The old Acknarian blinked his narrow eyes. "This is the only way to protect the past and the future. Do we have an accord?"

Javex hesitated. Could he destroy his only hope of fulfilling his life's mission? He didn't have the strength to answer. He regretted coming here. His primary goals, his life's journey, now threatened.

"Do we have an agreement?" The Great One asked again.

Aaro put a hand on Javex. "There are others, Captain. There's still hope." Aaro addressed the Acknarian. "Yes, we have an agreement."

"Very well." The old Acknarian relaxed in his seat.

Javex's heart constricted with bitterness and loss but was grateful to Aaro for having the strength to say what he struggled to. Even he must sacrifice something for the greater good. Aaro excelled to keep things in perspective when his own heart failed to make the right decision.

"As promised, we will provide the planet's location to the sage. Watch your step," the old Acknarian said.

Javex, Aaro, and Cade took a few steps back from the circle.

The elders placed their hands on the armrests of their stone chairs. Beams of light shot out from the base and met together at the center of the council where a stone lay. The light-energy transferred into a storing crystal, activating a hologram above it. A projection grid formed from the white light and took on the shape of a cone. One by one, planets of diverse cultures and climates appeared on the white projection. The Acknarians served as the biological key to unlock the hidden information.

A highlighted strobing planet drew his attention.

"The planet's name is Arimas, where you may find help. May your quest be successful."

Javex hoped it would be. Saving Cade depended on it.

Aaro stepped forward. "Permission to copy the information?"

"Of course."

Javex nodded for Aaro to start.

Aaro pressed several buttons on his gauntlet and pointed his arm at the display. A scan commenced, capturing the data when the display disappeared.

"We thank you for your time, Great One," Javex said, bowing respectfully. "Where will you go when we destroy the temple?"

The Acknarian's face settled into a thoughtful visage.

"We will remain on the planet. Who knows, maybe one day we can rebuild." The Great One bowed and stepped down from his chair. "For now, I must say farewell," he said with a toothy smile. Then, with a tremendous leap, he entered the trees, followed by the others.

Javex grimaced. "Farewell, Great One," he said to himself. He wished he didn't have to destroy the ruins, but their knowledge was no longer safe. He activated his comm. "Seraphina, we're ready for pickup. Meet you at the drop off coordinates."

"*Copy that, Captain.*"

Cade sauntered over towards the tree to get out of the rain while Aaro knelt to share a few words with Nava. A shrilling laugh left the creature, startling whatever stupor Cade had slipped into.

Aaro stood as Nava disappeared into the foggy trees, his bony white body becoming a lost memory of the fog.

"Ready?"

Aaro wiped the fog from his visor. "Yes, Captain. I think I'll be good if I never have to come back here."

Javex grinned. "What of Harves?"

"Well, he's the exception, but I won't go out of my way to see that little twat. Wanted my helmet just now. I threatened to shoot off one of his toes." Aaro stifled a laugh. "Then he laughed and jumped away. I swear he likes trouble."

Javex grinned down at Aaro. "So it would appear."

The three left the ruins and mounted their waiting dovtors to begin their return trip. As they rode away, Javex glanced back to the ruined temple. The pain of destroying it returned. Hope and despair flitted through his mind, along with the faces of the loved ones he'd left behind on his planet. His wife, his child, his duties. It proved difficult not to feel like he chose Cade over them. It wasn't like that, but his heart persisted, growing sore in his chest.

He glanced at Cade, who rode beside him. For once, a light shone behind his eyes rather than fear and terror. He wished the Great One shared more about the stranger's history. If he succeeded in helping Cade, perhaps one day he would share of his own accord.

"Coming up to our drop off point," Aaro said through the group comm.

"I'm ready," spoke Seraphina.

Javex dismounted his dovtor, eager to be off the animal's back. He gripped the tree and hoisted himself closer to the rich smelling bark and began his assent. The effort to climb the massive tree revitalized him, but also helped to lessen his frustrations. Sinking his claws into something always helped to process his intense emotions.

The *Dauntless* drew near, throwing the canopy of treetops into a disarray. Cade and Aaro stood beside him atop the massive tree limb when three lines appeared through the greenery.

Javex grabbed hold of a line and turned to assist Cade.

"Remember to keep your arm up this time!" Aaro cautioned, tugging on his line to ensure it was secure.

Javex grinned at the unamused expression on Cade's face. Above them, the *Dauntless* hovered, pivoting until it steadied.

"Ready?"

Cade's face glistened with sweat. The entire process was foreign to him. Cade nodded.

"Alright, hoist us up."

"Copy that. Grootie is standing by to aid," Seraphina said.

Aaro snorted. "Oh, is he now? Well, hopefully he's been practicing cause last time he—"

Aaro's breath flew out of him when his line suddenly jerked, propelling him off his feet and towards the ship at an unsafe speed.

Seraphina's mischievous giggles came over the line. *"I may have bribed him, Captain. Sorry."*

"Seraphina, we don't have time for games. Aaro has our next set of coordinates. Upload them into the computer, but don't leave the planet yet. We have one more task."

"Standing by."

When he boarded the ramp with Cade, Aaro was cursing Grootie, whose smug expression said it all.

"Aaro, to the bridge," Javex said, his stern tone a reminder of what still needed to be done.

With a few well-balanced strides, he entered the bridge with Aaro and Cade close behind.

Aaro approached the navigation console where Seraphina sat.

"How was your trip?" She asked.

Aaro glared at her as he pulled up his sleeve. "How do we transfer files from my gauntlet?"

The Shrovon technology differed from that of the ancient ship, but under the guidance and genius of Noro, Seraphina learned how to adapt it.

Seraphina scowled at his deflect. "Like this."

She took out the small crystal from his gauntlet and placed it in a port and closed the top. Soon, information began downloading and displaying onto the screen before them.

"Now we . . .?" Aaro asked, scratching his head.

"The *Dauntless* will do the rest." Seraphina motioned to the screen as it began locking in the coordinates by itself. "What would you do without me?"

"I'd have Noro." Aaro grinned, leaving her proximity before she could swat him.

Javex smirked at their interaction and thought better of correcting it.

"Are we ready?" he asked, breaking their moment.

"Yes, sir," Aaro replied, sliding into the weapons terminal seat. "I have the location of the ruins locked in."

The planet below spun as peaceful as ever. Its surface lush with bountiful shades of green jungles and speckled with bodies of water. So peaceful yet so unaware of what was about to happen. It broke Javex's heart.

"Fire."

It took a split second for Aaro to register the command and initiate the firing sequence. The *Dauntless'* cannon released a bombardment of projectile fire towards the planet. The energy soared with intense velocity, streaking the blackness of space with a blaze of piercing white light. Upon impact, a shockwave rolled through the jungles, followed by the rise of a mushroom cloud.

"Direct hit, Captain," Aaro reported. "I am also picking up an energy signature on the planet."

Javex perked his ears. "Is it Nevo?"

"No sir. Larger. A shield is covering the entire village."

Javex smiled, and a weight lifted. He should have known the Great One wouldn't sacrifice his patrons.

"Set course for Arimas. Our mission here is done," he said, and leaned back in his seat.

Chapter 17

ARIMAS

The *Dauntless* dropped out of hyperspace. Red lights flashed warnings and sirens rang through the small bridge. Kaytrix braced himself as Seraphina piloted the ship around the forward section of a destroyed ship.

"Sorry about that, Captain," she called as she directed the ship around another piece of debris. "I wasn't expecting this."

Aaro switched off the alarms as the *Dauntless* came to rest.

The planet before them was enormous. Finding the sage without a clearer idea of where to start would be an overwhelming task. Rugged terrain stretched across the planet's surface, but that's not what stopped Kaytrix's heart. Littered around the planet's atmosphere where the bones of destroyed ships.

Kaytrix released his breath. The devastation brought up familiar feelings, but he didn't know how it tied to his past.

Javex approached the viewport. "Is there any way to know what happened?"

Atara shifted in her seat beside Noro. They'd never seen something like this before.

Atara cleared her throat. "It appears to be a graveyard of ships, but I can't determine what destroyed the vessels. Whatever it was, it left no survivors."

"Anti-air turrets?" Aaro guessed.

"Possibly," Noro offered. "But it would have to be monstrous to have this level of effectiveness. My scans aren't picking up anything that size in the atmosphere or on the planet."

"Is there Nevo activity?" Kaytrix asked.

Noro observed his screen and pressed a few buttons. "None. Though I've identified a few of their ships among the debris. The rest are from varying classes of Varanus war vessels."

The atmosphere of the bridge shifted. Grootie huffed, his tendrils twitching in agitation. The Varanus stood at the corner of the bridge with his arms crossed. His arm muscles bulged, threatening strength Kaytrix only wished to possess.

"There seems to be some recent activity near the mountains, Captain. A settlement," Atara said, moving one of her braids behind her pointed ear. "A few hundred population."

Javex breathed a sigh of relief. The captain hadn't taken his gaze from Grootie since the mention of the Varanus.

"Take us down, Seraphina. Let's hope whatever destroyed these vessels is long dormant or destroyed."

The ship moved and a swell of pain radiated through Kaytrix's head. He closed his eyes while Javex chatted on with the crew.

Flashes of mountains raced through his vision, faces, the smell of a cake. Every time he endured this pain, another piece of the puzzle fell into place. Javex's voice brought him out of his pain-induced stupor before he figured out what the clues meant.

"Cade, I know you are not well, but you will join Grootie, myself, and Aaro on the surface. Seraphina will remain aboard with Noro and Atara in case we need a pickup," Javex said.

A look of worry flooded Noro's face while Atara tried to be brave.

"We will be back before you know it," Javex said, wrapping his arms around each of them. "But we must hurry."

Kaytrix stood to leave, catching a cautionary glance from Grootie and Aaro. He tried not to imagine what he looked like or what was happening inside his body as he followed Javex to the cargo bay and readied alongside them.

The ship below their feet groaned and a type of hissing reverberated through the empty hold.

"Alright, Captain," spoke Seraphina through their joined comms. *"I've landed a distance away from the settlement, out of sight. Just in case. Be safe."*

"Thank you, Seraphina," said Javex. "We shouldn't be long."

Grootie punched the release button, lowering the rear cargo hold door of the *Dauntless*. Cool air met them in a rush, whisking away the stale smell of repurposed air and replenishing it with new. Kaytrix absorbed the freshness but resisted taking a step.

Javex led them out, his ears flicking forward and to the sides, listening. He drew his bow as he took two steps forward and waited again. Aaro stood beside Kaytrix, weapons drawn, the creak of his leather holsters the only sound besides the fading whirr of the engines. Javex raised his hand and motioned them forward.

The steel of the ship surrendered to a new range of sounds. Songs flitted through the tops of the tall coniferous trees with whistles and flutters. Whatever creatures inhabited the forest, they were oblivious to the surrounding ruin.

To his left, large, cracked pillars lay splayed on the ground. Smaller pieces littered their path, pressed into the dirt as a permanent reminder of the destruction. Walls crumbled into heaps everywhere. Tools and barrels lay scattered at their bases and thrown in disorder.

Shreds of cloth flapped in the breeze where faces once peered out of windows. Further from the broken town, vertical heaps of smaller stone formed patterns. Kaytrix's heart sank when he recognized them to be graves. From that point on, the rocky terrain demanded most of his attention.

Navigating rocks proved trickier than walking on the sands of Rehnna. Aaro's boots tapped the firm surface of the ground with skilled silence, while Grootie's long claws scratched every rock he walked over. His steps were sluggish, and he tried to hide it between the footfalls of the others.

Javex rose his hand, and the group stopped. "Someone watches us." He growled.

Kaytrix searched the endless heights of trees, and the large ferns sprouted between the rocks for potential foes.

Aaro tensed beside him, his fingers switching off the safety on his blaster. "Orders?" He rasped through his helmet.

Javex's tail flicked, but the bowstring in his hand remained slack. "We will continue to the settlement. Stay alert."

Kaytrix navigated down the steep terrain of the mountainside. The scuttling rocks below his boots and the warmth from the stone bore a familiarity for him.

They followed the worn path through a ravine of rock that ended at a meadow. Green grass swayed in the slight breeze, stirring up the warm smells of the forest. In the distance, smoke rose from the settlement on the other side.

A memory of a field surfaced. A platoon of courageous soldiers plowed across to destroy a revolving turret, only to be massacred by a dark-robed figure.

"Hey." Aaro grabbed him by the shoulder, interrupting the memory. "Let's go."

Javex started across the clearing, but Kaytrix hesitated. "Shouldn't we go around? This feels like a trap." He didn't enjoy the revelation of his last memory, nor did he care to make it a déjà vu.

"If they wanted to kill us, they would have done it by now," Javex said, motioning him forward.

The wind rustled through the grass. Kaytrix struggled to shake his instincts. Walking through the clearing compromised their position.

"Come on, Cade," Aaro said.

Aaro's calm demeanor settled him, and he proceeded. At the end of the clearing, a worn dirt path cut through the remaining forest where, through the trees, a variety of pitched tents stood situated. Javex froze and gave a hand signal.

"Form up!" Aaro said.

Kaytrix formed up with Aaro and Grootie just as ten armed men rushed from the forest's edge, aiming their weapons at them. The leader stood in front. He was short, with a red bandana folded around his brow. Black markings smeared his under eye, his skin a rich brown from many hours in the sun.

"Drop your weapons!" the man demanded.

"You expect me to be that unwise?" Javex growled.

"You travel with a Varanus. We're at war with them and their sadistic leader, Lord Khelveliz!" His finger tightened on the trigger. "Now drop your weapons!"

Javex stepped in front of the man. "He is our friend, not your enemy. We trust him, as can you."

"I'll trust him when he's dead at my feet," snarled the man. "Did you not see the debris field when you approached our planet? The atmosphere is nothing but a graveyard for their kind."

A wildness blazed in the man's eyes. Did war or seclusion turn him crazy?

"We are here for the sage, not your war," Javex said, holding his bow ready.

The men wore mismatched armor, but each bore a yellow symbol. One on his shoulder pad, another on his chest plate. Whoever these rogue soldiers were, they fought together for the same cause.

The leader scrutinized them with his head tilted upwards. "Take their weapons!" He leaned towards Javex. "If you seek the sage, you will respect our demands."

Kaytrix held his breath, trying to navigate another wave of nausea.

"Very well," Javex said, giving up his bow.

The soldiers surrounded them and seized their weapons, wrenching Aaro's guns from his grasp.

"I won't be taking any chances with that one." The man sneered towards Grootie. His men aimed their weapons on the tall Varanus. "What's your name? I am Warren."

"Javex."

"How do you know the sage?"

Warren stared past Javex to peer at him and the others, his eyebrow rising at the sight of his skin.

"The Great One sent us."

Warren hid his surprise with a thoughtful expression. "So, it was you who destroyed the Nevo outpost on Acknaria?"

Javex stiffened, but his face remained composed.

They'd destroyed the Nevo outpost while leveling the ruins?

"Word travels fast. That was not our plan. Is the sage here or not? We're in a precarious situation and cannot wait."

Warren hesitated, eyeing Grootie. "If the Great One sent you, I'll be courteous. But mark my words. Do anything obnoxious and you are as good as dead. Read me?" He motioned for them to follow when he elbowed another soldier. "Summon General Reatz."

Two soldiers left their group and Warren led them to a tent located further in the encampment. How could Warren and his troops be responsible for the carnage lingering in the atmosphere above them? Their camp was unimpressive and hand-built, their weapons not more advanced than theirs, with no visible anti-aircraft turrets.

Warren welcomed them inside the tent and stood around the remnants of the morning fire. The sun warmed the tent, filling it with a rich smell of canvas and wood. Warren beckoned them to sit with him. Kaytrix sat with Javex, but Aaro and Grootie remained standing and on guard, reluctant to join.

"You said you were at war? For how long?" Kaytrix asked.

Warren snatched a cloth from his belt, soaked it with water, and wiped his face.

"Since I was a lieutenant, so, a few decades. Short compared to the suffering of others. Arimas has been fortunate. We can't complain about what little we have."

"Forgive my ignorance, but how have you lasted against the Nevo for so long?"

Warren ignored his question and instead said, "This planet is home to one of the toughest substances known in this region of space. We must protect it. Otherwise, the Nevo will create stronger ships and weaponry. We can't let that happen."

"Is the sage helping you?"

Warren poked the fire. "You are here to see the sage. Why?" He raised his gaze from the fire.

Javex huffed. "We have an urgent need for their skills."

Warren's face fell into a scowl. "They have not visited in a couple of solar rotations, but if you can help us, maybe my commanding officer can arrange for you to meet."

Kaytrix rubbed a temple and held his breath. Two solar rotations?

Javex stroked his chin. "What is it you need from me?"

Warren stumbled over his words. "Well, not you, but this one," he said, pointing to Grootie.

The tendrils on Grootie's head stiffened and his eyes narrowed. A chill tingled Kaytrix's spine. He'd never witnessed Grootie so irritated before today.

Grootie hissed. "I will not help you."

Javex stood and faced Grootie. The captain said nothing but shared an expression with the Varanus when a rolling growl came from Grootie.

"If you help the captain, then I will do what I can to aid you," Grootie said, his voice rumbling with a dark edge.

"Excellent." Warren beamed, but Grootie did not reciprocate his gratefulness.

"Commander Warren!" bellowed a voice. "You better have a reason for this!"

Warren smacked a hand across his forehead as a taller and older man entered the tent.

"General Reatz, sir! These travelers are responsible for the destruction of the Nevo outpost on Acknaria. They seek the sage."

"We claim no such thing," Javex corrected, though they were responsible.

General Reatz approached, his hand on his sidearm. Broken and worn armor graced his shoulders with a crude shape of a yellow painted helmet on his chest plate. A tattered red cloak hung by two clasps at his shoulder, the coppery color rubbed and worn.

"I don't care who they are or what they have done. Why did you allow this *thing* to enter our camp?" Reatz pointed to Grootie.

Warren took a step forward. "Sir, in exchange for help, the Varanus has agreed to translate the messages."

The general paused, but his livid eyes bore holes into Warren.

Javex bowed. "I am Javex. We seek only the sage, then we will leave."

General Reatz snapped a salute to Javex. "I am General Reatz. I oversee these soldiers and this base." He paused. "I regret to inform you I have not seen the sage in several solar rotations. All I can do is try to contact her, but it may take a half solar rotation."

Kaytrix's stomach dropped. That was a long time to wait.

Javex's ears flattened. No doubt he felt the same disappointment. "We appreciate anything you can do."

"Now, the communications," General Reatz began. "Since our translators passing, we've been on edge not knowing what the Varanus plan to do next. Your ability to translate would help us strategize."

"The language is Varanus?" Kaytrix asked.

"Precisely."

A guttural growl came from Grootie. "I will not aid you if this causes the death of more of my kind."

"I think in your case," began General Reatz, "it would be wise to aid us. The fall of this planet only ensures the continued slavery of everyone's world."

A snarl split Grootie's lips, revealing his fine teeth. It was true, but that didn't mean he liked it.

"Now, if you are still willing to help, follow me or leave immediately." General Reatz glared at them, waiting.

Grootie relented and nodded, but his hands remained balled at his side.

"Very well. This way."

The general guided them through the camp until they came upon the entrance of a cave. Several torches lit the entrance. Inside, the cave opened to a large carved round room. In the middle, several stations stood erect, with soldiers sitting and analyzing information. The general approached a station where a soldier sat with a pinched brow. Scribbles of foreign lines and symbols marked pages scattered around the man. His eyes widened as they approached.

"General!" He snapped a salute.

"Linc, these people are here to help with the translations."

Linc's knit brow softened. "Thank goodness you are here. I can't understand any of it," the soldier said.

Linc pressed a glowing button on his terminal. It pulsed green as a faded recording played, the sound of it distorted.

Grootie's eyes narrowed, and his brow furrowed. His upper lip curled into a snarl and a hiss seethed from between his clenched jaws.

"What is it?" Kaytrix asked.

Grootie paused for a second, listening to the rest of the recording. Once the distorted message of growls and grunts ended, Grootie stood tall, taking in a deep breath.

"The message is about a ground attack. They are planning to drop troops and surround the settlement to take the mine."

The words weighed on the men.

Grootie growled, startling him. "The attack is for today."

Commander Warren's face fell, his eyes widening. "Everyone, prepare—"

General Reatz rose his hand, silencing Warren. He raised an eyebrow at Grootie.

"Why should I believe you? We know your kind are deceitful."

Grootie lowered his gaze to be eye-level with the general, the tendrils on his head vibrating in a controlled rage.

Javex tensed.

Aaro's hands hovered near his holstered blasters.

Grootie could easily rip the man's head from his body, but whatever respect he had for the captain kept him from doing so.

"I do not represent my kind." Grootie hissed. "It's unfortunate the loss of your camp will never repay the countless lives of my brothers in the planet's atmosphere."

Bumps crawled along the surface of Kaytrix's skin at Grootie's display of anger. The general continued to stare at the Varanus, creating uncertainty.

"Ready our defenses at once!" General Reatz shouted. "And get these people out of here!"

"Wait, you promised to message the sage for us," Javex said.

The general turned to him, his weapon already drawn. "If we survive this, I will keep my word. You should evacuate."

"We could help if we had our weapons," Aaro offered, who then received a scowl from Grootie.

"No offense, but I don't trust you. Commander Warren, this is your mess. Get them out of here!"

"This way," Warren encouraged with an open hand.

Once outside the cave, soldiers rushed to the mouth of the mine and into the cavern like a rush of water. Two turrets sprang up from the mountainside, their large cannons retrofitted to attack ships in orbit. They whirled, creaked, and groaned as they sought targets.

"I will guide you back to your ship," Warren shouted over the racket as he handed them their weapons. "We best get moving."

"Very well. I will take point with you," Javex said. "Aaro, you and Grootie take the back. Kaytrix," he paused, "you're in the middle."

The middle. Why not the lead or cover the others? Still, he appreciated Javex's thoughtfulness.

A storm rolled in, forcing the sun into hiding. The swirling thunderstorm enveloped the mountain tops in thick, dark clouds, perfect cover for an invasion. The forest provided some buffering from the hard rain, but the cold drops forced themselves through the branches and down Kaytrix's back. Something about the falling rain caused an irritation in his soul.

He hated rain.

He also hated it would take half a solar rotation to hear from the sage. By then, this "two souls" problem would be just that. With every episode, the intensity of his sickness increased, leaving him drained. Was it even relevant he regained his identity? If he couldn't stop the Nevo symbiote from taking over his body, did his past even matter?

They traveled through the forest and approached the mountain's base. Their pace quickened as they drew closer to the *Dauntless*. The adrenaline coursing through Kaytrix's veins invigorated his body, but the feeling vanished as a deafening boom tore through the silence.

The terrible rumble filled the pass with a reverberating roar. Above them, through the thick black clouds, a piercing white light streaked across the sky. The light blazed overhead, plowing through the ancient trees.

"Take cover!" Aaro shouted.

Kaytrix ducked behind a boulder with Aaro. On the opposite side of the path, Grootie, Javex, and Warren took cover underneath the boughs of a large tree.

Large branches snapped from overhead as the object scorched a path through the treetops. The echo of a crash sounded through the mountain pass. A shockwave rumbled the ground beneath them, causing the joints in Kaytrix's knees and ankles to rise and fall.

"What was that?"

Grootie growled. "A ship."

"I know you want to leave, but I need to investigate," Warren said, griping his rifle tight. "If it is a Varanus vessel, I can't risk leaving them alive."

Grootie eyed the man with a ferocious glare.

Javex offered a reluctant nod. "We will go with you. Then we will leave."

Warren grimaced, withholding what would have been a thanks if Grootie's eyes didn't burn a hole into him.

They followed the trail of charred trees and debris from the ship's crash. It led them further into the mountains and into a thick forest, which extended into a glade. A cloud of smoke plumed into the sky ahead.

Javex's heckles raised, and his tail twitched. The Zaguarz's broad shoulders blocked his vision. Whatever Javex sensed wasn't good.

"Stay alert." Javex said, stepping into the clearing.

Besides the growing howl of the wind, all Kaytrix could feel was the thud of his heart beating against his ribcage. He readied to follow as Grootie and Warren proceeded ahead of him.

The wind blew against him and tossed tree branches back and forth. He found it impossible to rely on his senses to detect movement. A powerful gust of wind blew through the glade changing the direction of the smoke. Like something from a distant memory, the ship lay ahead in plain view.

He froze, recognizing it.

The pilot crashed the ship by skimming the surface of the ground and somehow kept it intact. The cockpit faced away from them while the engines still whined, continuing to burn at a low level.

Warren strode ahead, his gun tight against his shoulder. "Well, it is not Varanus," he said.

Grootie huffed, sounding relieved.

"But this *is* a common vessel used by bounty hunters," Aaro said, his tone cold and muffled by his helmet. He, too, froze at the sight of it.

There was no mistaking the ship. It was the same one from Rehnna.

"We need to find the body," Warren announced. "Make sure they are—"

"There!" Kaytrix pointed.

Close to the prow of the ship, a body lay in the tall grass.

Chapter 18

CONFRONTATION

The massive storm moved in, darkening the sky and the rain fell heavier. It dripped off the end of Javex's nose and beaded on his whiskers and fur. The crashed ship delayed their departure, but leaving Warren alone to investigate went against his morals. He wasn't expecting a survivor, and the glade was so open.

He listened to the forest, scanning for the faintest noise. The only thing detectable was the rustling of the wind in the trees and the sway of grass. He focused on the body.

"I will investigate," he said before the others could protest.

The last thing he needed was this kind of altercation. Bounty hunters are killers with a thirst for success and profit.

Javex stepped further into the clearing with his bow drawn and ready. With each step, the water soaked between his toes. He rotated his ears, focusing on what lay ahead: the sounds of the forest, the beating hearts of his companions.

The chest of the body rose and fell. The person was petite, frail, about the size of Seraphina, however fit and muscular. Overwhelming emotions clouded his mind as he stopped a few feet away. His ears pricked forwards. As he studied the figure, his predatory instincts switched to that of a father.

The woman lay on her back; her face held in a contorted state of anguish, half covered by her dark hair. The crash cut her in several places. Green blood ran over her rich yellow skin. Scorched and tattered clothing revealed charred skin and the mark of a slave branded on her hip.

Javex stepped closer. A weapon lay near the woman's hand. He froze and smelt the air, but she remained motionless. Cautiously, he drew his bow to its full length and flicked his tail at the predicament.

"Wake up," Javex said, hoping she could stand on her own.

Beyond the smell of smoke, another scent entered the glade. A branch in the forest snapped. He twitched. From the woodland, he returned his gaze to the woman. Her eyes were open and staring down the length of his arrow.

"Go ahead. Shoot me. You would be doing me a favor," she said.

Javex eased the tension in his bow. "I have no reason to kill you, but we are in a precarious situation at the moment."

Aaro and the others moved in on his position. Confusion contorted the woman's face as she glanced around. She reached for her weapon but recoiled.

"Curse whoever shot me out of the sky," she said, clutching her side in agony.

"Come with me and we will help you," Javex said, offering her his hand.

"Who's we?" Her amber eyes blazed suspiciously.

Javex was about to answer when the rest of his crew encircled him and the alien woman, their backs to them.

"Captain," Aaro began, "we have a bit of a situation."

"I smell them, Aaro," he acknowledged. "Remain in formation. We are not what they came for."

"Aye," Aaro said, bringing both of his sidearms up to bear.

Emerging out of the bush, four Varanus soldiers approached. A tall Varanus led them, but compared to Grootie, he lacked the muscle and width. The Varanus stalked towards them on large, clawed feet. His strapping torso moved with a lizard's grace while his column-like neck supported his long head with ease. The thick, whip-like tail moved with his body in a rippling pattern, and the spikes atop his head flowed in a dangerous dance to his apparent mood of anger.

Grootie stood on the defensive, posing for a pounce. Such aggression was unwarranted given how he reacted to the rebellion killing Varanus. Why the sudden change?

A deep, menacing growl escaped Grootie's clenched jaws, stirring panic in Javex.

"Grootie. Whatever this is, now is not the time," Javex said. "We need to work together if we are going to survive."

"They are high on Lord Khelveliz's power," Grootie began. "We won't walk away from this."

"That's comforting," Aaro spat.

Grootie stalked forward and a louder, challenging growl rip from his throat. The sudden display brought back stories from Javex's father on Zaguarz. When the Dark Ones left, they put the Varanus in charge of his people. Often the Varanus would challenge each other for higher positions of power, to gain favor from their masters. Grootie's display was a challenge and Varanus only challenged someone they had a quarrel with.

The approaching Varanus stopped, the leader stepping ahead from the others to distinguish himself.

"Oh, please. Is that how you greet an old friend?" came the snaky and shrewd voice from the lead Varanus. His purple scales shimmered in the rain.

"Friend?" Grootie huffed. "You are no friend of mine, Sirion."

Sirion's red eyes flared as he eyed the group. "How low you have stooped, brother," Sirion spoke mockingly. "A band of misfits as company."

"Grootie, you know this ugly bastard?" Aaro asked.

Grootie growled. "In another life, I commanded him and others as the right hand of Khelveliz."

Javex winced at the revelation. The crew did not know about Grootie's personal servitude to Lord Khelveliz, a truth he was content to leave un-known.

"Until you got too weak," Sirion spat. "But no matter. Now I can kill you and your *friends.*"

"Careful, you red-eyed sucker," Aaro snarled. "I doubt you're fast enough to dodge hot plasma."

Sirion regarded Aaro, his eyes flashing in recognition. "Ah, the last of the Red Sky Alliance, indeed a band of misfits."

Aaro raised his weapons.

The Varanus sneered. The look of fearlessness was familiar. Too familiar. A pain from Javex's past tightened his chest, causing his bones to quake. He couldn't lose his family, not again. There must be a way to win against the Varanus. But the longer they stood, the greater the silence grew, the clearer the truth. Not everyone would walk away from this fight.

Sirion's gaze locked with his, his tendrils flowing in chaos. A low hiss reverberated out of the Varanus' jaws.

"I may kill you just for the pleasure!" Sirion said, his body vibrating. The power from Lord Khelveliz was a spell impossible to resist.

"We will see," Javex said calmly. He readied his bow.

Sirion advanced by a step, but Grootie matched it, blocking the advance.

"You would die for your enemy?" Sirion hissed.

Grootie stood tall, his height and size more apparent. "I would die for a friend."

Sirion let out a boisterous laugh, a barking sound. "Right. What about your own kind?"

Grootie anchored a foot into the wet soil. "I didn't abandon my brothers, Sirion, only Lord Khelveliz. I intend to free my brothers. All you are doing is getting them killed!"

Sirion laughed again. "How do you intend on doing that? Begging? Freedom costs blood. That's why you're not leading us anymore, Grootie. You're weak."

A growl came from Grootie that made Javex's heckles rise.

"Let's put it to the test then, Sirion. Only this time, it will be a fair fight."

"Kill them all," Sirion spat.

A weight dropped in Javex's stomach as the four Varanus charged them. He drew his bow and let loose the first arrow. It whizzed through the rain, cutting droplets in half before sinking into the first Varanus's skull. The Varanus soldier fell to the ground, leaving Sirion and two others left. He would not be so lucky with the rest.

Grootie launched at Sirion. The Varanus collided with brute strength and terrific force. Each of them possessed the power of several men each, but their execution and skill would determine the winner. Claws scraped over scales in the brutal clash, but Javex faced other problems.

Javex threw down his bow and drew his short sword. The remaining two Varanus soldiers split, one heading his way, the other towards his crew.

Warren, Aaro, and Cade stood tight together, using part of the ship's wing as a barrier. They responded to the assault by firing their weapons. However, as agile creatures, the charging Varanus avoided their fire with ease.

Javex turned from the crew, unable to aid them to focus on the Varanus storming him. The creature was dark green with a crimson belly. It slowed its charge and eyed him, letting a wild hiss escape his fine-toothed mouth.

"I will give you one chance to walk away," Javex said, tightening the grip on his short sword. "You do not have to die today."

The Varanus roared, tossing his head. Its large hands quivered at its side, craving blood. His blood. There would be no talking this creature out of its orders. It would die before retreating.

Javex hissed, bearing his own canines. He hated fighting. He hated bloodshed. Not a victim fell whose face he did not remember. But if there would be no peace, then there must be war.

The Varanus charged. Its massive frame closed the distance in seconds. Javex jumped, missing the attack, and slashed the Varanus's tail.

The Varanus roared as the blade sliced through scales and cut the tail in half. The Varanus would be off balance now. With one less weapon to worry about in the fight, Javex focused on the remaining claws and teeth.

The Varanus swung around, swiping its arm at him, and grabbing with the other. Javex dodged the attack by leaping once more, but the Varanus's jaws snapped and tightened down on his arm. A crushing pain shot through his arm and to his shoulder.

Like a wild beast, the Varanus shook him only pausing to breathe. Javex took advantage of the moment, dropping his sword to catch it with his other hand. Desperate to free himself, he swung at the lizard's legs only to miss.

The Varanus clamped down harder. Javex roared, the pain unbearable. He lifted his sword and slashed it across the Varanus's face, but the creature only tightened its jaws further. Its massive arms grabbed him and held him still, the rage in his eyes not yet satisfied.

Javex dared a glance at his crew in search of help. A Varanus held Aaro by the throat while Warren took a blow to the head. Cade rose to plunge a knife in the Varanus to save Aaro, but the beast tossed him across the field. The robed woman attacked, her mango skin striking as she raced between the Varanus's stance and slashed its legs with her blades. The Varanus whipped her down with its tail.

Grootie held Sirion down by the throat, having won the fight against his former comrade, but now surveyed the battlefield.

Javex took in a sharp breath. The pain was too much. A drowning darkness overtook him. He wanted to succumb to the black veil of unconsciousness, to close his eyes and rest. Then, out of the forest, multiple beams of energy flew through the clearing. The energy struck the Varanus soldiers, sending them to their knees in chaotic spasms. Aaro kicked free and shot his attacker, while Grootie abandoned Sirion to writhe in pain on the ground.

Javex blinked, feeling odd and light. When he opened his eyes again, the sway of green grass danced in his vision. A tingling sensation coursed through his body. He was thankful for the numbing sensation.

"Captain!" Aaro crouched over him, his helmet off. The concern on Aaro's face deepened his brows. Aaro rummaged through his utility belt when he stabbed Javex in the arm.

A stabilizer. A medical concoction meant to calm the body and encourage fast healing. Sometimes it worked and sometimes it didn't.

"Ow."

"Sorry, Captain. You're in terrible shape."

"The others, is Cade . . .?"

"I think they're okay. Miraculously. But we lost Warren."

The news brought a heaviness to his heart.

Aaro wrapped his arm. "But you? What were you thinking?"

Javex winced at Aaro's lack of tenderness. "I guess I wasn't."

Aaro tsked. "Again? That's getting you into a bunch of trouble, Captain. You best retire."

Javex wanted to laugh, but it hurt too much. "What happened?"

Aaro took a break from wrapping his arm to look around. "Some kind of energy weapon stunned the Varanus. Not sure where it came from, but it saved our lives."

"Help me up."

With Aaro's help, Javex stood. The stabilizer aided his energy levels, taking away the pain of his injuries. He managed a couple steps when his gaze rested on a figure standing—no floating—at the wilderness edge.

Aaro raised his weapon while holding Javex. "What *is* that?"

The figure's body pulsed. A buzz like sensation ebbed from its form and in its hand, a glowing swirling light. A pearl black visor shielded its face. The being's blue unstable, shifting body of energy then transformed into a contained shape the likes of which resembled a humanoid.

Javex's jaw fell slack. "It can't be?"

"Can't be what?" Cade asked.

"A Shargan."

Aaro struggled under the weight of holding him up. "Is it friendly?"

The being slipped back into the forest and out of sight.

"Not sociable anyway," Javex said. "This answers how General Reatz protected this planet for so long. Come, we must leave before more Varanus arrive."

"What of the woman?" Aaro grunted.

Javex examined the woman. Her face locked in a fierce scowl, but her eyes were empty. "I already promised to help her."

Aaro shook his head. "Dammit, Captain. A bounty hunter, no less."

"I know. Last time."

"Ugh, fine, but we do it right this time."

Javex nodded and activated his comm. "Seraphina, we need a pickup. Have Atara ready the med bay and have Noro prep the secure cell. We have more company."

Chapter 19

TRUST

Kaytrix rubbed the back of his neck as he stood in the observatory. The bounty hunter slept restrained with straps all too familiar to him. It shouldn't surprise him to see her, and yet it did.

He leaned against the glass, braced his head against his forearm, and observed the bounty hunter's anguished face as she slept. Why was she here? Who hired her? He wanted to ask her these questions and more, but one stood out from the others since Rehnna: why did she save him?

The events of Acknaria played in his head. He did not expect to fight Varanus and now that he had, he understood why the Nevo used them as soldiers. They were lucky to leave Arimas with their lives. Javex's arm injury would heal, but it would take time and extensive medicine. Somehow, he and Aaro walked away with just a few scratches.

A surge of guilt rushed through him. If it weren't for his predicament with this spawn, Javex wouldn't be suffering from injuries. He could say the same for Traven and Clarr. Everyone who helped him became injured or got in trouble. Searching for answers to his problem was costing more than it should.

Kaytrix withdrew his arm and punched the thick glass. Pain shot through his knuckles. He clenched his jaw and tightened his hand. He sighed and continued to watch the bounty hunter sleep. Since the beginning, she didn't care about him, abandoning him on Rehnna with Traven. So why would she show up now?

Kaytrix closed his eyes as the pain in his head returned. He rubbed his temples. He didn't have time to wait anymore. If he didn't do something, fate would seal him with this symbiote.

A war cry ripped through the preceding silence.

"You will never find him!!" the bounty hunter shouted.

Her wild hair framed her face in knotted tangles and loose strands. Her wild eyes darted around the room as her dream faded.

Kaytrix activated his comm. "The bounty hunter is awake."

Aaro's voice came to him in a hurry. "We're already on our way."

The rush of the door opening drew his attention from the woman struggling in her restraints. Aaro and Grootie entered, followed by Javex, who relaxed with his right arm bandaged. Aaro, however, fidgeted with his gloves and stared through the glass. This bounty hunter issue posed a threat to the security of the *Dauntless*, but also Aaro's life.

"Is this your idea of helping me?!" the woman shouted.

"Has she said much?" Javex asked, his tone calm.

Kaytrix withdrew from the glass. "Not much, but I have a lot to ask her."

"Why is that?"

He hesitated. Did it matter anymore how much they knew? Odds were that he would die, anyway. The last thing he wanted was lies to remain between them.

"This woman saved me from the Nevo. I don't know why, or why she left me on Rehnna."

Javex rose an eyebrow while cradling his bandaged arm. "Interesting that we should run into her on Arimas. Are you certain she saved you? She may have carted you off hoping to receive ransom?"

"That could be. She's got more pieces to the puzzle than I do."

"She may work for the Nevo," Aaro began. "Or like Javex said, playing a dangerous game by stealing from them, expecting a payout." Aaro looked from Kaytrix to Javex. "You realize this may not end well for her, for us? Let's get our info, bandage her, and get her off the ship."

"If she knows we won't help her, why would she tell us anything?" Javex asked, his brow furrowed. He did not agree with Aaro's approach.

"Captain, look at her." The woman continued to pull and fight against her restraints, screeching more war cries. "She already thinks we're keeping her a hostage. All that's left is her freedom to bargain or leave her for the Nevo to find."

"Aaro!" Javex snarled.

Aaro pointed his finger at Javex. "Listen, it's her or us. If we don't get answers, we're all done for! If not now, for sure in the distant future. Symbiotes and shit. Damnit, Captain. Time to realize we're on the brink of a second war. Only this time, no one is going to be left!"

Aaro's words hit home and hit hard. Javex turned from him, the emotions in his eyes hidden.

"Well, there are questions I need answers to. I'm going in there." Kaytrix turned to gauge the others. "Anyone coming?"

Javex and Aaro both nodded, avoiding each other's eyes.

Kaytrix approached the door to the secure cell and inputted the security code. The door released its seal and whizzed to the side. His hands shook at his sides as he entered. The woman's amber eyes pierced his soul, a look of betrayal.

"This is how you show me thanks!?" She tugged against the restraints.

Kaytrix crossed his arms. "Why did you save me from the Nevo? Is it so you could gain in some way, *bounty hunter*?"

Her lips curled back. "You should thank me! Release me at once!"

He dragged his hands through his hair and laughed. "Right! Thanking you? For what exactly? Since you dumped me on Rehnna, things have only gotten worse!"

"If it wasn't for me, you would be dead," she hissed.

"I'm still going to die!"

That froze her. Her chest rose slowly as she drew in a steadying breath. "What do you mean?"

Kaytrix paced the floor, wringing his hands. Saying it aloud felt different from thinking about it. As if the spoken word solidified his fate. Finally, he faced her and released the breath he was holding.

"There's a Nevo inside me. Changing me. I don't know how much time I have until . . ."

She pulled against her restraints again. "NO! That's not possible!" Tears welled in her eyes, something peculiar to him. Why did she care?

"I'll ask you again. Why did you save me from the Nevo?"

A tear rolled down her face. This was the first time he saw it uncovered.

She spoke, her voice wavering. "I . . . I saved you from that monster."

"Who? Lord Khelveliz?"

She scoffed, her voice gaining strength. "The actual monster, Vhulse. He's the one who did this to you."

Like many other things, the name and her actions held no meaning. "Why?"

She blinked and examined the ceiling as if viewing a hologram. "My story is long, but I'll get to the point. I don't know what Vhulse did to you, but I . . ." She stopped, seeming to redirect her line of thought. "The way you looked at me with such agony. I couldn't leave you there to suffer."

"So you *saved* me by dumping me on Rehnna?!"

"I didn't have much choice," she shot back. "I was required to report to Lord Khelveliz." The tears were gone now, but she wasn't telling him something.

"What am I to the Nevo? Why do they have a bounty on me?"

She shook her head. "I will say nothing more until I am released, and this infernal dress is *off*."

The corner of his mouth turned up in a smile. "I am sure we can work something out."

Her eyebrows furrowed. He still didn't know her name. "What can I call you, besides your title? That is, if I am allowed to know? I'm Cade."

"Cade," she repeated, pulling at the dress. "Alissia Rabb. I'm from Drenna. Perhaps you remember?"

Drenna. The word soaked into his synapsis, bringing with it the memory of heat and mockery. Long rotations of standing in the sun with fellow soldiers and laborious fields of crops stretched out before him . . . Pain surged through his head, and he fell to his knees.

"Are you okay, kid?" Aaro asked as he helped him to stand.

"Just the same pain as ever," he mumbled. "Just never that intense." He groaned and found his footing. Javex stood with him, his form rigid with worry. "I'm ok," Kaytrix insisted.

Alissia's eyes widened, her breaths shallow. "Side effects?" She asked.

He rubbed his temples as the heaviness in his head and chest subsided. "The Nevo must want more than their kin inside of me. What else is going on here?"

She sighed. "You are something Lord Khelveliz prizes, something he would kill to have returned."

"Or pay greatly?" Aaro murmured. "Hence the bounty on you."

It still wasn't clear. He was a nobody. A regular man. Flashes of green eyes and the words progress surfaced.

"This Vhulse. Who is he?"

Alissia rolled her eyes. "He's disgusting. A power-hungry scientist."

The door to the secure room whizzed closed. The sound caught Kaytrix off guard, pulling his attention from Alissia.

Grootie stood in the observation room, his penetrating glare boring holes into them. It took Kaytrix a minute to realize the significance of the moment until Aaro slammed against the door. Aaro's fingers flew over the keypad when an ornery tone beeped at him.

"We're locked in!" Aaro shouted.

"Grootie, what are you doing?" Javex asked, his tone pained.

Grootie huffed as the light behind him outlined his broad silhouette. "Something I should have done long ago. Sirion was right. I abandoned my brothers, but now Lord Khelveliz will listen to me. My people will be free."

"Grootie, Lord Khelveliz will only kill you! Let's talk about this," Javex said.

Grootie turned away. "It's too late, Javex. I have made my choice. My brothers will no longer serve under Lord Khelveliz. For many solar rotations I served, working to free them. Sirion betrayed me before I had a chance. Now Lord Khelveliz has no reason to ignore my demands."

"Grootie, don't do this!" Aaro pleaded, but the Varanus stalked away without a look back. "Bastard! I knew it!" Aaro slammed a fist against the door.

"He plans to turn him over to Lord Khelveliz!" Alissia hissed.

"We have to stop him from getting to the bridge," Javex said. "The ventilation system runs through the entire ship. If one of you can get through, you can release us from the outside."

Kaytrix studied the vent, the opening far too narrow for him or Aaro. He turned to Alissia. "Now's a chance to prove where your loyalties lie." He undid the straps across her body and gathered her clothes. "Crawl through the vent and open the door."

"We can't trust she won't partner with Grootie," Aaro argued. "Seraphina can let us out."

"And risk Grootie running into her or the others on their way here?" Javex asked, his brow furrowed. "We have to trust Alissia."

Alissia finished dressing and pushed herself between the three of them. "Give me a boost." She smiled at Aaro, who rolled his eyes.

Kaytrix joined in to help lift her and offered his hand. Alissia's weight pressed down on him as she smashed the duct covering with the hilt of her knife and hoisted herself into the narrow shaft.

"Let us out first. You can't take him on alone," Javex ordered.

"There's no time!" Alissia disappeared into the darkness of the duct.

Kaytrix caught Javex's worried expression. There was no telling what Grootie would do to Alissia in a confrontation.

"Send me up. I'll let you out."

Aaro put his hand up. "Not so fast, kid. I should be the one to go."

Javex exhaled. "It will take all of us to stop him, but I only have the strength to send one of you."

"Screw this." Aaro turned from the vent opening and drew his weapon. "Sorry in advance, Captain."

Aaro aimed at the door's keypad and pulled the trigger. Sparks bounced off the door, onto his armor and the wall. In a flash of smoke, the door whizzed open. Aaro tossed Kaytrix his other sidearm.

"Let's go, Cade!"

"Aaro! Stun only," Javex said, trying to keep up.

"No promises, Captain."

Kaytrix followed Aaro down the corridor, but something inside him stirred. It wasn't the nausea he'd become familiar with, but a deeper aching sensation in his limbs and chest, as though someone turned the power off to his body.

Aaro was out of view, and a commotion broke out. Alissia yelled. Blaster fire reverberated through the corridor. He stumbled and caught himself on the wall.

"You're weak without me," echoed a voice.

The hair at the nape of his neck stood on end. This was more than a memory. He pushed forward and stumbled through the bridge's smoking doorframe, unable to see anything. Sparks flew at him as he entered the bridge.

The smoke subsided, and in its wake, Grootie stood glaring at him.

"You should have stayed with the captain." Grootie rumbled. Blood dripped from his claws to the floor.

Kaytrix's stomach dropped. "What have you done to Aaro and Alissia?"

"Oh, nothing terrible," Grootie chided, flashing a toothy grin.

The Varanus took a step forward, forcing Kaytrix to take one back. He was in no condition to fight.

"Stay back!" He didn't want to shoot Grootie, but the Varanus left him little choice.

"Surrender, and I won't break your legs," Grootie taunted. His blue tongue slithered in and out of his mouth.

"Let me help you," came the voice from inside. "Together, we can take him." The sound irritated the insides of Kaytrix's ears like a scratch.

"No!"

Grootie roared. "Have it your way."

Kaytrix gulped. Grootie didn't know he was speaking to the Nevo symbiote, but it was too late now. Kaytrix remained steadfast as Grootie locked his stance, ready to pounce. What could he do? He scanned the room, but ideas evaded him.

"Let me in!" demanded the voice. "The Varanus will destroy us both!"

Time froze. Grootie's slit eyes filled with rage as he targeted him. Sparks flew in slow motion beside him, falling like stars. Fatigue saturated his limbs. The nuzzle of his gun shook. It had never felt so heavy in his hand. If it meant saving the others, he could let the Nevo in and fight for him. He'd experienced the strength before, allowing him to fend off Aaro in their sparing match. He inhaled, about to relinquish his control. The nape of his neck crawled in anticipation.

Grootie launched for him, hurling his massive frame towards him like a boulder.

A flash of motion on Kaytrix's right caught his attention. Javex flew into the room, pouncing the Varanus. Javex hurried onto Grootie's back, sinking his teeth into the raging creature's neck. Grootie staggered, roared, and clawed at Javex, but the bulk of his arms prevented him from reaching the skilled Zaguarz atop his back.

Javex tightened his jaws. Like the flick of a switch, Grootie's eyes rolled back into his skull and his body crumbled to the floor.

Kaytrix caught his breath. The weight of the weapon in his hand eased as he holstered it.

"Aaro and Alissia!" He vaulted over a sparking terminal to find Aaro slumped behind it, his head hung over his chest. "Aaro!" A ball formed in his throat, tightening. He reached for Aaro's neck. Desperation welled inside as he waited. And waited. "Come on, Aaro!" He pressed harder. A faint pounding met the warmth of his hand and relief washed through him.

Javex stood from the other side of the bridge with Alissia draped over his arms, wincing as his bandaged arm bore the weight of her body. Five trails of torn flesh marked her ribs.

"Try to get Aaro up. We must stop the bleeding." Javex activated his comm. "Atara to the med bay immediately."

Kaytrix struggled to lift Aaro to his feet. The man was heavier than he expected. Just as they were about to exit the bridge, Seraphina entered. Her mouth gaped, her eyes widening as she dropped her tablet.

"Captain, what happened?" She scanned the room when her gaze rested on Grootie's unconscious body. A sadness entered her eyes but soon disappeared.

Javex shifted again. "Mutiny. Aaro and Alissia tried to stop him, but I fear they were too late."

Kaytrix struggled to lift Aaro, who groaned as he came to, cursing in Shrovon.

"Let me help," Seraphina said, rushing to Aaro's side when one of the bridge consoles beeped.

Seraphina halted. "Captain," she began, sounding confused. "We're being hailed."

"No one can send us a message The ship's stealth shield is active." Javex snarled as he shuffled towards the viewport. The aging captain froze, his ears lying flat across his head.

Kaytrix followed Javex's gaze. There, against the colors of Arimas, a black ship loomed. Memories of battles against this ship surfaced with a terrible sense of hopelessness, destruction, and death.

It was the Nevo.

Chapter 20

CHANGE OF PLAN

The hackles on Javex's neck raised as fear rushed up and down his spine. How did the Nevo find them so quick? The Nevo ship floated dormant, but the evil from the Nevo race penetrated the space between ships. The computer chirped again. Another hail attempt. Javex's arm grew weak, and he shifted the weight of Alissia in his arms.

"Orders, Captain?" Seraphina asked, her eyes wide, coated with the threat of tears.

Javex summoned his courage. "Ser, get Aaro and Alissia to the med bay. Patch them up quickly and stay there. I will try to buy us time." He placed Alissia on Seraphina's arm. "Perhaps they are only passing through."

Seraphina gave him a weary look as she struggled to support Alissia's unconscious body.

Cade and Seraphina shuffled off the command bridge with the wounded, and Javex sat in the command chair. To his left, an array of small screens displayed information from all the terminals. He grimaced. The terminal commanding the stealth shield received damage in the fight. All other systems registered as green. A quick glance at his communications array sent a stab through his heart.

The *Dauntless* broadcasted a message. The language scrolled across his screen in Varanus. Grootie's pain for his fallen brothers cracked what little healing he'd done aboard his ship. The fight with Sirion damaging the single thread that kept him from succumbing to the darkness. In the end, no amount of friendship and forgiveness would ease Grootie's burdened heart.

Dedeep, dedeep. Javex pressed a finger to the flashing screen, ignoring the incoming message. He readied the engines and engaged thrusters.

"Come on, *Dauntless*. One more run. That's all I'm asking." He pressed the thrusters forward, turning the *Dauntless* around.

"Captain! I tried to stop him!" Cade called.

Javex whipped around to see Aaro staggering onto the bridge, Noro pulling on him with little effect.

Javex returned his attention to piloting the ship. "You need to be in care, Aaro!"

Aaro slid into the weapon's terminal seat and readied weapons. His bloodied smile highlighted his swollen eye. "I've had worse. The kid told me everything. I need to be here to help you, Captain."

Javex grimaced. He was grateful for the help, but hoped he didn't need it. The *Dauntless* would not survive an attack from a Nevo cruiser. No ship could. They might outrun it if they acted now.

"Be ready. If we can't get clear in time for a jump, we must be ready to fight."

"Aye," Aaro said, "and our old ship doesn't improve our odds." Aaro clutched his ribs as he stifled a laugh.

Javex grimaced at the reminder. "Cade. If you are what we think, it is imperative the Nevo do not know you are here."

Cade nodded and took a seat near the communications terminal, out of view. He appeared sicker than before, the veins in his neck dark and swollen. His ghostly skin was slick with sweat, as if death had passed over him.

The time to find help for Cade was running out. Yet another reminder of his failure to keep his promises, and now, to keep his crew safe from the Nevo.

"What's the plan, Captain?" Noro asked.

"Ensure the shields remain charged. We can borrow power from other systems if necessary. We can't let them fail. If they do, we're all victims to the wisp."

"Wisp?" Cade asked, his tone curious.

"The Nevo use a technology to steal victims from their ships, or to reclaim lost property from planet surfaces. It's why most people can never truly escape the Nevo. Our freedom is only an illusion."

Javex took in an even breath, struggling to remain calm as he readied the *Dauntless'* hyperdrive sequence. With only two cells left to charge, the hyperdrive system neared completion to initiate a safe jump.

"The Nevo ship is readying weapons," Aaro warned from his station.

Javex gripped the armrests of his chair. Only one cell remained. The *Dauntless* surged forward. A hyperdrive window appeared before them, sparkling and rippling. A surge of hope rose in Javex's chest. They were going to escape.

Green weapons' fire shattered the open portal, causing it to shrivel and disappear.

"No!" Javex roared. They were moments from being safe, only to have the possibility ripped away from them.

The *Dauntless* rocked to the side, sending Javex to the right. Red lights pulsed along the bridge ceiling, followed by a solemn wail.

"Hyperspace jump window collapsed. They're attacking our shields!"

The hyperdrive gauge bottomed out, leaving all the cells reading empty. What power remained they needed for the shields. Javex had little choice but to face them. Regret settled into his bones at this realization. He never should have allowed the crew to stay. He should have made them leave, find somewhere secluded to live. Now their fate rested in his capabilities as a leader.

Another blast shook the ship. The Nevo weapons tore through their shields like paper.

"Return fire!" Javex commanded, tucking the *Dauntless* into a nosedive to avoid another attack.

The ship lurched from another blast of weapon's fire. Wailing sirens and screeches warned of damage caused to systems.

"Weapons are offline, Captain!" Aaro shouted.

Javex struggled to hold his composure. He had nothing left to fall back on and no one to aid them.

"Let them have me!" Cade stood before him, his face slick with sweat.

Javex knit his brows. "I can't!" He stood to pace the bridge.

"Your crew's lives are worth more than mine," Cade argued. "They don't deserve to die because of me."

"There is more at stake here than just our lives!" Javex argued. Whatever Cade meant to the evil lord, he couldn't risk letting him go.

The *Dauntless* stilled as the Nevo ship ceased fire. Through the viewport, the immense vessel loomed above them.

Cade sighed. "I am not asking."

Javex turned to see Cade touch a screen at his command.

"Cade, no!"

A green energy emerged on the bridge, consuming Cade's figure like a flame. Cade dissolved into a green wisp and disappeared.

Aaro stood from his seat, his face white. "He . . . he deactivated the shields?"

Javex rushed to reactivate the shields when he sank into his seat. A hollowness emptied his soul. His failure crushed him. With a damaged ship, he couldn't hope to mount a rescue, and that was if the Nevo didn't obliterate them first.

He closed his eyes. This must be the end of everything. But when the *Dauntless* didn't wail more warnings, he surveyed their status.

"Sir, the Nevo ship is moving off and jumping into hyperspace," Aaro said.

The Nevo ship entered the green hyperspace window and disappeared. The colors from the jump dissipated, leaving the emptiness of space before them and the planet of Arimas floating in the background.

A voice echoed down the hall. Javex turned. A bandaged Alissia stormed through the bridge doors, clutching her side. She staggered onto the command deck.

Her amber eyes scoured the bridge. "What's happening?" The bridge lights danced across her skin, changing, and melding with the color. "Where's Cade?"

Javex tried to answer her, but his throat seized. The sense of failure consuming his heart.

"Where is he?" she screeched, losing her composure.

Aaro approached Alissia, his hands open to calm her. "He sacrificed himself to protect us," he said, his expression soft. "He deactivated the shields and," he paused, "he's aboard a Nevo ship."

Tears swelled in Alissia's eyes. She deflected Aaro's attempt to comfort her. "We're getting him back, right? We must get him back!"

Javex stood, but did not meet her gaze.

Alissia stepped back and unleashed her dual blades. "Where's that Varanus? I'll kill him!" She paused her fury to glare at them. "Where *is* the Varanus?"

"Seems the Nevo have taken him." Javex scowled.

As much as Grootie's betrayal hurt, he hoped they would spare his life.

"Captain." Aaro tapped a screen multiple times, growing visibly frustrated.

Something in his face disturbed him. The rim of tears building under his bloodshot eyes, unlike him.

"Aaro, what is it?"

Aaro swallowed and forced the words out. "T-t-they are," he struggled to continue. He cupped his mouth. "They're no longer aboard the ship."

Javex's heart stopped as he turned to Noro's station. The Lanks was gone. "What? What did you say?"

Aaro swallowed, tears brimming his eyes. "The bastards took them, Captain. The kids, Ser, they took them!"

Aaro stormed from his station, gripping his head as he paced the bridge.

Pain numbed Javex's extremities, and his world faded away. His children, Seraphina, gone? Grief rung his heart. The breath in his lungs rushed out as a cry, then an angry roar.

Chapter 21

BROKEN

Javex sat in his command seat, watching through the viewport at Arimas spinning. The *Dauntless* drifted, damaged and beyond repair. Its engines at half capacity limited their ability to travel far.

Aaro and Alissia busied themselves with tasks and repairs, but the truth was, they couldn't bear to witness his immense hopelessness. Why should they?

He stared out across the ruined ship. The *Dauntless* betrayed him in his time of need. His mercy and patience for Grootie wasted. Two solar rotations and what did it produce? Nothing.

Tears sought to surface, to relieve him of the ache in his heart, to give him peace, but his anger prevented them from falling. After all this time trying to make a difference, and what did he accomplish?

He growled and his mood darkened. And to think he could help Cade. He should have listened to his father and stayed with the tribe. It would have saved him the grief, the pain . . .

The familiar sound of Aaro's boots entered the bridge, their taps aggressive, purposeful.

"Are you done brooding yet?"

"Leave me. You do not understand what I have lost."

Aaro stood before him to block his view. "A heck of a lot more if you don't fight back."

A sudden spike of anger knit Javex's brows, and he rose from his seat.

"It's too late, Aaro. There's nothing that can be done. The ships a wreck and I failed! I . . ." A tear escaped, caressing his cheek.

"Javex, if we sit here and do nothing, then we have failed."

"There is no hope, Aaro. The Nevo have won!"

Aaro grit his teeth. "No, there's still time. I've been analyzing data with Alissia. We can use the remaining power in the engines to get us into the planet's orbit. We can try to land from there. It's not perfect, but it's something."

Aaro's eyes didn't waver from his gaze.

"Even if we make it to Arimas, then what? We don't have a ship or know where the Nevo are going."

Carefully placed footsteps tapped the bridge's smooth floor as Alissia entered. She braided her hair up into a pony and re-bandaged her wounds. Her fierce gaze rested on him.

"We will use my ship," Alissia said, marching towards them with her head held high. "We will return to Arimas to retrieve her. She may be a bit scraped up, but her shields kept her in one piece."

"We should get underway as quickly as possible," Aaro said, sitting at the navigation consul. "But where are going after we get to Arimas?"

"If," Javex corrected with a grumble.

"I know," Alissia said.

She touched one of Aaro's navigation screens and motioned for them to view the displayed hologram. A star chart bounced into the clearing and dictated a path.

"If the Nevo are heading anywhere, it will be Cordabo. That's their base of operations."

A chill ran down Javex's spine. Cordabo was the hive of the Nevo, the claimed kingdom of Lord Khelveliz. No one dared to venture there. He swallowed, willing to entertain her thoughts.

"How are we supposed to infiltrate a secure Nevo base?"

Aaro ran his hands through his hair. "Yeah? We can't just walk in." He grunted.

Alissia's eye glimmered with mischief. "That's precisely what we are going to do."

Aaro guffawed. "How?"

"I come and go from Cordabo as I please. You will pretend to be my prisoners. We'll walk right past the guards without raising a suspicion."

The idea was awful and too good to be true. Javex held his chin. "What if they recognize us?"

Alissia crossed her arms. "You're both injured. It should help with the bluff."

Javex hated to admit she was right, but his torn arm limited his fighting abilities. Walking into the Nevo lair maimed was a disaster waiting to happen. If the Nevo discovered them, they wouldn't be able to fight their way out. As unfortunate as their circumstance was, this plan was all they had. Their time to act dwindled.

Javex sat in the pilot chair and got comfortable with the controls. In one display, he verified the amount of power remaining in the thrusters. Aaro and Alissia were right. After a quick check of their calculations, they would have just enough energy to fly the ship to Arimas.

"Strap in. This could get bumpy."

Aaro and Alissia strapped into seats on the bridge, exchanging looks with each other. A silent hope their plan would work.

Javex gripped the controls and summoned his courage. He had to believe he would see his kids again, that they would save them. He directed the *Dauntless* around and headed for Arimas, giving just enough power to the engines to propel them forward.

"We might not have enough power to slow ourselves once we reach the planet. We'll be entering the atmosphere too hot."

Aaro allowed a nervous chuckle. "You mean we might actually crash the ship?"

Javex grimaced. "Yes. Not that I want to, but we may have no other choice."

"Better that than getting shot down," Alissia said with a scowl.

Javex agreed with her, which brought back an important detail he hadn't considered.

"Aaro, remember that being of energy in the glade?"

"You mean Mr. Antisocial?"

Javex grimaced. "Yes, him. The Shargan. Prepare a signal to send to Arimas. Let the general know we are coming back for an unplanned landing. We wouldn't want to be mistaken as a threat."

Aaro got to work readying the message. Javex turned to Alissia, her arms crossed as she stared out of the viewport.

"Thank you for not giving up on finding a way out of this mess."

Alissia rose her eyebrows. "Don't thank me yet, Captain. We're still a far way off from saving ourselves. Never mind saving your crew."

"You are right, but you did not allow yourself to consider quitting."

"Sometimes quitting isn't an option, Captain. I told myself long ago I would never let myself quit on anything again."

Javex considered this. For a bounty hunter, she displayed characteristics and a code unlike the typical morality of a person seeking monetary gain.

"In fact, Captain, it should be me thanking you for sparing my life," she said.

Aaro huffed at that. "You should, because I wouldn't have."

Alissia smiled, narrowing her eyes. "I know, Aaro Riffo, Supreme Commander of the Shrovon. I know a lot of things about you."

Aaro scowled and turned away from her.

The *Dauntless* shuddered, ending the banter between them. Arimas filled the viewport with her green boreal forests and vast mountain ranges. They approached the planet fast.

"You were right, Captain. She's coming in hot."

White light blazed across the bow of the starship. With their shields fried, nothing protected them from the heat of re-entry. Groans reverberated through the ship. The temperature of the cabin intensified. Pieces of the hull curled from the heat and flew off. Yellow strobe lights flashed around the bridge as warnings blipped.

"We're cutting it close, Captain," Aaro called. "Systems are going haywire. We'll lose our ability to control the angle of the *Dauntless* if we continue to burn like this."

Javex grit his teeth, staring against the brightness of re-entry. "A little more. Just a little more," he said to himself.

If the *Dauntless* didn't make it, that part didn't matter, but they needed to survive. If the ship lost its angle, it would be impossible to correct and land safe.

They passed through the atmosphere of the planet when the yellow lights of the bridge blazed red. The ship pivoted, beginning to rotate.

"We're going into a spiral!" Alissia called.

Javex pulled on the controls, but he wasted his effort. The ship acted with a mind of its own, tumbling and spiraling towards the planet.

The view of Arimas drew closer. In moments, they would smear across its surface. Javex was about to close his eyes and say a prayer when, beyond the viewport of the damaged ship, a blue light appeared.

"Aaro, look."

Aaro squinted from his good eye. "What is that?"

The ship's violent spiral slowed, the blue light becoming steady. The light grew closer and soon touched the ship. It floated across the *Dauntless'* hull like a star until it paused before the glass.

Javex stared, stunned. "It can't be."

A surge of energy trickled through Javex as the light passed through the window and onto his ship. The energy particles spun and sparkled until they drifted apart and reconstructed together. Before them now stood a person. Its body—a vivid blue armor suit—deepened in hues with a black armor skin beneath.

The Shargan bowed. "Greetings. I am T'vos."

"Hello," Javex said, heart racing with excitement. The tingling feeling surging through him subsided. This individual not only saved them from certain death, but represented an ancient race long-forgotten. "T'vos, thank you for saving my ship and helping us on Arimas."

T'vos inclined his head. "Sorry I could not aid you further. I had prior commitments." T'vos took a few paces further onto the bridge. "When I sensed the Nevo, I knew your vessel would not survive the attack. I tried to aid you. Regrettably, the conflict on Arimas kept me longer than I intended." T'vos glanced around the room. "Where is the one with the sickness?"

Javex caught his breath. "You mean Cade?"

"Is that what he calls himself? Then yes. A dark energy grows in him."

The reminder stabbed Javex in the heart, and he fought to find his words.

Aaro cleared his throat. "The Nevo used the wisp to take him and three of our crew. We are about to launch a rescue."

T'vos turned, his heavy footsteps thudding on the floor. "In this vessel?"

"Mine," Alissia said. "It's on the surface. You had something to do with that, didn't you?"

T'vos nodded. "Your ship approached with the fleet of Varanus. I did what was necessary."

Alissa eyed the soldier. "I forgive you. Had I not crashed, I may not have found Cade."

The *Dauntless* approached the surface of Arimas, performing a smooth landing on a rocky surface. Indeed, this was a Shargan, a noble warrior able to wield energy and many other untold abilities. If their mission was to be successful, they needed help. But would the ancient soldier be willing? He'd have to take his chances.

"We are going to Cordabo. Will you help me?"

The Shargan stiffened, a crackle of energy surging over his armor. "That is the claimed throne of Lord Khelveliz. It's impenetrable."

Alissia stood from her seat. "Not for me."

T'vos clasped his hands in front of him. "I can help you launch your ship, but I am forbidden to step onto Cordabo."

Javex bowed. The declaration was unfortunate. "I understand. Thank you, T'vos."

Aaro stood from his seat, placing his helmet back over his head. "Alright, then. Let's bring our family back home."

Chapter 22

PRECIOUS CARGO

Kaytrix blinked to adjust his vision of the surrounding darkness. Shrieks echoed around him, their barrage of pain and suffering. The air, moist and clammy, clung to him like a sickness. The stench of rot filled his nostrils.

Kaytrix stood and grabbed the slimy bars of the cell. He pulled on them, but the cold metal mocked his strength. Maybe this hadn't been such a great idea. The Nevo might have destroyed the *Dauntless* once they took him.

He hoped not.

A dim light emerged in the darkness, throbbing a pale dull green barred by blackness. Otherworldly details crept into his perception. Nevo stood guard across the fog ridden corridor watching him. To his left, tentacles slithered through the bars, oozing as they forced themselves through the thin spaces towards him.

The sounds of the ship flooded his focus, the shrieks, the creaks, the oozing tentacles relentless in trying to touch him . . . The ship represented death, but he wasn't ready to accept that fate, not yet.

He breathed in. *Focus.* Slowly, the darkness fell away, and, in the unlikeliest places, he calmed his mind. The fear, confusion, uncertainty—remained, but he distanced himself from those emotions and embraced his situation with a new clarity. Even the voice in his head stayed silent, as if retreating to the furthest corner of his mind. Why, he wasn't sure.

The cell of his door jerked open, the loud shrill of the metal shattering his meditation. Two Nevo soldiers stood in front of his cell and huffed. Their beady eyes peered from beneath twisted shapes of metal fashioned to their heads. When he didn't move, the Nevo drew their weapons. Green energy blazed them alive with threatening power.

"Time to go," the one said, a grimy, grating sound.

Kaytrix hesitated. He refused to follow these creatures anywhere. Something latched around his boot. He stepped forward in time to avoid becoming the tentacle's next meal, only for the Nevo to slap a set of cuffs on him.

They pulled him forwards and dragged him through the dark corridor. More green orbs lit the path, their light bouncing off the rolling fog. More prison cells lined the walls, stacked upon one another like a hive. Some poor souls hung strung from chains; others lay in their cell curled in the fetal position.

Kaytrix's boots thudded the grated corridor floor, echoing through the prison ward. It spanned as far as the eye could see, shrouded in darkness with an orb of light to give depth. The farther they walked, the louder the screams grew, and the more irritated. The foul smell of sweating bodies and corpses intensified.

Nevo soldiers stood in the distance. The blazing green of their weapons danced off the odd shapes of their armor. Beyond them, a horde gathered on a round platform, the center of what appeared to connect several cell blocks.

"Get them unloaded and ready for departure!" A Nevo roared.

He stood taller than the others, with a mid-length cape flowing down his backside. Around him, Nevo scrambled to the cells. Varanus servants obeyed the same order.

Cell doors shrilled open, and the Nevo began the terrible practice of removing the occupants. They pulled the prisoners from their cells and to the waiting hands below. Kaytrix winced as a Nevo lugged a prisoner out and let go before the next set of hands grasped them. The victim fell, hitting the metal of the rough enclosures and falling to their death into the depths of the ship.

"The next careless fool who damages the property of his Lord will die by my hands!" The Nevo with the cape roared, his eyes blazing.

Kaytrix assumed it commanded the smaller and underdeveloped Nevo soldiers. Their structure of power not dissimilar to the colonies of the insectoids on Rehnna.

A young and scared cry caught his attention. As he walked by, he glimpsed Atara, Seraphina, and Noro crammed into a cell.

Atara clung to the bars with Noro, tears streaked their faces.

"Cade! What's happened? Why are we here?"

Seraphina shook her head. "The Nevo used the wisp to take us, but there's no way the *Dauntless* lost its shields." Seraphina's eyes shone fiercely. "You lowered the shield, didn't you?"

"This wasn't supposed to happen. I was trying to protect you!"

Atara pulled back. "What wasn't supposed to happen?"

Before Kaytrix could respond, an unknown feeling set his nervous system on fire. The jolt traveled through his body, sending him to his knees in anguish.

"Get moving!" the Nevo soldier said. Its hands grabbed his arm and pulled him to his feet.

"Cade!" Atara and Noro called after him, but Seraphina's stare was bitter. He'd done the unspeakable, and now she was back in the hell she'd spent the last ten solar rotations of her life running from.

"I will figure something out. I promise!"

The sting from the baton worsened through his body, but it didn't compare to the sting of resentment from Seraphina.

"Silence!" One soldier ordered, smacking him across the back.

Kaytrix looked back to remember their location when a Nevo jerked the cell door open and threw Seraphina, Atara, and Noro out.

"These go to the lost property hold. Reactivate their chips and prep them for shipment," a Nevo said.

Seraphina fought to keep them off Atara and Noro, only to receive the same fiery shock. He soon lost them in the crowd of bodies. All around him, Nevo hauled their captives from cells and forced them to walk. They herded them down the corridors and to the open platform. More prisoners flooded into the room from other access corridors. Their faces blurred together. The intense smell from before worsened, as did the sounds of groans and sobs.

This had to be a nightmare.

Green lights throbbed along the perimeter of the hold. The rhythm quickened until it strobed as a single light. A shudder tested his balance as the ship beneath him moved. The wide platform was a cargo hold.

"Prepare to unload the prisoners!" A Nevo called out from the throng.

The Nevo standing next to him tightened their grasp, keeping him separate from the crowd. A loud metal groan reverberated throughout the cargo hold, causing a gasp from the crowd.

The green lights faded, leaving them in temporary darkness until a small, arching light appeared. A low whirr hummed and the angle at which he stood shifted down.

The group grew uneasy, pushing each other. Unrest broke out as they fought and scrambled, as if the growing crack represented their fear. The greater the light, the more real their fate became.

"Push them forward!" The Nevo commander bellowed.

Sharp zaps seared flesh with a crackling sound, forcing the unwilling crowd to descend the opening ramp. The smell lessened as cool, damp air rushed into the cargo hold. Awaiting them at the bottom of the ramp were Nevo soldiers. Their eyes were mere luminescent dots in the darkness. They stood as shadows. Waiting.

Kaytrix's escorts pulled him to the side as the other Nevo forced the prisoners into the waiting hands of their captors.

"To the holding cells!" the same Nevo called.

His voice grew louder as the cry of the crowd emptied from the ship. The commanding Nevo stood beside him now, taller than the others, a lieutenant if he had to guess.

"Take this one to Lord Khelveliz. He is expecting his arrival. Don't make him wait."

His escorts nodded with a subtle hiss and yanked him forwards.

The air grew chill, prickling his skin as they set foot in the blades of grass. He hesitated. Something about this planet was familiar. In the night sky, a visible ring arched over them. Flakes crusted the trees, grass, and buildings in a glowing dust. To the far right of him, the entrance of a cave and next to it, a passage carved through the earth to allow airflow.

His throat tightened; his heart raced. This was the planet where it all began, the planet Alissia saved him from. He slowed his pace, but the Nevo soldier shoved him from behind.

They approached the entrance of the underground base. Rows of ships lined either side, frightful looking pieces of metal, like demons in the shadows. They entered a lift and grated doors slammed shut across the front. One soldier pressed a button on a consul covered in solar rotations of dirt. A jolt disrupted his balance as they traveled down.

He counted the levels passing by. Soon, the sounds and smells from the surface fell away, replaced by the cold smell of steel and dirt. The lift jerked to a halt.

The underground base was not as crude as the ship. Soldiers, guards, and servants passed each other with only a glance. White lights lit their path. The floor wasn't dirt like he expected, but fine stone placed in alternating patterns.

He stalled, eyeing up the details. Crude tapestries hung staggered down the corridor, their black material worn with tattered gold edges. In the center bore a red insignia he didn't recognize. The gray stone walls stood tall and unpolished with an odd slash here and there. Beyond these details, he searched for an escape.

The Nevo soldiers sensed his intentions, and one grumbled to the other. Another shock passed through him. The jolt put more of a spring in his step, but it did little to dissuade him from raking in escape possibilities.

They spun to the left just as a potential exit presented itself. He feigned a stumble, but the Nevo behind grasped the collar of his shirt and pulled him forward. They entered another room and threw him face-first onto the floor.

A bone-chilling hiss split the pre-existing silence. It's deep rattle freezing his heart.

"Handle him like that again, and I'll reduce you to scrap!" roared a voice.

The sound of metal scuffing stone scratched his ears. Kaytrix assumed the soldier bowed and left, but when he opened his eyes, a taller, broader Nevo held the soldier by the throat.

"How fortunate for you I need your pathetic skin alive," spoke the impressive figure. The dark Nevo thrust the soldier away. "Leave! Before I change my mind!"

The soldier staggered backwards into the other and left in a frenzy, their footfalls echoing through the hall, leaving him alone with the menacing Nevo.

Kaytrix regained his composure and knelt on the floor, waiting. The glow of the lights reflected on the floor, shining as if he gazed upon a section of space.

"Rise," ordered the voice.

Something inside wanted to refuse the demand, but another part of him obeyed. A weird feeling formed in the back of his skull. Kaytrix stood, making eye contact with the voice for the first time. There, sat upon a throne embellished in tarnished black metal, sat a formidable looking Nevo. Its eyes glowed with a wicked flair.

A massive being of metal and flesh, this Nevo was the king of all others. Its height surpassed Grootie, its width defined with a large, dark cloak. Among everything else, the large crushing mechanical feet armed with sharp talons heightened his fear.

Then it spoke, and the power of his words froze him.

"After all this time, we stand face-to-face." The Nevo rose from the throne to tower over him. "Did you really think you could escape me?"

"I—," Kaytrix paused, trying to not let his efforts of concentration show. The stabbing feeling in his skull intensified. "I don't know what you are talking about. I don't even know who you are."

The evil lord paused, huffing through his grated mouth. "Do you expect me to believe your lies?"

"If I remembered, I would know," he retorted. "I don't think anyone would forget your face."

The Nevo lord remained silent, and he feared his comment stirred the already seething pot.

"I am Lord Khelveliz, conqueror of worlds, master of many. And you are the remnants of the race that tried to stand against me." Khelveliz walked around him, his body whirring and clicking with the movement.

The name didn't register, but the anger and hatred Lord Khelveliz exuded was real.

His skin crawled.

"Extend your arm," Lord Khelveliz demanded, frustration thick in his tone.

"Which one?" He chided.

Khelveliz snorted. "I see you still lack a proper sense of fear." He grabbed Kaytrix's arms backwards, almost pulling them from their sockets. "There is no mistaking who you are, though you try to hide it."

Khelveliz released him and returned to the throne. "You seem to have earned the loyalty of a Zaguarz with the five marks," Khelveliz said, waving his hand.

"Javex took me in as one of his own."

"And what of the Varanus who turned you in? Did the Zaguarz impart the same trust to him?" Khelveliz's eyes intensified.

"I don't know."

Khelveliz talked too much, something he already hated. He glanced around the room. Trophies covered the wall behind the Nevo lord's throne. His stomach churned, recognizing a Zaguarz hide, the skull of a Varanus, and the remains of what resembled an Acknarian. Other species he could not identify.

Alissia's words floated back to him: *"You are something Lord Khelveliz prizes, something he would kill to have returned."*

The words brought him back to where it all started, sputtering and naked as Alissia pulled tubes from his body. A startling realization stabbed his brain. He was Lord Khelveliz's trophy.

"I didn't sense fear in you before," Khelveliz spoke, making his heart skip a beat. "But I sense it in you now, Commander Torex."

Khelveliz's voice grated on his soul, deepening the paralyzing fear. Flashes of battles and death surfaced, causing pain in his temples.

Wait? He recognized that name from somewhere. Javex said it aboard the *Dauntless.*

"Something else about you . . ." Khelveliz knelt close, breathing in heavily. "Ah, I sense it now. A spawn. That explains your poor health."

Khelveliz rose to his full height and drove a fist into the clay wall. Cracks raced from the point of impact. A rattling hiss seethed from Khelveliz's grated mouth.

"So, Vhulse not only lied to me, but he's also betrayed me. Nevertheless," he hissed the words. "His task is nearing completion. Then his usefulness will end."

What task? Kaytrix searched his memory. Alissia mentioned Vhulse on the *Dauntless* and his mission. Kaytrix's fears escalated, his heart quickened.

"Who am I to you?"

Khelveliz yanked his fist from the wall and returned to his throne. The Nevo lord breathed in, a flare of pride in his eyes as if Kaytrix should already know.

"You are the last of the conquered. Now the key to furthering my race's existence. Finally, our path to becoming unstoppable is within our grasp." Khelveliz paused, his orbed eyes roaming Kaytrix's open-jawed expression. "It's a shame you will not live to see the glory the Nevo will possess."

Kaytrix shook his head. Maybe this dark creature could help piece together the painful void of his life with a little prodding.

"Not to steal your thunder, but I don't remember the Last Stand. Hard to impress me with your greatness when I can't recall our history."

Khelveliz flashed his eyes, his taloned fingers clicking on his throne. "Your pitiful mind won't be able to comprehend it, nor do I need it to. Soldier!"

Two Nevo soldiers entered the room and bowed. "Yes, my Lord."

"Take him to the lab."

Panic rushed through Kaytrix. He couldn't leave yet. Too many unanswered questions remained.

"Why are you doing this to the galaxy? To me? What did I ever do to you?"

Khelveliz's hands crushed the armrests to his metal throne with a deafening screech.

"What did *you* do?" Khelveliz stood, rising like an erupting volcano. "How quickly the arrogant forget! *You* destroyed my planet. *You* brought my kind to extinction! And now you will join your kin in death." Khelveliz motioned for the soldiers to take him.

Kaytrix resisted, but the soldiers dragged him away to his waiting fate.

Chapter 23

CORDABO

Alissia struggled to relax, crossing her legs only to uncross them. Even with the comfort of her ship and a solid plan, things could still go wrong. She released her breath and inhaled deep. Now more than ever, she needed her wits, her strength, but more than that, she needed to be clever. Her emotions were powerful. If she could channel them, they would succeed.

The dark and glowing Cordabo planet glimmered in the ship's viewport. Alissia tightened her gear and tightened it again. She'd walked among the Nevo for most of her life, but this was the first time she had something to lose. With that realization came the fear.

All this time, she convinced herself she hated Vhulse and wanted nothing more than to see Khelveliz kill him. She kept herself from admitting the real reason she'd saved Cade from Vhulse. It wasn't the thirst for revenge that she saved his life, but something much stronger.

Her stomach churned; her palms were sweaty. She was a fool for not checking on him sooner. Because of her negligence, the Nevo had Cade in their clutches. If she was right about what Cade meant to them, their future was on the line. This might be the last mistake she'd make, and what a deadly one it was.

"Doing okay?"

She jumped at the sound of Aaro's voice. "Yes," she said, her tone cutting.

"Mhm," Aaro sat in the cockpit beside her. "How long have we been out of warp? You know we're on a time sensitive mission."

"Not long. I was about to announce to Javex we arrived."

"Mhm," Aaro's soothing voice rumbled in his throat.

"Something the matter with you?"

He grinned at her, his face an annoyance to her vision. "Nope. I just don't trust you."

She smirked. "Yet here we are, aboard my ship, heading to a planet infested with Nevo. So, who exactly are we trusting?"

He waved her off. "Yeah, but one virtuous deed doesn't erase a lifetime of corrupt ones. You of all people should know that."

"What if I am not looking to erase my deeds, Shrovon? Only those who regret what they've done seek forgiveness. You think I am a bounty hunter, but there's more to me than my pretty face and knives."

His cold blue eyes locked with hers. "Whatever you've done, you are making the right choice today. Doesn't mean I won't be keeping an eye on you."

"I wouldn't expect anything less, Shrovon."

"Aaro," he corrected. "My name is Aaro."

She allowed herself a smile. "Very well, Aaro. Tell your captain we are here."

Aaro flashed her a smile and exited the cockpit to the cargo hold below. His voice carried the message and she let it drift away. She grasped the controls tighter and clenched her jaw. She hoped they weren't too late.

The ship sailed to the planet, towards Nevo patrol ships, towards uncertainty. A fervent beep followed by a flashing light appeared on her console. The patrol recognized her ship, but a second confirmation was required.

Her communique display flashed yellow. They wanted to talk. She flicked the switch and sat on the edge of her seat. Nerves bubbled in her stomach.

"Bounty hunter, state your business," demanded a gruff voice.

She gathered her nerves. "Alissia Rabb. I'm returning with a bounty for Vhulse. Destination: the underground lab. Permission to proceed with landing."

Static carried over the comms. She hoped her lack of contact with Vhulse, and their touchy history, didn't affect his faith in her to return. That's the last thing this mission needed. Otherwise, they were walking into a trap.

The comm echoed static. "Proceed," the voice said.

She flicked the communication switch off, relieved, but that was one barrier of many that awaited them.

"Get ready. We're landing."

A chorus of relieved sounds escaped Aaro and Javex from the cargo bay below. She was lucky—no, fortunate—that Cade found himself a decent group of people. Except for the Varanus, he could rot.

The ship eased through the atmosphere and touched the ground with grace, unlike the last time she landed. Arimas brought forth revelations she wasn't ready to handle. Everything was more complicated now.

"Excellent skill piloting this vessel," Javex said from behind her.

She turned to see him clung to the top rung, a slight smile to his face. Amazingly, the Zaguarz's spirits rekindled even after losing his children, his pilot, and his ship to the Nevo. It fascinated her to see the power of hope glimmer in his eyes.

"Thank you. Now we best hurry. Nevo will pass the information on as soon as they receive it. Fortunate for us, the process is slow. We need the edge while we have it."

Javex nodded and disappeared down the ladder into the cargo hold. When she came down the last of the rungs, she stood face-to-face with Aaro.

"Alissia," he acknowledged. He and Javex dressed in familiar robes. "I took the liberty of raiding your closet. Hope you don't mind."

"Disguises, excellent plan." She wrapped her robes around herself and over her head. "Remember. Stay close, stay quiet, and let me do the talking." She grabbed cuffs from a nearby shelf and handed them out.

Javex rose an eyebrow.

Alissia grimaced. "To make it look good. Place them on and follow me. This is our only shot. If we mess it up . . ." her voice trailed off.

"We won't," Aaro said as he put the cuffs on. "We can't."

Alissia punched the release to the cargo hold ramp. The overwhelming stillness of the planet grabbed at her as the flecks of glowing light fell. She didn't want the peace the planet offered. She had work to do, and with it, blood to shed.

The bright night of the planet lit their surroundings. Up ahead, the entrance of the underground base lay situated, illuminated in the light cast by the ring above them. Nevo fighter ships waited along the opening while a small group of soldiers stood guard. The grass yielded to her steps, its soft crunch announcing Aaro and Javex following her.

Alissia detected a potent scent, a smell she'd only ever encountered on a Nevo ship. The smell of decay, feces, and fear. Javex cleared his nose behind her. He smelt it, too.

"A dropship unloaded its prisoners not too long ago," she said. "We're on the right track."

She motioned with her hand for them to follow her as she approached the base.

"Where exactly are we going? What's the plan?" Aaro asked.

She led them to the side of the base where a lift waited. "This abandoned lift will take us to below the planet's surface where the Nevo have created an extensive system of levels. Once in, we will locate and extract your crew and Cade."

The two nodded and followed her lead. They entered the lift and closed the door, her face inches from Aaro.

"Kind of tight in here," Aaro said when he stifled a cough.

In the low light, his gloved hand gleamed, the bottom half of his helmet smeared in blood. It reminded Alissia of her own wounds buried beneath bandages. With Aaro and Javex injured, they couldn't afford to get into a fight, least of all with a Nevo, and hope to escape.

The grimy control panel glowed a pale light beneath the worn metal buttons. They wouldn't find Cade, Noro, Atara, and Seraphina by looking. That would cost them time they didn't have. She selected the sixth level. The lift jolted to life as it began its slow descent into another kind of hell.

"There is a terminal on the sixth level with a prisoner manifest. Once we locate the kids and Seraphina, we will wait at the lab for them to bring Cade. Watch out for any patrols."

"How many in a patrol?" Aaro asked, his voice muffled by his helmet.

"Lucky for us, one, but given the circumstances, we may run into more. They are smaller and weaker than Lord Khelveliz and Vhulse. Weaker than a Varanus even, but their weapons are powerful." She unsheathed one of her blades. "Your best defense is to stab them between their armor plates. Their shields repel energy, but blades sink through. But you must be quick and accurate."

The lift jerked to a stop. The grated door opened to the level of darkness and the foul smell from the surface met them with a warm wave. At first, she couldn't stomach the smell. Only after some time did she get used to it.

Alissia waited a moment, assessing the situation and allowing them to catch their breath. "The terminal is right around this corner."

Soft dirt gave way to clanging as they ventured down the first corridor. The floor and walls transformed into endless heights and lengths of prisoner cells like honeycombs stacked together. A sludge cascaded between some rows, a mix of blood, excrements, and vomit. Victims cried out in agony.

"What is this place?" Javex growled, his tone angry.

"Best you do not know, or you'll never sleep again," she warned.

Alissia led them around the corner to where the terminal stood against an unoccupied block of cells. The corridor was empty of Nevo patrols. She never had this kind of luck before. She stepped closer and fingered through the reports, reading the Nevo language with ease.

"Here, I have something," she said in a whisper. "Just before the interrogation block, three reclaimed pieces of property from a recent raid. It says two lost slaves belong to a certain mining operation and slated to be returned. The third, to be returned to active duty as a hostess?"

"That's them," Javex said, his tone sad.

A flash of Alissia's past surfaced, her brother and father protecting her while the Nevo burned and destroyed her home. The memory was too painful to recall, so she suppressed it. Now was not the time to remember that kind of love.

"How do we unlock one of these cells?" Aaro stood surveying one, his helmet's gaze fixed on the solid frame. "There's no structural weakness that I can detect."

Alissia stepped back from the terminal. "We need a key."

Aaro chuckled, muffled by his helmet. "Right, and let me guess. Only the Nevo have the keys?"

She wrinkled her nose. "You're so smart."

He shook his head and crossed his arms at her sarcasm.

She smiled and pulled aside her robe to produce a small round gadget half the size of a person's palm.

"The key is a frequency. I copied it some time ago, but it should still work. Never know when the Nevo will betray you."

The clang of footsteps reverberated through the corridor.

"Someone approaches. We must go," Javex said in a whisper.

Alissia motioned them forward. The next corridor ended at an intersection spanning boundless lengths and heights of grated flooring and prisoner hives. Just off to their right, another corridor entryway stood askew.

"We're almost there. Just through that corridor, then take a right to another passage. The manifest said your crew is on that block."

Aaro stifled another cough, his next breath a wheeze. The fight from Grootie damaged him more than he let on. Everyone was sacrificing something to be here, but it was imperative they stop Vhulse from completing his task for Lord Khelveliz.

They crossed the intersecting corridor only to come face-to-face with a Nevo patrol. Alissia froze as fear rushed from her heart to her limbs.

"What's your business with these prisoners?" the Nevo demanded, charging his weapon. He stepped forward and huffed. His black armor whirred with the motion, but behind the plates of his protective skeleton, shined the neon color of skin.

Alissia laughed to herself, remembering she'd cuffed and disguised Aaro and Javex. She had no reason to be afraid.

"I am taking them to a cell for Vhulse to examine."

The Nevo stepped forward, this time staring her down. "No one informed me of this," he hissed.

Alissia squared up with the Nevo and met his gaze. "I do not report to you! Do you know who I am?"

The Nevo guard remained steadfast.

She continued. "I am the personal bounty hunter of Lord Khelveliz. Your questioning is delaying your Lord's commands." Her heart raced in her chest. "Shall I inform him of your intrusion into my work? I am sure the lack of progress will displease him." Alissia summoned every inch of her hardened heart to stare daggers at the guard.

The Nevo took a retreating step back but waited. Alissia feared her bluff was less than convincing. She reached for her communique when the Nevo lowered his weapon.

"That won't be necessary, bounty hunter. Continue on your way."

"I shall." She yanked on the tether and pulled her prisoners close.

The Nevo soldier stalked past her, his eyes flashing when he rounded the last turn in the hallway and disappeared.

Alissia glanced back at Aaro and Javex. "Come, we are almost there."

They traveled down the aisle and took a right where the prison cells continued. In a lower section, the familiar sound of Atara's voice cooed.

Alissia approached the cell, readying her device to open the door. Atara's wild and terrified face peered through the encrusted bars. Seraphina sat holding Noro in her lap, but her green eyes burned with anger. Unlike Atara, Seraphina was not pleased to see her.

Alissia motioned for them to keep silent. "Back away from the door."

Alissia squeezed the trigger on the device and waited for the security system to recognize the frequency. After a moment's delay, the bolt retracted from across the door, shrilling through the prison. She winced, hoping it did not alert the Nevo.

Atara wiped a tear from her eye and shook Noro. "Brother, wake up."

"No. I'm done, Atara. I have no fight left in me." His voice was raw and weak.

"Brother, look. Please."

Noro lifted his gaze, his eyes red and swollen from the horror they'd already endured from the Nevo.

"Am I dreaming?" A smile split across his bruised face.

Alissia smiled, but her heart burned with anger at his wounds.

"Come, friends. It is time to leave. We must hurry and rescue Cade."

Noro and Atara lifted themselves up, but it wasn't long before Javex reached in to help them.

"Father!" they said in unison, their voices hushed.

Seraphina crawled out of the small cell next, her hair matted and dirty, but more prevalent was a fresh cut across her face.

"It's Cade's fault we're here. Let's leave while we still can."

Javex did not answer her, but instead reached to pull her up. Aaro moved into comfort Seraphina, taking a clean medical wipe to dab the cut on her face.

Alissia turned from the tender moment as Atara and Noro embraced Javex and cried tears of relief. The moment stung her heart, knowing she would never feel the embrace of her father again. Anger replaced sorrow as she recalled the day her slavery began at the hands of the Nevo.

A hand touched her shoulder, and she turned to see Aaro's helmet gazing at her.

"Are you ok?"

She brushed his hand away. "When every Nevo is dead, then maybe. We need to keep going. It's doubtful our disguises will continue to work with all of us now. Be ready to draw your weapons."

The crew ended their reunion and pressed together behind her. They traveled down the corridor and made a left turn where a different cell appeared. Victims hung from chains secured around their wrists, their arms pulled taunt from the weight of their body. These cells were for interrogation. Alissia witnessed many brutal deaths in these cells, many she would never forget. As they passed these torture chambers, a familiar figure hung.

"Grootie?" Javex whispered.

The large Varanus hung strung, his head lowered as his arms bore the weight of his massive frame.

"Leave him!" Alissia hissed. "He's the reason we're in this mess, not Cade." Her eyes darted to Seraphina.

Javex hesitated. The grief on his face hinted at the difficult decision he faced. Noro and Atara squeezed his hands. To hold him back or to remind him they were the reason he came?

"Captain, we don't have time for this!" Aaro said, his tone harsh. "Grootie made his choice."

Javex sighed. "Indeed."

For a moment, he released the children's hands and clenched his fists. His brow furrowed into a deep crevasse when his countenance softened, and he stepped closer.

"But he deserves a chance to redeem himself."

Alissia wanted to pull her hair out as Javex struggled to release the Varanus. After several attempts, the chains remained taunt.

Alissia glanced around for patrols. She hated to help the vile creature, but if she didn't, Javex's stubbornness to save Grootie's unworthy skin would doom their entire mission.

"Step aside."

She entered the chamber and grabbed a lever disguised as a chain anchor. She wished she didn't have to do this. Grootie above any other deserved to die. She pulled down and after another persistent yank, the chains released the Varanus into the debris below.

She glared at Javex. "The rest is up to him. We must leave now, or we will find ourselves in the same predicament."

Javex nodded and regrouped with the others.

Relief washed through her. They may still make it out of here. "Just around this corner. C'mon," she said, taking up the lead.

She quickened her pace, keeping her footfalls silent. They rounded the last corner leading to the lab. The light from the entrance cascaded into the corridor, revealing two Nevo soldiers standing guard. Her heart sank, and she paused alongside the corridor wall.

"Why have we stopped?" Aaro asked.

"Those Nevo guards aren't usually there. That means Cade is inside and they won't let us in. We will have to feign walking by and spring a surprise attack."

"What?! You can't be serious?" Aaro pulled his knife out even as he argued with her.

She withdrew her blades. "We'll be discreet. Remember, between the armor."

Chapter 24

THE LAB

The Nevo soldiers brought Kaytrix into a dark room, the center lit with bright beams of light. In the center of these lights, a chair with metal restraints faced him. Kaytrix resisted, digging his heels into the metal grated floor only to have his strength foiled once again. He fought as the Nevo slammed him into a seat and secured restraints around his wrists, arms, legs, and feet. The cold steel seared his skin.

The lab.

The smell brought back every inch of his pain when Alissia pulled him from the darkness and offered another chance at life, albeit a confusing one. Faint beeps and squirting sounds filled his ears as the stomping and whirring bodies of the Nevo soldiers left. A cold sensation prickled his skin.

The bright lights prevented him from seeing much at first, but soon adjusted. Tables filled with rotting carcasses littered every available space. On the far wall, three preservation tanks, one smashed, another with its contents slumped at the bottom . . .

Kaytrix forced himself to look away. This wasn't what he pictured when he told himself he wanted answers. Despite his attempt to ignore the tanks, he took a breath and faced his dark beginning.

Beside the smashed tank, a human form slumped at the bottom of the second, its resemblance uncanny. The third tank remained full of fluid, bubbling green bubbles. Tubes floated inside, waving as though jeering at the coming torment. He shuddered. The realization they might put him into the last tank terrified him. He needed to escape.

Kaytrix struggled against the chair, looking for a weakness when a voice spoke. It delved deeper into his soul and consciousness than anything he'd seen so far.

"Trying to go somewhere? You've only just returned after your little gallivant in the galaxy."

The voice cut through him, angering him more than he thought it would. It was a snide, proud tone. He could only guess to whom it belonged.

"Vhulse. What makes you think I came back on my accord? I didn't miss *you*," he said, forcing the words out with as much menace as he could muster.

The throbbing pain in his head resurfaced, more intrusive than before. Was the creature in his body more at home here?

"Come, come," chided the voice again as it rounded his right side. "After everything we've been through together. And we were making such substantial progress."

The phrase struck a chord. His nightmares were full of chants and promises of *progress*. The Nevo stood before him. Compared to Khelveliz, his appearance was like a juvenile. However, something about him appeared more sinister than Lord Khelveliz. Was it the metal shaped around his head, or the narrow eyes that didn't blink?

"What is it exactly you are trying to do? Khelveliz was less than helpful."

"Trying? Goodness. That's the wrong word to use, my friend."

Kaytrix grit his teeth. "I'm not your friend."

Vhulse closed the gap between them in a burst of speed. The Nevo locked its cold metal hand on his jaw, forcing Kaytrix to look at him.

"I am your *only* friend here." Vhulse tossed his face away.

Kaytrix recoiled from the smell of Vhulse's rotten, pungent breath. The Nevo strode around him on his left, circling him like a predator.

"What I have done is synthesize a cure for our race. An acceptance serum."

Kaytrix reflected on his conversation with Lord Khelveliz. It didn't sound like they had much of a race left to cure. "Enlighten me."

"So you've forgotten?" A boisterous laugh erupted from his metal-platted mouth. "No doubt when you came out of the tank—" He stopped short.

The silence was dreadful. What was this monster thinking now?

"There's no way you made it out of this place alone," he chided. "You would not have the strength to walk, to stand . . . Someone helped you."

"I asked about the serum, not how I escaped. You insult my resolve."

He hoped his bluff was enough, but a wicked flare ignited Vhulse's eyes as he disappeared behind him. A rattle broke the lengthened silence as Vhulse prepared something on a tray.

"Doesn't matter now," Vhulse finally said. "You are here, and I am going to finish my life's work."

Without warning, a sharp needle stabbed Kaytrix in the neck. Vhulse drove the needle deep until the coldness of his metal hands rested against Kaytrix's skin. The pain intensified as the needle withdrew his blood.

Kaytrix struggled, feeling helpless.

"Aagghhhh!"

"Oh, shut it. That didn't hurt."

Vhulse removed the sharp needle, and a warmth crept down Kaytrix's neck and seeped into his shirt. Vhulse stood in front of him, holding a vial of blue blood. His blood.

"This is what I've been waiting for. Thanks to my spawn in your body, the perfect chemical balance exists. From this, I can create a serum. With a single injection into any specie, it will allow us to inhabit any race without the threat of death."

Kaytrix forced himself to swallow down his bile. He was dying just so his body could create this chemical balance. His death would mean the continuation of an evil race, but not only that. The Nevo planned to infest every known race. It meant a galaxy-wide death sentence. A genius, but an awful plan. He couldn't let Vhulse complete his work, but how would he stop him? His last weapon was time. It was imperative he delay Vhulse as long as possible.

"Speaking of your *spawn*, can you get him out of me now?"

Vhulse chuckled. "Unfortunately, it's too late for you. Let the symbiote in. It's the only way for you to survive. Of course, your consciousness will fade and the Nevo will take complete control of you. What's so bad about that?"

Kaytrix recoiled. "You call that surviving?!"

"Suite yourself, but I will not perform such a procedure. It's your fate to become like one of us, Commander Torex. Such irony, especially when you fought so hard to stop us. Now it is your blood to doom everyone."

The vial disappeared into Vhulse's cloak. What else could he say to keep Vhulse from leaving? Strategies eluded him when a commotion outside the doorway drew his attention.

Slashes and groans filtered through the closed door, followed by the scuffling of feet and heavy thuds. The noise settled, and the door flew sideways. In strode the familiar black robes of Alissia, her amber eyes burrowing into Vhulse.

Relief flooded Kaytrix, but also sadness. If what Vhulse said was true, he wouldn't have long before the Nevo took over.

"Ah, Alissia." The anger in Vhulse's tone was thick.

"Save your words and give me the vial!" Alissia demanded.

Vhulse lifted his hands. "What vile?"

Alissia took a step further into the room, spinning her dual blades in her hands. Green blood covered them. Behind her strode Javex and Aaro, their blades also bloodied.

Vhulse huffed.

Alissia blocked Vhulse's escape. "Do not mistake me for a fool, Vhulse. I can see the blood running down Cade's neck."

"Cade? Is that what you call him? All right, as you wish. It's just inside my cloak." Vhulse reached to retrieve it, but far lower than his hand needed to be.

A pit formed in Kaytrix's stomach.

Aaro inched closer to stand beside Alissia. "Steady now."

Vhulse withdrew a blaster from beneath his cloak and fired at them, forcing the crew to duck for cover. Vhulse seized this opportunity to slip past and to the door.

"He's getting away!" Kaytrix called. "He can't escape."

Javex moved in to remove his restraints as the skirmish continued.

Alissia hurled her blades, striking Vhulse's hand holding the blaster. Her other blade sliced past his leg, just missing. Vhulse continued to move towards the door. Alissia cast her robes aside, revealing a harness of blades. She whirled them with a deft swiftness, but she wasn't quick enough. Vhulse was a stride away from the door when Alissia released another onslaught of blades, this time pinning each of his appendages to the wall.

Vhulse thrashed like a caught fish. "You!!!" he screeched.

Alissia strode up to him, smirking. "Do shut up," she said, reaching into his cloak to recover the vial.

She held it before his eyes before smashing it onto the floor. The contents spilled everywhere, spoiling the sample.

Vhulse flashed his eyes, the anger unmeasurable, and said nothing more.

"We must hurry," Javex said as he finished undoing the last of Kaytrix's restraints.

Aaro and Javex helped him to his feet.

"Don't follow us, Vhulse," Alissia hissed, backing away. "Or I will kill you."

"You would be wise to kill me anyway," Vhulse taunted her.

Alissia twirled her blades. "I should. But I think facing Lord Khelveliz for your failure will be a much better fate."

Vhulse's eyes widened. For the first time, fear entered the eyes responsible for so much terror in others. Kaytrix didn't feel pity for this creature. Now Vhulse would feel the same horror he incited in others. Justice has a funny way of coming around.

Kaytrix hobbled along with Javex and Aaro towards the exit. Atara and Noro rushed in to help, and relief eased his heavy heart. He was happy to see them safe. Seraphina was here too, though she kept her menacing gaze to herself. A rush of ecstatic hope swelled in his chest. The crew was safe, the sample of blood destroyed. Now they were about to escape. The worst was behind them.

The door to the lab whizzed opened, and they entered the corridor.

"We'll take the nearest lift," began Alissia. "I don't think they know what's—"

A deep growl rumbled in the silence.

The group stopped as a green scaled foot entered the light. Following it, the familiar and massive frame of Grootie. He was beat, bleeding, but his rage remained.

"Going somewhere?" Grootie's voice rumbled. The flesh around his teeth curled back in a snarl.

"Grootie." Alissia hissed. "Back off." She lifted her blades, but her actions came too late.

Grootie swung his left arm, tossing her into the corridor wall. Aaro prepared to fire his guns, but Grootie's right hand clamped them together, then he hurled him to the ground.

A hollowing feeling deepened in Kaytrix as Javex struggled to steady him while also shielding Noro and Atara.

Javex roared, pausing the Varanus in his tracks.

"How could you do this, Grootie? Not once, but twice?" Javex was beyond the point of grief, anger the only emotion in his voice.

Grootie snorted. "Once I've reprimanded you, Lord Khelveliz will reward my efforts and release my planet from his control. Varanus will be free once again." A wicked glare flashed in Grootie's reptilian eyes.

"You're a fool," groaned Aaro from the floor. "Better yet, a puppet." He wheezed.

"You know nothing," Grootie spat.

"He's right." Kaytrix struggled to find the strength to stand on his own. "Vhulse told me what he plans to do with the serum he's making. They're going to infect the entire galaxy with their race. No one will survive."

Grootie paused, his tongue flickering.

"They're lying to save themselves," Vhulse called from the lab. "Look at them. Pathetic. I shall reward you. I will make sure Lord Khelveliz knows of your bravery."

"More like treachery," Alissia said from the ground.

Grootie growled, holding them there in the stalemate. A clashing sound of screeches reverberated through the corridor.

"Let us go, Grootie. I don't want to fight you, but I will." Javex snarled.

Grootie lifted his head, remaining firm in his stance. Their time to leave dwindled. On the corridor walls, shadows danced, chaos growing louder. Nevo soldiers rounded the corner, led by Lord Khelveliz.

A scream from Atara drew Kaytrix's gaze from the oncoming horde.

Javex and Grootie stood toe-to-toe, fighting each other. Fur flew from Javex's body in tufts, but he blocked most blows. Despite Javex's apparent skill, his injuries were a disadvantage to Grootie's power and rage.

Javex paced himself, waiting. The agile Zaguarz pounced. Grootie side-stepped, anticipating the bite Javex would deliver to his neck. Grootie caught Javex by the throat and lowered him to his knees with a triumphant guttural growl.

Kaytrix caught the pain in Javex's face, the blood on his body as he sank to his knees. The fight was over. The Varanus solidified his choice after everything the captain tried to do for him.

Resentment turned Kaytrix's heart cold, his fists tightening. How could a creature deny forgiveness not once, but twice, for someone as wretched and evil as Lord Khelveliz?

Kaytrix rose his hands to fight. Alissia shared the same sentiment as she engaged Grootie with a warrior cry.

"Cade, here!" Aaro tossed him a blade and joined in the assault.

Kaytrix caught the blade as Grootie slammed Aaro and Alissia to the floor. Kaytrix tightened his grip and targeted where Javex sank his teeth on the Varanus's neck. If he stabbed him in the same place, he'd fall unconscious again.

"Get out of here!" Alissia screamed.

He stood ready with the blade in his hand as Atara and Noro cowered in Javex's shadow.

"Take the kids with you!" Aaro said, rising to his feet.

Kaytrix hesitated. He couldn't leave them in Grootie's grasp, but he also wanted to help the kids escape. He took a step towards the kids when Grootie whipped his tail against his hand. Kaytrix recoiled, dropping the blade.

The Nevo flooded the narrow corridor and swarmed them. Something sharp slashed his wrists and a blow to his knees sent him down. Above the chaos, Lord Khelveliz bellowed orders as his soldiers behaved like frenzied animals. The Nevo quieted, and in its wake, Lord Khelveliz stood over them all, his green orbed eyes scanning the situation.

Kaytrix and the crew knelt side by side, facing Lord Khelveliz. The Nevo's gaze focused on Javex, then rotated through all the faces until they rested on Alissia. His shoulders slumped, but he corrected the motion.

"This is most disappointing." Khelveliz hissed, placing a claw under Alissia's chin.

She pulled her face away, but kept her gaze locked on him.

"And you," Khelveliz breathed, focusing on Grootie.

Khelveliz's voice crawled up Kaytrix's spine as if he laced the words with an invisible poison.

Grootie knelt. "I stopped them from leaving, my Lord. Even after they released me from—"

"Traitor!!" Aaro roared, rising to his feet. A Nevo soldier clubbed Aaro across the back of the head.

Khelveliz turned from Grootie and faced Aaro. "I recognize those helmet markings," he said. "Remnants of the Red Sky Alliance, and the armor—" Khelveliz dragged a claw across the metal "—belongs to a Shrovon deserter, Aaro Riffo."

Deserter? That didn't sound like the Aaro he knew. Aaro proved he was a leader, a fighter. Loyal to his companions.

"Take this one to the arkross. Send him back to Shrovon to face the penalty waiting for him," Lord Khelveliz said.

"No!" Javex rose to his feet, jerking out of his captor's grasp to stand toe-to-toe with Lord Khelveliz. "If you send him there, they will kill him."

Khelveliz threw his cloak to the side and squared up with Javex. "Precisely," he hissed.

"What of these?" A soldier asked, motioning to Atara and Noro.

"Their owners at the mines have missed their labor. Send them back to Sadishka to work." Khelveliz stared at Javex as he gave the order. "Send this one with them. He can watch the children's bodies deteriorate under the whips of the slavers. And that one," Khelveliz pointed to Seraphina, "She also has a master to answer to. Send her back to them."

Javex's lips twitched, his bound hands shaking. Tears soaked the fur of his face as judgment passed on his family.

Kaytrix couldn't imagine what Javex was feeling. In his own body, a deepening helplessness hollowed him out. He regretted leaving Rehnna. He should have listened to Traven, then none of this would be happening.

"And the traitor bounty hunter?" Another soldier asked.

Kaytrix observed Alissia. Her fierce gaze hadn't left Lord Khelveliz's metal face.

"I'll deal with her!" A voice called from the lab. Vhulse pushed through the crowd of soldiers. "I'll make sure she never betrays us again."

Khelveliz ignored Javex's withering visage to focus on Vhulse. "What interest is she to *you*?!"

Vhulse trembled, but his greed prevented him from retreating.

Lord Khelveliz flashed his eyes and the air between them intensified. "I'll decide what becomes of her later."

Vhulse persisted. "My Lord—"

"Silence!" Khelveliz roared and motioned for two larger soldiers to step from the swarm. "I am aware of your treachery, Vhulse. Planting your own symbiote into my prize." Khelveliz's fists vibrated at his sides. "You are no longer free to move on this base until you complete the serum."

Lord Khelveliz whirled to the soldiers holding the individuals Kaytrix came to call friends. "Take them away!"

Atara screamed again as the soldiers pulled them down the dark corridor. Alissia fought every step of the way while Aaro's limp form disappeared in the other direction. Amidst the thrashing, Grootie stood with his gaze frozen forward.

The Varanus's blank visage enraged Kaytrix. These events weren't his fault. Everything was fine aboard the *Dauntless* until Grootie betrayed them.

"You!" Kaytrix cried, fighting to be released when he, too, found himself dragged back into the lab. "Let me go!"

Kaytrix pulled against the sharp metal of the Nevo's hands as they slammed him back into the chair and secured the restraints.

He ground his teeth. "When I get out of here, I'm—"

A chuckle stole his next words. Vhulse stood ready with another needle. "You're never getting out of here. Now, to finish what I started." Vhulse turned the needle around in his hands.

Kaytrix thrashed against the restraints.

"Hold him!"

The four soldiers rushed in, their clammy metal hands securing Kaytrix's head, torso, and legs.

"Aaaagggghhhhhhhh!!"

The needle pierced his neck again, only this time, his world grew dark.

Chapter 25

SYMBIOTE

A splitting headache woke Kaytrix with a start. A breath of damp air and the familiar sounds of torture floated to his ears. He was in a cell again. His head hurt like hell, throbbing, as though his heartbeat were there instead of in his chest.

"It's only a matter of time," said a small voice inside him. "Why not make this easy on yourself? Let go."

A rush of memories flooded to the surface. Khelveliz splitting up the crew of the *Dauntless*, sentencing them to cruel fates and Vhulse's words of his doom.

"There's still a chance to save them," he argued.

He found it odd to say the words aloud. No one was there, but the Nevo spawn taking over his body.

"Is there though?" The voice replied. "Even if there was, in your state, you could never save them. Let me help you. We will save them together."

Kaytrix recalled the strength the Varanus possessed on Arimas. Whatever the Nevo did to their subjects, it not only empowered them, but it damn near made them invincible. Better yet, fearless. If he wanted to save the crew, he needed that kind of power, the power of the Nevo.

A weird sensation crawled the back of his skull like fingers prickling nerves as he considered it.

"That's it," the voice encouraged.

A chill traveled his spine and his body quivered. He summoned his strength to push back the sensation, fighting its advancement. There had to be another way. But was there?

While he weighed his options, Vhulse worked to create the most dangerous weapon known to the galaxy using his blood. The acceptance serum. The terrible future awaiting them played through his mind. Races forced to receive an injection then subjected to become Nevo hosts. The plan would turn the galaxy into a horde of Nevo. Certain details, like how Nevo created spawn, and how they implanted into people, remained a mystery. One thing was certain, the experience was awful.

Why wasn't he strong enough to stop the spawn? Lord Khelveliz called him Commander Torex. He revered the name, this warrior from the past, but Kaytrix didn't feel powerful, or like a warrior. All he felt was failure.

Failure.

Something about that word plagued him. The fear of being a failure laced the glimpses of memories in his dreams. He studied the markings on his forearm. The veins there bulged a grotesque black. Enlarged and gorged like a feeding leech. The black, intricate lines of his markings faded into his now graying skin.

"You will die without me," the voice tempted again.

Why not? Why couldn't he use the Nevo power to do something right for a change? Maybe his destiny was to use their power against them? His rage flared. Anything he'd ever done ended in failure. If he embraced it, he might change how his story ended. But even as he led himself to believe that, would he follow through, allowing the darkness to have him? To trust darkness to do good?

"You *are* the reason I am dying," he growled, forcing himself to stand and face the reality of his situation.

Before him sprawled the hives of cells inhabited with whimpering prisoners. What use they were to the Nevo he could only guess. If Vhulse had any part to play in their capture, they would end up in his lab, dissected and rotting.

Pain shot through him as the symbiote thrashed against his spine.

"Aaagghh," he howled, his voice carrying through the cells like everyone else's scream.

Kaytrix fell to his knees and clutched his head to rid himself of the intruding pain. Even this fight was like a failure. His life drained out of him. Fire tore through his veins. The symbiote was winning. He could feel his consciousness slipping away. His brain ceased to throb as the moment froze.

He could hear the Nevo symbiote cackling, or was it him? The fire continued through him, tightening all his muscles, locking them under the control of the Nevo symbiote. The laughing stopped.

"Let me in!" The symbiote demanded.

Kaytrix floated in his brain, waiting for the Nevo to knock down the doors of his consciousness and steal his body, but something stood between him and the symbiote. A barrier pulsing and rippling like a shield.

The Nevo screeched in his ears and thrashed his body against the cell. "You're protected!" It fumed.

Protected? How was that possible? Wasn't he about to die? Kaytrix looked out across the prisoner ward once again, only this time a face framed in black hair met his gaze.

Alissia, he thought. But how could that be? She must have escaped her cell.

"It's too late," the symbiote spoke through his teeth. "His body is *mine!*"

Kaytrix experienced the horror of the Nevo symbiote as Alissia reached through the bars and grabbed his throat.

"Not if I have anything to say about it," she snarled.

Through the bars of his cell, she thrust a control rod and sent a jolt through him. The symbiote recoiled, but its tethers throughout his body remained strong.

"Hold on, Cade," she pleaded. Alissia released her hold on him as she fidgeted with something on her belt loop.

The name she spoke was foreign. A lie. If he was going to die, he needed to set it straight.

"Kaytrix," he croaked. "My name is Kaytrix." An internal relief washed through him at the sound of his voice. Whatever she hit him with sent the Nevo symbiote in retreat—for now.

Alissia activated something in her hand, and the door to his cell opened.

"Hurry," she hissed. "We have little time."

Like before, she guided his weakened body from his cell and down the corridor. She walked fast, but her stride wobbled, injured.

"I knew your name wasn't Cade," she said finally.

He allowed himself a chuckle—an odd thing to experience as they traveled through what could only be hell.

"This way," she said, walking with care. They entered a new corridor, and he recognized it led to the lab.

He resisted. "Why are you bringing me here?"

Alissia struggled to hold him as her hands slipped from around his body. "It's not what you think," she insisted. She pointed to a dark tunnel hollowed into the dirt just opposite of the doorway to the lab.

"It's the air vent." She wheezed. "It's what we took last time when I saved you."

He grimaced. "That's a bad habit you got there, saving me all the time." He caught the corner of her mouth pull up in a smile, but then it vanished.

"I can't find the others," she said. "Lord Khelveliz already sent them away."

Kaytrix's anger returned. He clenched his jaw at the injustice of the situation. How was it fair that they suffered the consequences of helping him? He couldn't leave. Not with his blood in Vhulse's hands. Not with the sacrifice of Javex, Aaro, Noro, Atara, and Seraphina. No, this would end here.

Alissia gasped. "What are you doing?"

He forced himself towards the lab. "I'm finishing my mission. Will you help me?"

Alissia took a step towards him, reaching. For the first time, the fight in her eyes vanished. "There's no escaping this fate if this is what you choose," she warned.

"I don't have much time left. I don't want to spend it running away."

She lowered her hand and squared her shoulders. "I'll help you," she agreed. "What's your plan?"

"You got a couple of extra knives?"

Alissia pulled back part of her robe to expose her thigh lined with thin, sharp blades. "Always." She grinned, handing him two.

"I'll cause a distraction while you destroy the serum."

Alissia nodded and unsheathed her blades. "Ready."

Kaytrix drew in a breath and prepared to face Vhulse. The door whizzed open. He rushed in, ready to stop Vhulse's evil plans, only to find the lab empty. On the floor, two Nevo soldiers lay mangled. Green blood pooled around their corpses.

"He's not here," Alissia said, observing the bodies. "Looks as though he's trying to make a run for it. Coward."

"To the hanger topside?"

"It's the fastest way. The arkross is within the city of Cordabo. It would take too long to reach it."

"Then we head to the surface and try to stop him."

Alissia strode to the doorway. "We best hurry. We'll take the lift."

Kaytrix turned to follow Alissia, grateful she knew where to go. With all the twists and turns, he'd already forgotten which way led where, but more unnerving was his growing weakness. He couldn't afford to collapse or lose his body to the Nevo . . . again.

When they reached the lift, a brim of light strobed across the top of its shaft, signaling its return to its port.

Alissia gnawed on her bottom lip, her foot tapping with impatience. He caught her glance at him sideways. What did he look like compared to when she first saved his life?

"Why did you leave me on Rehnna?"

Alissia looked at him, her eyes wide, as if she feared answering the question. Strange for Alissia. Fear never resided in her eyes.

"I did it to protect you from Vhulse."

"Yeah, you've said that, but why? So many others suffer from his voracious experimentation. Why risk your life for me?"

She chewed her lip and fidgeted with her swords. Finally, she sighed, and her amber eyes met his. "I've known you since before the Nevo plagued our galaxy. Before you became a hero, before you lost everything. Before I lost everything. On my world, Drenna, your leaders stationed you there as a protector."

Kaytrix nodded. "On the *Dauntless* you asked me if I remembered Drenna. I recall parts of it, but not you."

"That's right. We didn't meet officially, but I haven't forgotten you. Even after everything." She blushed and focused on the blinking lift.

His cheeks warmed, finally understanding what drove her to such lengths to save and protect him.

"I'll do the fighting," she said.

"What? No. Did you see those mangled Nevo? You are going to need my help." What was Alissia thinking?

"Kaytrix—"

"This is my fight. Don't ask me to stand aside. That monster needs to be stopped. Regardless of what happens to me."

Alissia frowned, then nodded.

The strobing lights along the top of the lift glowed a steady orange hue. The door opened, but the lift wasn't empty.

"You two!" Grootie hissed.

Kaytrix forced the door shut while Alissia pinned a knife into the mechanism, jamming it.

"I swear I will tear you to pieces!" Grootie snarled through the grated opening.

The words created an unpleasant visual—the crew being pulled apart from each other. Kaytrix threw a fist through the bars and hit the Varanus in the temple.

"Haven't you done enough?"

Grootie's slit reptilian eyes narrowed, and a deep, guttural hiss escaped between his jaws. Grootie wrapped his clawed hands around the bars and snorted. His rage was pure and undeniable. The Varanus wanted to dance, and Kaytrix was ready for a fight.

Alissia pulled on him. "He's delaying us. We need to get to the surface. Now!"

How he wanted to bust the Varanus's jaw and tear that smug look off his face; to make him pay for screwing up the crew's only chance to escape, at having everyone back together and on their way to the ship. Dammit but Alissia was right.

Kaytrix shrugged her off, but Grootie's fixated gaze unsettled his resolve to back away. If they let Grootie live, who was to say he wouldn't try to capture or kill them?

"Kaytrix!" Alissia said sharply.

"He needs to die." He snarled.

Alissia rushed to his side; her face pressed against his. Her breath was hot as it flew across his skin.

"He will. One day. But not now. Let's *go*." Her words were firm, commanding.

Another day then. Kaytrix turned and followed her to a different lift. His bones quaked as they boarded and selected the surface. He was sure he would regret walking away from Grootie, but this was the first and last time he would show mercy.

The surface brought a welcomed chill to Kaytrix's feverish skin as he followed Alissia through the thick grass. Each step stirred the fine dust, creating whirlwinds of floating particles.

They crouched near the opening of the hangar. Rows and rows of ships parked inside, but only one had activity. Vhulse was trying to escape.

"We'll try to keep the element of surprise," Alissia said.

Kaytrix was ready to follow Alissia into the hangar when a long-forgotten feeling tingled over his skin. He caught her wrist as they squatted.

"Do you feel that?" He whispered.

Alissia caught sight of something behind him. Instead of a grimace, she smiled.

Curious, he glanced over his shoulder. Amidst the light and shadow cast by the planet and plant life, a figure stalked over towards them. A black visor reflecting the large ring of light above them. Kaytrix recognized the being from the planet Arimas. Javex called it a Shargan.

"T'vos," Alissia greeted, her tone surprised.

"A friend of yours?" Kaytrix asked.

T'vos crouched to be with them. "And one of yours," he said.

"Why are you here?" Alissia questioned quickly. "Thought you couldn't touch the soil of Cordabo?"

"I received orders to retrieve Kaytrix."

Kaytrix examined the being. How did he know his real name?

"Sorry, but I'm not going anywhere. Vhulse has my blood. We can't allow him to escape."

T'vos nodded. "I see your stubbornness hasn't left you. Very well, I will help."

A terrible roar escaped the mouth of the cave. Instinctively, they melted into the tall grass to hide.

"The bounty hunter helped him to escape!" an enraged Grootie roared.

Kaytrix grit his teeth. There was the regret already.

"What!?" screeched a voice in reply. "Find them!"

T'vos laid a hand on Kaytrix's shoulder, sending an electric tingle through his body.

"I need to get you off the planet."

"Not with Vhulse right there!"

Alissia turned to him, her sweet smell floating in the cool grass. "I'll finish this. You need to go. *Now!*"

Pain twisted Kaytrix's heart, but it wasn't from the symbiote, or any other ailment. He didn't want Alissia to face Vhulse. Not alone.

"Forget it. I'm staying here."

T'vos stood, and a hum began thrumming through Kaytrix's body. In the Shargan's hands two bright lights of energy floated around itself, gaining in speed and intensity.

"There they are! After them!" Vhulse shouted.

T'vos brought his elbows back and threw the energy into the hanger. The surge hit the first ships in either row, then rushed to the next, creating a chain reaction of explosions. Vhulse couldn't escape with the ships destroyed.

"Now let's go," T'vos said, his voice steady.

The rampaging Varanus exited the hangar and drew closer, his panting growing louder.

Alissia pulled Kaytrix to his feet and removed his cloak. "Go on ahead with T'vos. I'll draw Grootie off your trail and meet with you back at the arkross. Promise!"

Kaytrix hesitated when Alissia turned his face towards her.

"You need to live." A tear rolled down her cheek when she pressed her lips to his.

Her flowery scent encompassed him, the warmth of her touch welcomed in the cool evening. Kaytrix wanted to object, but he couldn't reject her passion. He embraced her, wrapping his arms around her delicate frame to drink in the moment.

"Don't worry," she said. "Fate seems to pull us back together, no matter the distance." She pulled away, and the fire returned to her eyes. "Now, T'vos!"

"Wait! Wait!" he called.

But Alissia was over the mound of grass and running for danger.

T'vos sent a surge of energy through Kaytrix's body and pulled him into the glowing jungle. His adrenaline spiked.

"Run," T'vos said.

His legs obeyed, carrying him with a speed with as much foreignness as the planet. They moved into the dense vegetation, brushing through the ferns and vines, and crossing a creek. They propelled themselves over twisted roots and stumps, avoiding large glowing webs and hungry Cordabo wolves feasting.

His heart thudded in his chest, his breathing ragged. He focused on the ground below his feet, and the sadness that Alissia's kiss left with him.

They entered a clearing with a hill of tall grass before them. Just beyond it, a soft hue of light glowed in the sky from the lanterns of the village. A frustrated roar tore through the silent floating flakes behind them.

"He's figured out he followed the wrong trail. He'll be coming this way now," T'vos said.

They began their ascent and were at the top of the hill when Grootie broke through the jungle, surging with strength and anger.

"There is no escape for you!" Grootie bellowed from below, tearing through the vegetation with his massive hands.

Before them lay a village, outlined with the glittery glowing substance. In the courtyard separate from the buildings, the arkross stood upon its stone-like base, its arms arched and ready for activation. A group of Nevo swarmed towards it from the opposite direction.

"Quick, we have to make it before they beat us," T'vos said, nudging him forward.

They entered the village, and the buildings grew taller and darker. The lit lanterns in their red silhouettes danced as if in synchronization with his heartbeat. Passing through the buildings, their view of the arkross became obstructed. Did T'vos know where he was going?

They rounded the sharp corner of a structure at the end of a street. The cobblestone echoing not only their panicked run, but the sharp claws of Grootie as he gained ground on them.

"We need to move faster!" T'vos said.

Around the next corner, the arkross came into view. Grootie panted behind, mere steps away from reaching them. In front, Nevo soldiers flooded the open courtyard where the arkross stood.

T'vos emitted a ball of energy from his hand and threw it towards the Nevo horde. They recoiled like bugs and scuttled away. Next, he threw one at Grootie.

Kaytrix looked back. The Varanus couldn't dodge the blast at such a close distance. The energy raced over his scales and sent burning veins of energy throughout his massive frame.

"Get on the arkross!" T'vos bellowed.

The swarm of Nevo returned, this time following a bigger Nevo.

A pit formed in Kaytrix's stomach.

"C'mon! We can make it!!"

Kaytrix followed T'vos onto the platform. The energy within the arches began to spin and form a ball around them.

Agitated screeches from the Nevo intensified as they clawed and clambered over each other like a possessed wind. The hum of shifting metal and screeches seized the swarm as they launched themselves at the activating arkross. While in the beginning stages of creating a wormhole, the arms, heads, and legs of Nevo entered through the energy, only to have them severed from their bodies.

"What are they doing?"

"They are trying to disrupt the wormhole!!" T'vos said.

The swirling energy burned brighter and brighter.

"Will we make it?" Kaytrix asked.

T'vos remained silent.

Through the blue energy surrounding them, the haunting Nevo silhouettes swarmed outside, tearing apart the ancient machinery to get at them. The energy increased intensity and picked up speed. Kaytrix groaned as the machine prepared them for the journey, whisking them into a de-materialized energy across time and space.

Chapter 26

A Cruel Fate

Alissia perched on a cliff of trees and vines, waiting. After Grootie stormed after T'vos and Kaytrix, she returned to the hangar to finish business. Nothing moved inside the darkness except for the smoke from the destroyed ships wafting into the night. It ruined her visibility.

T'vos destroyed the ships, but Vhulse may still be alive. Anger twisted her stomach. She wanted him dead before she would consider leaving this dreadful place.

Alissia dropped to land on some soft plants and moved towards the mouth of the hangar. Once at the entrance, she removed Kaytrix's cloak. It worked to throw Grootie off Kaytrix's trail if for a while, but now the iridescent glitter acted as a highlight for her silhouette, the last thing she wanted.

With care, she entered the darkness yet again. How many times would she return to this place? She hoped this was the last.

"Welcome back," a voice greeted, igniting the rage in her.

"You must really want to die," she spat.

The smoked cleared to reveal Vhulse standing in wait for her.

"I was about to say the same about you. Especially after what you did. Did your hard heart finally soften? And for some poor excuse of a hero, no less." Vhulse mocked her as he stepped forward. "Did you think you would get away with sabotaging me?"

"Are you blind? I did get away with it." She ground her teeth, stalking into the hangar as she observed her surroundings.

Vhulse's eyes flashed. "Did you?"

"I guess we're going to find out." Alissia hissed, twirling her blades.

Vhulse scoffed as she approached. "You really hope to defeat me with just two blades?"

"These *blades*," Alissia snarled, "I designed. Not only will they tear through your shield, but they will slide through your armor and shred your flesh."

Vhulse survived the hangar explosions because of his shield repelling the energy. Shield or not, her knifes could penetrate his defense and kill him. She just needed to get close enough.

For the moment, she didn't care if she lived. If what happened to Kaytrix was going to stop, so would the heart of Vhulse.

Vhulse detached his cloak and let it fall to the ground. His only weapons, the talons of his hands and the powerful grip of his razor-clawed feet, but that is all any Nevo needed when they towered over others.

Alissia made the first move, charging Vhulse with a shrilling war cry. Vhulse prepared himself, anchoring a foot, and readied to strike her. Instead of the jump he would expect, she slid on her knees past his massive arms and struck both his legs from underneath. Her blades sliced through the hydraulic tendons of his mechanical limbs.

"You witch!" He screeched, turning to grab her.

Alissia rolled and ducked the sharp talons of his hand as they whizzed by her head. Fluid splashed to the ground. Vhulse tried to catch her in his grasp.

She whirled on him and slashed one of her blades across his fingers, severing them from his hand. She was about to retreat to plan her next move when Vhulse grabbed her in his crushing grip.

A sick gurgle left his throat as he laughed. "You stupid bounty hunter, thinking that you could take me on," he said with a dark edge to his voice. He raised her to be eye-level with him. "No one is coming to save you. You will die by my hands."

Alissia squirmed in his grasp; her arms clenched at her sides. She tried desperately to hang on to her weapons as the crushing worsened. She must escape his grasp, but how?

"You're pathetic," she said. "You will never be mightier than Khelveliz while you scheme and plan in the darkness, afraid to confront him."

The crushing intensified, constricting her ability to breathe. That was it. Vhulse's last shred of patience, gone.

"I was going to spare you, but now I've changed my mind. I have greater plans for you, *Alissia*."

Alissia's eyes drooped. She couldn't breathe. Her bones popped out of their sockets. Her ribs crushed her lungs, stabbing them in betrayal. The world darkened with Vhulse's green eyes, the only light she could see. God forbid.

"What is the meaning of this!?"

An angry voice echoed in her mind. The crushing pain stopped, but the damage to her body was complete. The oxygen rushed to her lungs but escaped. Blood trickled in, drowning her. She heard Vhulse trying to be coy while answering Khelveliz.

She smiled, tasting blood. A shadow crossed over her and struck the face of her killer.

Good, she thought. Her death would not be meaningless.

"Get her to the lab immediately, you fool!" Khelveliz ordered. "If she is as valuable as you insisted before, we will use her to our advantage. She found him once. She will find him again."

What did it mean? Would she see Kaytrix again? She prayed she died. She prayed this was the end.

No.

This *would* be the end. With her last breath, she would decide her fate, not the evil scheming of the enemy. She lifted her blade and plunged it into her chest as deep as it would go.

Chapter 27

OLD FRIEND

Emerging out of the transport's energy instilled a distinct feeling in Kaytrix. The sense of victory vanished as he stumbled down the steps of the arkross and onto the planet.

Alissia remained on Cordabo, the captain and the crew disbursed. Aaro faced a death penalty. Yet here he remained alive. Well, for a while.

The familiar faces of rebel soldiers distorted upon seeing his appearance. Death was certain, but when remained the question. How long could he ignore the crawling plea of the Nevo inside his head? The battle of vying for control?

A hand reached around his torso while another grabbed his shoulder.

"Walk with me," T'vos pleaded.

Kaytrix stumbled, his boot hitting a rock. Anger surged through him. What was the purpose of it all? Vhulse possessed his blood, and he was going to die. The sting of failure pierced his heart. He stepped away from T'vos and sat down.

"What's the point if I die here or lying over there?" He grumbled. The fresh mountain air blew against his slick skin, a welcomed change to the pits of Nevo captivity. "This view is better than any stuffy tent."

"Kaytrix," T'vos began, kneeling beside him. "We must make it back to the settlement."

T'vos' visored gaze held steady and though Kaytrix couldn't see his eyes, the stranger's presence felt familiar.

Kaytrix lifted his gaze to the mountains surrounding him. Their mighty faces were old and wise, yet the peace he sought from their beauty escaped his soul.

"Now," T'vos said, his tone commanding.

Kaytrix forced himself to stand and suffer through the agonizing descent of the mountainside. The last few steps weighed on him. The smoke of the settlement danced around as T'vos led him further in. Children's laughter echoed through the settlement. He glanced around. Last time he was here, he didn't see any children.

Memories of Noro and Atara playing Colorz surfaced, driving his regret deeper into his soul. Their hopes and dreams lost now because of him. The fire the children danced around was massive, surrounded by large stones. A chain of silhouettes danced around it while others stood by. Was it a celebration? He hoped not for him.

As he approached the growing gathering, a silhouette turned to face him. The broad shoulders bore a hooded parka. A pair of gold eyes gazed at him. A rush of air flew to his lungs as he recognized the figure.

"J-J-Javex?" His words stuck in his throat when two forces smacked into him, one at his waist, the other at his chest. He wheezed.

"Cade!" the voices sang in unison.

His hands trembled as he stroked the backs of Atara and Noro. Tears flooded his vision. He looked up to the kind eyes of the captain and to Seraphina by his side.

"Javex? You guys are here? How?"

A knowing smile rose Javex's whiskers in a wave of happiness as they embraced.

"T'vos arrived at the arkross before the Nevo sent us through. He saved us and sent us here to safety."

Kaytrix examined the crowd, hoping to glimpse the one person he hadn't spotted yet.

"Aaro isn't here," Javex admitted with lowered ears. "The Nevo sent him through the arkross first."

Seraphina let a finger glide under her eye before pulling her cloak closer together. She nodded along with the conversation, the red streaks of her eyes remnants of tears long lost.

Kaytrix frowned. A part of this reunion was incomplete without the man who became like a brother. Was Aaro lost then? Part of him didn't want to believe the teasing swash buckler was gone. In fact, he wouldn't. If he survived another night, his first mission would be to save Aaro. For now, he wanted to address some unfinished business, in case tomorrow didn't come.

"Captain, I never thanked you."

Javex raised an eyebrow. "For what?"

"For risking your life and your crew to help me. You lost everything because of me, your ship, Aaro, your chance to continue your mission. For what it's worth, I'd rather die here than, well, anywhere else."

Javex smiled. "No one said you have to die."

Kaytrix crumpled his brow. Could Javex not see the grotesque black veins popping out of his arms? "I'm not letting the symbiote take control."

T'vos placed a hand on his shoulder. "You won't have to. Come. Someone is waiting to meet you."

"Me?"

"Yes. This way."

T'vos led him from the firepit to walk amongst the rest of the settlement. Many fires scattered throughout the small settlement, with more people dancing and singing. Their voices cheerful, full of hope. What song did they sing? He didn't know the words to these songs.

T'vos approached another fire, but only one person stood near the tall flames. They held their shoulders back, their head high as they sang along to the songs. A strange sensation began thrumming through Kaytrix, the same sensation he recognized from T'vos.

The woman stood with her hands folded in front of her. The light of the fire danced across her face, illuminating it in a glow warmer than the fire itself. Striking white hair floated past her shoulders. Beneath the layer of poncho fabric, a hardened black and blue suit of armor. The features of her face were soft and kind, revealing the shimmering opaque of her eyes.

"Hello Commander," her warm, melodic voice greeted.

He stumbled closer to the fire. "Hi. You are?"

She glanced to T'vos, then her eyes glimmered back at him. "You truly do not remember your life? The captain said as much."

"Nothing. Flashes, nightmares sometimes. I get minor revelations, but less now with the symbiote in my head."

The woman nodded and motioned for him to sit. "I heard you've been searching for a sage to help you."

He nodded, taking the seat. "Yes. The Great One from Acknaria said they may be here, but the soldiers haven't seen them for a while. Guess I am doomed." He forced a chuckle.

The woman sat on a stump next to him. The humming in his body increased and a light danced in his head.

"What is that? Why is my body pulsing?"

"My presence has that effect on people," she said with a smile.

Kaytrix had never seen someone so perfect, to his knowledge. "Who are you?" Nothing was making sense. He'd like to spend his last moments with the crew.

"We've met, oh, some odd solar rotations ago in a galaxy different from today. I'd like to help you remember. To remove the symbiote." Her hands remained folded on her lap, the poncho still draped along the sides of her face.

"How?"

She lifted her hands to touch either side of his face. "May I?"

"Will it hurt?" Not that it mattered. Everything bloody hurt.

"It will feel intrusive, but clarity will follow."

"I'll try anything," he admitted, wringing his hands.

The woman smiled. "Very well. T'vos, hold him. Be ready for the symbiote."

Kaytrix wanted to ask another question, but he was too late. The moment her hands touched him, pain thrashed inside of his head. The crawling sensation of the Nevo symbiote returned with desperate force as it clawed and flailed.

Something hot seared the back of his neck.

"No, no, no!!" The Nevo screeched. Its voice was loud, penetrating. It slipped further away as if pulled down an echoing tunnel.

A crushing wave of coolness cascaded through Kaytrix's temples, down his spine, and raced through his extremities. The chill traveled through his veins to every part of his body chasing the darker presence.

An odd sensation writhed up his spine in the wake of the cool sensation. Something at his neck wiggled out. Warmth crept down his neck as the creature's body slithered in escape.

"I have it!" T'vos exclaimed.

The silhouette of T'vos's skilled hand clenched the shadow of some hideous creature as it writhed in his grasp. Without hesitation, T'vos tossed the symbiote into the fire where the tormented screeching continued.

Searing pain returned to Kaytrix's neck, surprising him as the woman closed the wound. Kaytrix groaned when another phenomenon followed. This one peaceful and calming, expanded from his mind to disappear like a popped bubble.

His furrowed brow relaxed as a memory of two older faces came to the surface. They offered him a piece of cake. His dad made it, a proud smile on his face. Ma looked good for being sick.

Kaytrix opened his eyes. A tear surfaced and graced his cheek. His first memory of a time he cherished, a life he'd forgotten.

"Kaytrix." The woman smiled. Her thumb caressed his cheek, removing the tear.

"Queen Rayla, it's you." Kaytrix embraced her, his arms bringing her small frame close. "Oh, sorry, your majesty."

Was it proper manners to hug a queen? When did he see her last? A battle scene surfaced in his memories: his last attempt to destroy Khelveliz's ship while Archaria, his home planet, burned.

Another swell of emotion rose to the surface. Grief. Anger. A choking sob tightened his throat as he fought the onslaught of memories. His crew dying in service, his last goodbye to his parents, the betrayal of the council which led to their races' ultimate failure and destruction.

He clenched his teeth, fighting the urge to roar. "H-how long has it been? How did I survive?"

Queen Rayla lowered her gaze, then looked at T'vos. She was as young and graceful as he remembered.

"The Last Stand happened sixty-eight solar rotations before you awoke. The way Vhulse preserved you, kept you alive and slowed the aging process."

The number punched his gut. "It happened sixty-eight solar rotations ago!?"

Queen Rayla nodded, not looking at him.

"Gee, I . . ." His gaze fell on T'vos, who stood off to the side quiet like always. Memories of his bravery aboard the *Ro'arck* battleship surfaced. "T'vos! You're better!"

T'vos chuckled. "For a while now. Commander Torex, about not returning to aid you in the Last Stand—"

"T'vos, you don't have to feel guilt. That was a lifetime ago."

T'vos said nothing, but the incline of his head hinted at a deeper sorrow.

The delicate pitter-patter of feet approached, followed by the soft footfalls of boots. The crew approached the fire, gazing at him. Javex's face especially held a curious expression. What did he hear?

"All went well?" Javex's eyes were warm as he smiled and sat with Noro and Atara under each of his arms. Seraphina stood beside him, warming by the fire.

Queen Rayla nodded. "Yes, Kaytrix is symbiote free and his memories restored, though it will take time for all his memories to return. The Blessing of Life protected his mind, but his body must cleanse from harboring the symbiote for so long."

"The blessing?" Kaytrix asked.

Flashes of the Queen offering him a gift flew through his mind. So that is what she bestowed upon him. A shield for his mind. As if she knew he would need it.

The queen nodded. "Correct."

"So you are not a sage," Javex began, "and your name is not Cade?"

Guilt squeezed Kaytrix's stomach. The captain and crew underwent so much for him, and only now were they learning his real name. They deserved to know the truth about who he was and so much more.

"My real name is Kaytrix. Cade was a pseudonym given to me on Rehnna. I'm sorry to have misled you."

Queen Rayla bowed. "As am I sorry for being deceptive. Sage was a title to keep the Nevo from discovering I am Queen of the Shargans. Had they discovered me . . ."

A snap from the fire drew the group's attention as small sparks flew into the air around them and fizzled out.

Javex smiled, his golden eyes forgiving, but something in his eyes hadn't settled. "I understand," he said.

For the first time, Kaytrix recognized Javex and the regal markings of who this captain was to him a lifetime ago.

"Chief Kovex." Kaytrix whispered.

Javex's ears twitched, having heard the name. His jaw opened, then shut. Pain surfaced in his eyes.

"That's a way cooler name than Cade," Noro chimed in. He snuggled closer to Javex and yawned. "And you energy people are cool too," Noro mumbled.

Atara shushed him. "Cade is a cool name, too." She smiled. "What's your second name?"

"Torex," Javex said knowingly.

Kaytrix met the Zaguarz's gaze, sensing a shift between them. "Yes, that's right. Kaytrix Torex."

Of course, Javex made the connection first. He overheard everything said between him and Queen Rayla.

The fire snapped as the sounds of celebration carried on in the settlement. The story of the Last Stand was common knowledge, but the realization of his identity hit Seraphina first.

She glanced from Javex to Kaytrix, and her brow furrowed. "From the stories?"

Javex nodded.

The correlation then dawned on Atara and Noro.

"What a minute," Atara objected. "You are the Commander? The one from the Last Stand who faced the fleet of Nevo ships?"

Noro's smile was wide, his nose crinkled. "You're old!"

They all shared a laugh.

"I suppose I am." Kaytrix chuckled. He spared a look at Javex. Those same golden eyes he encountered in the tavern on Tarwi now gazed at him with a deeper understanding, but also expectation.

Seraphina caught their exchange. "Captain, this means you've found what you've been looking for." Her voice bubbled with a hint of excitement.

"Yes." Javex nodded, continuing to gaze at Kaytrix. "I suppose it does."

Seraphina warmed her hands over the fire before sitting down. "What will you do, Kaytrix? Now that you remember?"

The sorrow in her eyes lessened, glimmering with hope. The same hope that twinkled in Javex's eyes, and that pulsed through T'vos and Queen Rayla.

Lord Khelveliz's seething voice haunted Kaytrix, followed by the fresh events of their time on Cordabo. The horrors, the smell, the cruelty. It needed to end. He was one man who just came out of hell. He wasn't so keen on returning.

This wasn't about him any longer. Others still suffered the torment of the Nevo. This was larger than him or any alliance, as his leaders once led him to believe.

His bones quaked as he answered. "I have an oath to uphold. A responsibility to protect and to give back what I received. There are many who suffer without the hope I had. Lord Khelveliz and Vhulse possess my blood. I intend to stop their plans of domination, but I can't do it alone."

T'vos bowed. "I will fight with you as I did in the Last Stand."

"As will I," spoke Javex, standing.

Noro and Atara cheered, hugging Javex tighter before plowing into Kaytrix. "You can be our new uncle!"

Seraphina struggled to smile at him. "I'm in, but I have one condition. Aaro is in danger, and as much as I don't like Alissia, we don't know what happened to her."

The same thought weighed on Kaytrix's heart throughout the entire evening. Not knowing if Alissia was safe or what fate awaited Aaro, kept him from celebrating the return of his memory.

"Saving Aaro is my first mission. After that, I'm going after the Nevo."

Atara and Noro cheered and danced around the fire. They grabbed Javex's hands and convinced him to join. T'vos joined in too, creating imagery of energy from his hands that delighted the younger ones to no end. Seraphina stayed off to the side. Her gaze lingered on him.

"Thank you," she mouthed, before she joined the others around the fire to sway.

Happiness crept into Kaytrix's heart. Surrounded by people he cared about, he no longer walked alone in the darkness. For the first time the echoes of destiny rang true.

Acknowledgments

I would like to thank my sister, Marlena, for listening to every chapter of this book under every title its had since we were twelve and thirteen. Your enthusiasm and passion for my characters is rivaled only by me.

Thanks to my dad and stepmom who continue to encourage me and my dreams.

To my husband, Steve, who endured many a night and day with his wife locked away in her office. Thanks for the desk. It help motivate me in the last stretch of the race.

Thanks to my beta reader, Nicholas W. Fuller. Your insightful comments (and gushes) helped me approach Echoes of Destiny differently and appreciate my writing in a way I hadn't yet.

To my Advanced Reader Copy (ARC) team. Thank you for giving Echoes of Destiny a chance.

Thanks to the team at Miblart who delivered a phenomenal cover.

Thank you to every amazing author/reader in my community on Instagram. Your endless support and understanding of this craft made the journey feel more like an adventure. The community we've built means more to me than anything else.

About the Author

Ericka Evren is the author of the *Archarian* series, a sci-fi space adventure that delivers emotional gut punches and challenges the deeper meaning of heroism and morality. She attended college for Early Learning and Childcare and now teaches at a preschool where she gets to be a big kid daily. Ericka wrote her first story at thirteen and published her debut novel, *Mission of the Ro'arck*, in 2022. She and her husband live in Alberta, Canada, with their two tabby cats, where they enjoy camping, family time, and nature.

Connect with her on social media: @erickaevrenauthor

Find more about Ericka and her books at: erickaevren.com

Connect

STAY UP TO DATE

If you loved the story and want to see what happens next, consider joining my monthly newsletter. There you will get one-on-one interactions with me, opportunities to become an ARC reader, sneak peaks to future projects, and much more! You can sign up for it by scanning the QR code below.

Newsletter Sign Up

Thank You

Thank you for reading my book! I can't tell you how much I appreciate it. It's readers like you who are vital for indie authors. Good reviews are also vital for indie authors and help readers find new adventures to experience.

If you enjoyed this book, would you help me reach more sci-fi loving readers by taking a minute to leave it a review? I can't tell you how over-the-moon I would be!

Below is a convenient to the best places to leave a review and help readers find a new sci-fi adventure to enjoy.